The Day of Calamity

by

H.B. Berlow

The Wichita Chronicles, Vol. 1

The Day of Calamity

Cover Art by *Tina Lynn Stout*

The Wild Rose Press, Inc.
PO Box 708
Adams Basin, NY 14410-0708
Visit us at www.thewildrosepress.com

Publishing History
First Edition, 2023
Trade Paperback ISBN 978-1-5092-5166-7
Digital ISBN 978-1-5092-5167-4

The Wichita Chronicles, Vol. 1
Published in the United States of America

While Central was a broader intersection, there was hardly any traffic coming through. I picked up my pace to a jog to cross it. Even though I stayed on the west side of the street alongside the ornate Sedgwick County Courthouse, the regular pace of those footsteps continued, the faint echo now growing a bit louder. I crossed the street quickly, without warning, right at the house with the two white lions standing guard. This time the pace of the footsteps quickened and were about three to four feet behind me.

"Best keep your nose out of other people's business." It was the baritone voice of a colored man.

"But it is my business," I uttered. "A wife is looking for her husband. That's all."

"She be better off without him."

I stopped suddenly. He did as well. My shoulder started to twitch, turn inward toward the right.

"You don't want to be turning around. You got nothing to look at here."

I hadn't gotten a line on Alonzo Washington enough to judge whether he carried a gun or not. I stayed still out of an abundance of caution.

"I can help you." I didn't intend to sound as pleading as I did.

"Ain't nobody can help me, mister. I seen too much."

"Let me try."

There was no response. Was he thinking about the proposition or eliminating me as a possible threat? Two or three minutes went by. There was no breathing or movement.

Dedication

To George Berlow (1922-2012) and Joseph Entin (1890-1984), my father and grandfather, who stood with me at my bar mitzvah. From both of you, I learned a great tradition.

To me belongeth vengeance, and recompence; their foot shall slide in due time: for the day of their calamity is at hand, and the things that shall come upon them make haste.

Deuteronomy 32:35 KJV

Chapter One

There was no need to think too hard on it. I was quite certain it was not my extensive work on divorce cases that brought me to the attention of Albert Whitman. A wealthy businessman like him who lives in ritzy Eastborough could easily go through a divorce between lunch and dinner without breaking a sweat or even being overly concerned. It was likely the discreet assistance I provided a former city councilman in retrieving his kidnapped daughter from a desperate ex-bootlegger. The notion in certain high-income circles was I was trustworthy enough to keep the dirty laundry of the well-to-do under wraps. As Falstaff said, discretion is the better part of valor. I often wondered if I was more detached than discreet.

In the brief time in my newfound career, nothing resembling my war experiences came before me. No bloody do-or-die situations with the clarity of Good versus Evil or even Us versus Them. It was while in Europe I learned any man could develop a taste for killing. There are those who eat it up with a spoon. Others choke on it and spit it out. When I returned home, I simply could no longer accept the old-fashioned notion of Law and Order and return to being an officer with the Wichita Police Department. For the same reason, I was not able to bring myself to following my father's dream for me of becoming a rabbi. I split the difference and became a private investigator.

As usual, I called upon Richie Mayer to give me a lift over to 50 East Norfolk Drive. I didn't own a car, didn't want one, and hadn't found a need for one so far. The Selective Service Board rejected Richie on account of his asthma, so he wound up driving a hack for Yellow Cab. I threw business his way every chance I got. He had a lot of gumption in his slight hundred- and twenty-five-pound frame. Probably read too many comic books.

"How's the foot today, Hirsch?" Richie had the mistaken notion 'Hirsch' was the Yiddish nickname for 'Harold' and called me that since I got back. I hated to tell him otherwise considering it drew us closer as friends. Besides, there were a lot worse things you could call a Jew.

"The weather is warming up. But I'll know if it rains." Ever since I took a couple of bullets in the leg and foot during the Battle of the Bulge, I've been better than a barometer. Because of the injury, I was out of commission for the rest of the war. When the fracture didn't heal properly, I wound up with a bit of a limp. The cold and damp brought on a small measure of pain and my ballroom dancing days ended in ignominy.

We meandered slowly through Eastborough per the restricted speed limits. Richie let out a long whistle when we reached our destination.

"Geez, Hirsch, that's one big house."

He didn't get too many fares for this part of town. The occasional phlegmy cough and unsyncopated wheezing did not endear him to the swells. His whistle was a sign he was highly impressed.

The joint was a Tudor-style brick home but considerably bigger. The only thing missing was a moat. I never really understood the rich Americans' fascination with that architecture considering most of them felt the British were too stuffy. Maybe it was because most of their type were criminals at heart and had no real taste for anything. Then again, their money made it so they didn't need it.

The telegram I got rather early that morning indicated a request for my presence on this day at this time regarding an 'urgent matter' as though there were any other kind. Those with hefty bank accounts prioritize their needs and expect the rest of the riff raff to be of an equal mind. However, I figured Whitman's money and stature were worthy of my best black pinstripe suit with a freshly ironed and starched shirt and black tie. I even went so far as to polish my shoes. If I only had a hat and a couple of *payos* in front of my ears, I would be the perfect likeness of a Hasid. My contrary nature excluded me from inclusion in that blessed group. Instead, I looked as though I were attending a funeral. For all I knew, maybe I was.

"Richie, you got anything like a note pad or receipt book?" I leaned over the front seat from the back to gather my thoughts.

"Yeah. Why?"

"Make out a receipt for five dollars."

"A fin? What gives? That was a buck and a quarter, tops, a buck fifty with your usual tip."

"Don't worry. The man in this house has money to spare." Perhaps I was pre-judging a person I had never met but I certainly knew the type.

Richie reminded of a young kid back in

penmanship class scrawling out a refined looking invoice. I appreciated his efforts.

The brick walkway snaked its way through an immaculately manicured lawn, which was devoid of anything like mature adult trees to impede the majesty of the house. While many others preferred privacy, the owner of this house was not afraid of showing off his wealth and subsequent importance. The flowerbeds circling the front contained an abundance of yellow and lavender flowers. The petunias and crocus gave off a sweet fragrance and also exuded a regal elegance. The first day of Spring always felt like a coronation. I was about to meet a king.

Between bureaucrats in the police department, high-ranking officers in the army, and several local politicians, I personally encountered many men who strove for power and would do anything to hold on to it. They used intimidation as a first weapon before moving on to extortion and then physical violence. Avoidance was the best tool to stay out of their way. But as written in the Sanhedrin: *Even when you're minding your own business, your enemy feels threatened.* And to me, all men of wealth and power could be the enemy if they wanted to.

The ominous bronze lion head that greeted me at eye level held a large iron ring. Doorknockers were more elegant than bells. It was everything I could do not to sound like a police officer at the door executing a warrant. A mostly bald man wearing a suit akin to a tuxedo answered my clunky inquiry. The only other time I went to a house with a butler was when I was a policeman responding to a trespassing call at the Wey Mansion over on Park Place. This time it was before noon on a beautiful spring day.

"Harold Bergman for Mr. Whitman."

Like an automaton, he turned forty-five degrees toward the foyer and, with a flattened hand and an extended index finger, wordlessly pointed in the direction of the parlor. He made no effort to escort me, so I meandered on my own.

There wasn't any soot in the shallow fireplace. Either the bald butler recently cleaned it immaculately or it was nothing more than a showpiece to further impress. Atop the mantel was a Staffordshire clock surrounded by bronze wolves. The cherrywood paneling throughout gave the impression of a library more than a parlor although there weren't any books in sight. Perhaps Mr. Whitman was too busy to read. A decidedly uncomfortable looking settee was on the opposite side of two equally uncomfortable chairs with an extremely low coffee table in the middle. You would strain your back reaching down to pick up or put down a cup and saucer. The room was for appearance and not use. It was saying, "Here lives a man of wealth and stature. Please do not stay too long."

Albert Whitman walked into the room silently, whether that was his intention or not. My years on the police force and in the war made me attune to the slightest of movements. He was tall, perhaps approaching six feet, and was in between slender and average build. He combed back what little hair remained. It was the yellowish side of gray, quite like his eyes. He wore a gray pinstripe suit, deep blue shirt and tie, and cordovan wingtip shoes. There was no wedding ring, only an area showing more pale flesh. An unidentifiable signet ring sat prominently on his left pinkie finger. I placed him in his late fifties. He may have been older. He may have been Dorian Gray for all I knew.

"You're Bergman." It was less of a question and more of a statement, as though he were reminding me who I was. Fortunately, I hadn't forgotten. "I don't allow smoking in my home."

"I don't smoke," I responded, slightly surprised at the comment.

"I suppose you don't drink either. I thought all you detectives had a bottle of cheap rye in your office desk drawer." He had obviously acquired his impression about private investigators from Humphrey Bogart or Dick Powell. He hoped I would justify his biases. I simply remained quiet. "You any relation to Jay Bergman of Bergman Oil?"

"No, sir." I waited for him to continue but he simply stared at me. "Nor am I kin to Arthur Bergman of Keep Klean System or Ben Bergman, the linotype operator at the *Eagle*." I got both those names from the Polk directory on a whim.

I expected him to make a comment about the impetuousness of my youth or another melodramatic retort. "Tell me about yourself," he blurted in staccato.

This was the typical start of conversations with the rich and powerful when they required the services of an individual they believed beneath them. Such dialogue was a pretense, an opportunity to display their superiority even though they had few powers of perception. If nothing more, it gave them the feeling of control.

"I would have thought a man of your business sensibility would have a thorough dossier on me."

"I would like to hear it from you."

"I was a cop, then I was a soldier, and now I'm a private investigator." I hadn't rehearsed it, but it came out sounding that way. All of it was true. Perhaps he was wanting a more glamorous recitation.

"That's all?"

"Yep."

A raised eyebrow showed the disappointment at my brevity.

"And…you're Jewish."

There it was. The comment designed to indicate he may or may not have umbrage against the Jews. This guy was no Pharaoh. However, like others before him, he came across that way. In my experience, it didn't matter what else I might have done in my life. Being a Jew was the thing that made me different.

"My religious beliefs do not impact my professionalism. So before you start wondering whether I work on the Sabbath, the answer is I do."

"That limp. From the war?"

Apparently, he had seen me walk into the room prior to his grand entrance. The pleasantness of the weather only made it less bothersome. However, it was a constant reminder of a dangerous time. A man like him would look upon any defect as a character flaw. Somewhat like my religion.

"I had to give up my aspirations for the hundred-metres in the Olympics." We stared at each other, neither blinking. Showing him his wealth and stature couldn't overwhelm me more than made up for my limp and Judaism. Maybe he was looking for an impetuous private detective after all.

"What do you know about me?" The follow-up

7

question was one of ego and capability. Guys like Whitman had a need to know two things: how important they were in my eyes and how much research I had done on them.

"You own Whitson Import & Export and apparently make enough money to own a house in Eastborough. You make philanthropic donations to the museum and a few other charities of note but nothing that puts you in the spotlight of the social section of the newspaper. Or any other section, for that matter." I paused for a moment to determine if he would challenge my assertion. "So what is it you import and export?" I popped out. The answer was of less importance to me than to him.

"Anything that will make a profit." He smiled gleefully. The tension melted from him as I apparently passed his test, whatever that might have been. With a gracious hand, he directed me toward one of those uncomfortable chairs while he sat upright in the settee.

"I need you to find my daughter."

I'd learned not to ask too many questions right up front. They're eventually necessary to fill in the blanks but initially it is best to let a prospective client tell his story. In Whitman's case, I played dentist and started pulling teeth. After fifteen seconds of silence, I realized I had to do all the work.

"When did you last see her?"

"Here, two nights ago."

"What was the purpose of her visit?"

"No visit. She lives here."

"She comes and goes as she pleases?"

"She's a junior at Friends University. I give her a little leeway on the weekends but expect her to maintain her academic standing."

"So it's Wednesday and she hasn't been home since Monday," I responded, restating the facts we had so far. "Is that enough to worry about?"

"Whether it is or it isn't, I want her found."

As a private investigator, it was good enough for me. My sensibilities and beliefs had nothing to do with those of a client. Whitman wanted his daughter found, that was the job as stated, and he was willing to pay for it.

"It would help if I knew what she looked like."

He searched around the room desperately, finally setting his sights on a small baby grand gathering dust over by a bay window shrouded in heavy curtains. Several framed photos stood there providing the musical instrument with an alternate function. As we walked over, I saw pictures of a matronly woman with a lot of pride, two immaculately dressed men one of whom was Whitman, and a young woman with a passionate fire in her eyes that closely resembled those of her father. He removed the photo from its frame and handed it to me.

"The university has been instructed to provide any assistance they can."

"Do you know any of her friends or who she hangs out with?" He shook his head negatively. "Does she have any hobbies?"

"None that I'm aware of."

"What about a car?"

"My driver brings her to and from school."

There was a whole line of questioning attached to that one response. Did the driver take her somewhere the past weekend? If not, who picked her up? Did she say where she was going? Instead, I nodded because there were no viable answers forthcoming and nothing more to do at the time. I've had jobs that started with less. It was more about how I finished.

"I get twenty-five dollars a day plus expenses."

"I expect itemized receipts."

I pulled Richie's paper out of my pocket and handed it to Whitman.

"We'll start with this. I don't have a car either. This is for my driver."

Whitman reached into his pants pocket and pulled out a fiver as though he expected me to ask. I gave him one final look in the eyes, searching for an inkling there that could lead me in a direction. There was nothing. I merely nodded as I headed out the door. The butler wasn't around to show me out which was fine because I knew my way by now.

I plopped down into the back seat of the hack and handed Richie the bill.

"Looks like I'll need you for a couple of days. And the money will be good."

Just as long as we both came out ahead.

Chapter Two

The housing shortage after the Second World War was not expected. Apparently, aircraft manufacturing remained strong, and the influx of workers made it difficult for returning veterans like me. This was true for employment as well as places to live. It would have been feasible to live with my father, especially since my mother had passed away shortly after my deployment. As it was his religious beliefs countered with my new profession, and it wasn't my intent to be the cause of friction. We were all each of us had left in the world. While I visited him regularly, I still sought my own abode.

It was practically a miracle I found an opening at the Arch Plaza Apartments, a sturdy two-story building at 730 N. Market with eleven total units. Constance Hanover was the gracious landlady in her seventies who had difficulty renting the front unit due to unfortunate circumstances as well as a bit of unsubstantiated gossip.

"Mr. O'Malley died suddenly and, well, that gave the appearance of a curse of some sort," she explained to me in the early fall of 1945. The prior resident, Padraic O'Malley, was a long-time bartender at Tom's Inn over on North Seneca. According to various stories passed around, he had a colorful way about him, claiming at one time to be a leprechaun, among other things. You either embraced his Irish charm or avoided him entirely.

"And those cats!" she added with disdain.

The first-floor apartment contained a main room looking out over the street and pocket doors separating the quaint kitchenette, the bathroom, and the small bedroom. The cats of which she spoke were two Manx, one an elegant tuxedo named Lady Mittens and the other a bright orange fellow called Sir Pounce. None of O'Malley's co-workers would take them in, and Mrs. Hanover didn't have the heart to evict them, being the good Christian woman she was. That I was willing to move in with a guaranteed one-year lease and maintain the feline residents allowed her to offer me a reduced monthly rent. The place was in proximity to everywhere in downtown I needed to be. I did not believe in curses and had no aversion to felines I was aware of. I just didn't know what I was getting myself into.

Richie dropped me off after my visit with Whitman. I indicated I would head on over to the university late in the afternoon and he should pick me up at three. I reminded him to have spare receipt books available. His eager smile indicated he was ready for an adventure. His labored breathing due to the excitement had me worried.

Mrs. Hanover placed a small bench outside my front door so prospective clients wouldn't have to wait on the stoop or in the street. It was done as much for propriety as for privacy. She allowed me to put a sign on the door itself, reading H. BERGMAN, INVESTIGATOR, with the caveat I would not be entertaining clients at all hours and disturbing the neighbors. At the time, I was barely making ends meet and did not think that to be a problem.

Patiently waiting like a penitent member of a congregation was a colored woman, perhaps in her mid to late forties, with smooth skin and thin lines around her bloodshot eyes. She sat delicately with her hands in her lap.

"Mr. Bergman?"

"Yes, ma'am."

"I need your help." It was a respectful supplication that struck my heart immediately. It was contrary to the dispassionate inquiry of the morning.

I unlocked the door and waved her in silently. I had the pocket doors closed to keep the cats from rummaging around in the parlor when I was out. We had plenty of time for play and ear scratching when my day ended. While I didn't have as much furniture as the house in Eastborough, I was proud to say it was far more comfortable. She sat in the love seat, and I opposite in one of the upholstered chairs.

"My name is Althea Washington. I'm concerned about my husband, Alonzo."

"How so?"

"He hasn't been home for four days."

In the span of only a couple of hours, I encountered people whose loved ones had gone missing, likely for two entirely different reasons.

"Is that unusual?"

"Oh, yes."

"Does he work?" She nodded affirmatively. "Where?"

"Cudahy Meat Packing. Up on North Broadway."

"What does he do there?"

"Night watchman. Goes in at six of an evening and

13

comes home four, maybe five the next morning. He's there Monday through Friday. Sometimes more."

"Is that all he does?"

Even though we looked directly at each other, her eyes held a vacant stare, seeing something not in this room. It was the kind of gaze I observed from soldiers in the war. Men were alive, physically, but had lost their willpower, their motivation, their very soul. Althea Washington had a husband. More than likely the struggles of life dried him up.

"Mr. Bergman, Alonzo is a good man. Takes care of me real fine."

"I'm sure he does, ma'am."

"There are times he has more money than a night watchman ought to have, you know?" She didn't have to spell it out for me. "He always comes home, though."

"But not since Saturday?" She shook her head negatively. "Was he working at the plant that night?"

"Left about seven of an evening. Said he had business to take care of that'd mean a few extra dollars. I told him I'd wait up for him." She hung her head. "He hasn't come back since."

"Any chance he left you for another woman?" It was a painful thing to ask. It implied she wasn't good enough in an unidentified yet palpable manner, wasn't pretty enough, submissive enough, giving enough. I asked this question countless times before, and it never got easier, sticking in my throat like a shard of glass. When you have a necessary question to ask, it's best to just ask it.

"He ain't like that."

I gave her my best reassuring smile. It was really

all I had to offer.

"I can check with the plant, maybe talk to his supervisor, and see what he knows. Does your husband have any friends or close associates?"

"Randy Mason and he grew up in Topeka. Alonzo and me moved down here when Randy got him the job three years ago. There's also a white man named Johnnie Pajak he mentioned a couple of times. I never met him."

I nodded my head, thinking I had more information from this sad woman than from a rich man who hired me by telegram. In both cases, it didn't really matter. It was my job to do what I could when asked regardless of what I received.

"I'll ask around. Who knows? Maybe he'll come back on his own. Where do you live?"

"North Cleveland. Two blocks down from New Hope Baptist Church."

"I know it."

She smiled at my awareness of both her people and her religion.

I stood up, forming a notion or two in my mind.

She stood up as well, head still hung.

"I don't have all that much money..." Her voice was barely a whisper.

"We'll work something out."

She lifted her head and smiled.

For me, it was a *mitzvah,* to do a service out of duty and human responsibility without thinking in terms of personal gain. In a single instant, Hope had returned to her heart. As I escorted her out, uncertain as to how she got here or how she would make it home, I had another realization.

"Mrs. Washington, why me?"

"I don't understand."

"I'm white. I'm Jewish. I can't imagine there isn't a colored man who could assist in this for you."

She smiled graciously.

"I consulted with my pastor."

"I see."

She smiled again. This time there was a touch of whimsy to it.

"My pastor said he had his watch repaired by your father. Referred to him as a man of integrity. Figured you'd be the same."

"Yes, ma'am." With such a proclamation, she bestowed upon me the honor of respect.

As I approached the pocket doors, the meowing became incessant. It was as though the two felines were galley slaves seeking their freedom. Sir Pounce immediately jumped up on my lap as I sat back down in the chair while Lady Mittens rubbed up against my pant leg. For this one moment, the whole world was right here in this room.

Outside of a soft purring, a stillness returned to me. Certain cases made me question how the world worked and what Adonai supposedly had in store for us. As a policeman, a beat cop working his way toward becoming a detective, it was solely about facts, a logical chain created to lead you from the question to the answer. Then, the District Attorney gets the case to determine whether to bring it to trial. As a rabbi, we speak of Divine Providence, perhaps as enunciated by Maimonides. *"This Universe remains perpetually with the same properties with which the Creator has endowed it... none of these will ever be changed except by way of miracle in some individual instances."*

The problem for me was I witnessed so-called Laws broken during war but did not hold fast to the notion of miracles. As a private investigator, I always saw the gray in between the black and the white. Perhaps both other professions had firm beliefs that did not perplex a man's soul and make him shudder.

When I considered these two cases, it was as though we simply had a wayward daughter and a mischievous husband both on the prowl for whatever it was intangible to me. The thing to consider was whether they would find what they sought and if it would satiate them enough to return home or stay away even longer. It was merely a personal thought. For the moment, my goal was simply to find them.

There was still a bag of Spratt's dried cat food in the pantry, but I opened a can of Kit-E-Kat instead. I divided it into two equal portions, although Sir Pounce had an attitude in that regard, he being slightly bigger and thinking he required more sustenance. The relative calm of their feeding frenzy accompanied a peacefulness of satisfaction, thus achieving their happiness. I always wondered why it wasn't so easy for humans.

At three on the nose, Richie was in front, and the cats returned to the cozy confinement of the back of the apartment behind the pocket doors. We headed over to Friends University to find out about the academic life of Caroline Whitman and whatever else might be meaningful.

The Davis Administration building was an impressive structure with a tall clock tower that stood out over the city like a stoic watchman. Perhaps you could call it a lighthouse on the plains. There was a kind of grandeur to it that hid the darker aspects of those who occupied such buildings. Whitman referred me to the registrar, a man by the name of Branford Cooper. He was a slender gentleman, short in stature, likely approaching sixty, who appeared consumptive. Despite his professional wardrobe, his eyes were set back with a bit of a reddishness as though he were feverish. He continuously licked dry lips while rubbing his hands to get warm even though it was a little over sixty degrees. With such a slight frame, a strong Kansas wind would likely have blown him over. His handshake reminded me of a wet fish.

"I'm sorry you came all this way," he said as though I were one of the Three Magi. "However, I previously advised Mr. Whitman Caroline had not been attending classes for about a month, maybe two." The warble in his throat was a clear indication he was afraid of telling the truth both to Albert Whitman and to me. His high-pitched squeal of a voice was decidedly more defensive in nature, even though all I had previously said was my name.

I stood in his office stunned, wondering why Whitman suggested I come here for information he already obtained. It made it appear as though Caroline Whitman's disappearance was less of a mystery to him. Now it was more of one to me.

"Do you know any of her friends?" I asked quietly to allay his fears.

"No."

"Can you check her class schedule and see if she has the same classes with any of the other girls?"

The sigh that emerged was slight and almost

dismissive. It took several minutes for Cooper to contact an assistant who then had to retrieve the files and further compare names. Two young ladies shared three classes with Miss Whitman: Annette Copeland and Arlene Guthrie. They were both finishing up their Social Sciences class on the third floor. The assistant escorted me as much out of decorum as to identify them.

Annette and Arlene were both fresh faced and innocent looking gals, brought up correctly by their parents, and were likely regular attendees at church. Their pure demeanor relaxed after they notified Cooper's assistant it was okay to speak with me alone. The façade melted as quickly as a block of ice on the Fourth of July.

"Caroline was only here because of her dad," Annette began. "It's not like he was going to let her be a secretary or a teacher or anything like that."

"Then why go to college?" I asked.

"It was a status thing," Arlene responded. "A gal with a degree is a lot more appealing to the proper suitor."

"Oh? And what makes a guy a 'proper suitor'?"

"Well, certainly not a colored jazz musician." Giggles from the two of them followed Annette's comment. I stood there non-plussed. "Caroline spends most of her time in the clubs."

"She's a real hep cat."

"She's down with the jive."

"One sweet frail."

"A serious mop."

My head swiveled back and forth as if I watched Jack Kramer and Fred Parker at the U.S. National

Championships. I couldn't really tell if these girls used the slang sarcastically or if they embraced it as well. Suddenly, their expression changed to one of determined protectors, scowls followed by finger pointing, figuring I was an as-yet undetermined enemy.

"Look, mister," Annette said with a deeper tone in her voice, "Caroline is not interested in her dad's business or her dad's house or her dad's anything."

"She doesn't even care about his money," Arlene chimed in.

With that, they walked away, not giving a thought to looking back or noticing my reaction. While I was certain Caroline Whitman was somehow missing, it was not as Albert Whitman implied. If what these girls said had any resonance to it, the father's desire to retrieve his daughter might not have been as paternal as it first appeared.

Chapter Three

It was pushing five o'clock by the time we got back downtown making it too late to try to reach out to Alonzo Washington's supervisor at Cudahy. Those kind of guys work nine to five and leave the trivial tasks to stiffs like Alonzo. I figured I'd put on decent threads and head out in search of Caroline Whitman a little later in the evening. It was a crapshoot considering it was only Wednesday night. There was just a slight chance of success unless boredom or restlessness overtook her.

Most of my experience with jazz came by way of the radio whenever I could pull in a station from Topeka or Kansas City. The musicians' strike of '42 and '43 never much impacted me as I was in Europe. Nightlife was only significant when I drew late night beats on Douglas or Broadway as a cop before the war. Even to this day, the early rising soldier's life was still in my blood. On those occasions when the job required me to be a night owl, I felt distinctly out of sorts, a stranger in a strange land. This would take a concerted effort.

"Say, Richie, feel like going nightclubbing tonight?" I asked as we pulled up to a hack stand on Douglas and Market.

"Sure, Hirsch." Heavy rapid breathing intermingled with a wheeze impacted his voice. It was at least an octave lower. Having heard that sound many times before, I recognized it as the onset of an asthma attack. It had been a busy and exciting day for him, one filled with the kind of stress he didn't sign up for even though he was always willing.

"I guess I better call it a night, huh?"

I nodded like a Jewish mother.

Parked right in front of us was Charlie Argento, leaning against his hack and reading the morning edition of the *Wichita Beacon*. In early 1941, I found him passed out drunk waiting on a fare. I told him in a rather pointed way I thought it better he finish his shift at once. Another arrest would have lost his medallion making it that much harder to support his wife and two young daughters. A minor act of discretion made me aces in his book.

Dark haired, almost black, always slicked back, and deep olive skin gave him an exotic look, like a character out of an Italian opera. He was the least foreign acting guy I knew. Our eyes met after my whistle.

"American Airlines announced the purchase of eight Stratocruisers for service on its trans-Atlantic routes," he practically recited from the newspaper article. "Probably make it easier to get a flight overseas."

"I've already been there," I replied.

He had a blank look on his face for a moment. "Oh, yeah," he responded with a smile when he took my meaning. "So what gives, Mr. B.?"

"I'll be hitting the clubs tonight. Want to be my chauffeur?"

"What was up with Richie?" He knew I treated Richie Mayer like a kid brother and didn't mind all that much I threw a lot of business in Richie's direction. Charlie was a stand-up guy.

"He was having one of his episodes. Needs to sack out for the night."

"Well, I'm up for it. I live with three gals that are always looking for a new dress or shoes."

I glanced up at the Woolf Brothers clothing store not a half a block behind us.

"Must be quite a temptation parking the hack so close."

"You know it," he responded, shaking his head in dismay. "So when and where?"

"My place. Seven o'clock. Oh, and you'll need to make out a receipt for the job."

"This a case?"

"Yes, it is. And the man wants receipts. So make them hefty." Charlie smiled knowing new clothes were right around the corner.

I let Richie drop me off at home just so I could check on him. He often shrugged off the notion his condition impacted his life in any fashion. A while back, I passed along my father's recommendations based on Talmudic writings, but Richie was content with the aminophylline tablets the doctor gave him as well as large amounts of coffee. I had to laugh to myself when he would say, "I better call it a night," figuring he'd be awake until past midnight.

I had a little over an hour and a half to relax and figure out how to handle these two cases. The first thing I did was make sure I filled the bowl in the kitchen with dry food as well as two shallow saucers of milk for Lady Mittens and Sir Pounce. Demanding cats do not allow for deep introspective thinking. The funny thing was my parents did not have any pets when I was growing up. While I had no innate love or hate for dogs or cats, somehow caring for these two had given me a purpose in the quiet times, when there were no jobs and the world and its madness swirled around in my ever-thinking skull. The love and devotion of these cats put everything into a proper perspective.

My head lay against the cushion of the sofa, one leg up and one leg on the floor, not necessarily sleeping posture, just enough of a recline to close my eyes and let images float. It was easy to recognize a defiant young girl, fortunate enough to come from a home of privilege and perhaps resentful of the control she granted her father to maintain it. Then, finding other aspects of the world that thrilled her, previously forbidden heretofore, and deciding, at least at this moment in time, these sordid desires were more important than a lifetime of culture and refinement. Certainly, Albert Whitman was nothing like Mildred Pierce.

Then again, to my way of thinking, he was neither cultured nor refined. His wealth afforded him the opportunity to buy the trappings of both. It was largely possession without appreciation. Nevertheless, as it is with most parents, he wanted more for his daughter than he had and would do whatever it took to ensure it. In this regard, I gave him more credit than when I first met him. Perhaps this was presuming a lot, but the man was paying me for a job. Naturally, this earned him the benefit of the doubt. For the time being.

I changed into a plain white shirt, striped tie, and a gray wool jacket that didn't match my trousers. Anyone looking at me would assume I was a complete and utter nebbish. Slickly dressed investigators are not as successful in making inquiries as a guy no one would give a second thought to if they even considered it enough. People needed to see me and then forget me just as quickly.

Charlie waited outside my building when I strode out at seven. Knowing him, it was likely he had been there for at least ten minutes. Opportunities like this were not as abundant for him, and his daughters were now older and often asked for newer clothing more frequently.

"Where to?" he asked as I hopped in the back.

"I'm looking for the jazz clubs."

"Well, that'd be Broadway, north or south. For the most part anyway."

I pulled out a quarter.

"Heads, north. Tails, south."

"So that's the way you professional investigators do it."

It came up tails.

I told Charlie to drive slow and easy, not make it look like we were in any kind of rush, and, if anyone asked, to act as though he had a sucker with dough as a fare. This could very well be a late night considering Caroline Whitman no longer had to get up early for classes.

We started at the Play-Mor, which was largely just a ballroom with mostly delicate music wafting through the air. The clientele was far too elegant to accommodate the high times and swinging crowd I assumed Annette and Arlene referred to earlier. It didn't take much more than standing in the doorway and scanning the crowd to realize this wasn't the place.

There was, however, wild music coming out of Mutt's Place as we pulled up. I was aware of a musician performing as Mutt & His Eight Ball Band, Mutt and His Cotton Club Orchestra, and Mutt's Five Piece Rhythm Band. I had no idea who Mutt really was, if he even existed, or if this place was his. Nevertheless, it gave me my first sign of hope.

It was a colored band, colored waiters, a colored hatcheck girl, and a colored bartender. The patrons were all white and seriously moving their bodies whether it was in their seats or on the tiny dance floor. The place was like a hypnotic ride at Joyland. It was the kind of music one could not ignore. I leaned clumsily on the bar, ordered a bourbon Manhattan as though I had no idea what it was, and watched a skilled man measure, shake, and pour. He smiled broadly as I took my first sip and then raised the glass in salute to his skills.

"Looks like a big hit with the kids." My voice grew louder as though the music was getting to me.

"Them kids dig the sound," he responded in a normal tone, implying I should do the same.

"My younger sister told me about this place. Said I might find a like-minded lady."

"Why didn't she just fix you up herself?" There was nothing to his comment one way or the other. Either it was casual conversation, or he wasn't buying my story. I told him I would see what I could find. Wandering around aimlessly, I kept my eyes peeled for the girl whose photograph I committed to memory. In reflecting back on my conversation with her friends, I couldn't be sure if she was fond of black musicians personally or for their music. That might be obvious whenever I found her.

I struck out at Idlewise, which was largely a beer parlor with a sweaty old tone-deaf white guy in a ragged tuxedo on a tinny piano. I walked into the Kaliko Kat, closer to Mutt's Place in terms of style and music, just as Dixie Cobb was blowing a mean trumpet solo. I met him in the summer of 1940, impressed by his poise and sense of sophistication. He had left town shortly before my enlistment. Our eyes met and he nodded.

Right after the set, I met him just off the stage. He nodded in remembrance while he wiped the sweat from his brow. He was the best-dressed guy in the room.

"Rabbi," he said, reminding of his nickname for me. "Seems you ditched the blues."

"I've gone private," I responded. "Where have you been?"

"New York mostly. I took any gig that came along and worked with some real hep bands. Came across this cat last year, name of Miles Davis from St. Louis. Kid's got chops. I mean, serious chops."

"Like you?"

"No, man. He's got something real special."

I laid down my story, told him what I was looking for. While he had his share of lady admirers, white and colored, none of them matched the description I gave him. He did indicate he'd keep an eye open.

It was about eleven o'clock when I walked into Martin's Blue Bonnett. The ad out front indicated an exclusive appearance by Junior Johnson this forthcoming Friday and Saturday evening. Tonight, however, the three-piece combo (piano, bass, and drum) put down a tight set. The toes tapped, the fingers snapped, and the crowd was lively.

Fortunately, I ran into Tiny Taylor, a musician I almost arrested one time on possession of reefer back in 1939. He tipped me off to slot machines at the Grapevine Inn so I let him walk, advising him I would be on his tail if the info proved false.

I let him know what I was working on, figuring it was best to be straight considering I no longer had the backing of the Wichita Police Department. The description I gave him of Caroline Whitman resonated. He was aware of several young white college girls making the rounds in the last few months but didn't get the impression they were all that hep to the music.

"It's like they come in and put on a face and make like they real cool. Then they go off."

"What? Like other clubs?"

"No, man. Somewhere…else. And then they come back later. Much later. Dig?"

I was never one to accuse a musician of making sense, given the English language is not their first choice for communication. I could only guess he was mugglin' in the back before I met up with him.

I felt like Cinderella and thought it was best for my head to plop down on my own pillow before midnight. Even though I gave him a sawbuck, Charlie wrote me a great receipt for twenty dollars. He told me he was ready for one of these jobs again, and I reminded him there was still North Broadway to consider.

Neither of the cats was much interested in my return, both comfortably ensconced at the end of my bed, each of them far apart from the other. I slid under the covers without disturbing either. What struck me most as I drifted off to sleep was where these college girls were going once they got to the clubs and what held their attention more than the music. I felt out of touch with the world now or at least young people barely past their teenage years.

Chapter Four

There is nothing to compare to waking up with a cat lying on your chest and staring at you with another sprawled across your ankles and pinning you down. If they were hungry, there would have been unremitting howling and perhaps a few well-placed claws. This morning, Sir Pounce had a disaffected look on his face and Lady Mittens acted as though she had nowhere better to go. This was tantamount to medieval torture. Either that or a rather expressive way of showing their love.

A shower preceded my first cup of coffee. I was fortunate to discover two eggs and half a loaf of bread remaining in the icebox. There was obviously no bacon or ham. It wasn't I kept kosher, per se. But I did make a concerted effort to maintain a degree of respect for my religion. While I sat in the cramped chair and table of my kitchenette, it occurred to me to visit Cudahy Meat Packing plant to determine exactly what the husband of my other client did there. It also would be helpful to get a line on Alonzo Washington from others who may have known him.

My acquaintance with Sullivan Starks, the barber at the De Luxe Barber Shop on East 9th Street, was due to a divorce case involving his cousin. He still wasn't all that comfortable with me being inside his store asking about another colored man.

"Yeah, I know Alonzo. So?" It was matter-of-fact but it had an air of caution to it.

"Just asking around, Sully. That was all."

"Ain't seen him in a while." With that as his final word, he returned to cleaning combs and scissors.

The nice counter lady at the Lu Grand Store was far more deferential and just as evasive.

"Althea does most of the shopping for the household. The times I've seen her with Alonzo he seemed bored to be here. Like most husbands. You know what I mean?"

If I didn't know any better, I would have sworn everyone was covering up for him. For what reason I couldn't tell.

It took me talking to a security guard at the gate and one at the front entrance to find the person who supposedly was in charge. The tall and big boned redhead named Aaron Lautenberg was the man Alonzo Washington reported to, although he never provided me any kind of a title or even so much as announced himself as a supervisor. His air of supremacy was supposed to indicate a level of importance, regardless of the salutation. Gruff, disinterested, and uttering as few words as possible in response through a gritted unlit cigar, Lautenberg was not annoyed with me as much as the world in general and all who might intrude upon his domain. He had the air of an Albert Whitman type, just without the money or the accoutrements. In my mind, that made him insignificant.

"Bergman?" he said while squinting his eyes possibly passing for deep thought. "What kind of name is that?"

"American." I heard the question thousands of

times. It bored me to tears.

"You Jewish?" he asked, the word tripping on his tongue like pronouncing the name of a foreigner.

"Yep."

"Didn't know there were Jewish private dicks." There was the briefest notion of playing games with him by listing Shmuel Spadestein and Phillip Marlowvitz, but I had little patience and less time. When I didn't respond, he continued. "Look, guys are always running out on their wives," he responded dismissively to the explanation for my inquiry. "It's either a skirt or some hooch, and they both run out pretty quick. Guaranteed he'll be back." He winked reassuringly.

"You married?"

"Nah. My wife ran out on me." He laughed uproariously at his own comment. I sat there non-committal, understanding what he took time to understand.

"What can you tell me about Randy Mason?" I finally asked him after the humor waned. He cleared his throat and returned to a more serious attitude although his acting was along the line of Huntz Hall or any of the Bowery Boys.

"He comes to work on time, doesn't get in any trouble, and then goes home."

"Can I talk to him?"

The clock above the door to his office captured his attention.

"He gets out of work in fifteen minutes. You can probably grab him at the front gate."

I thanked him for his time because that was literally all he had given me. It wasn't as though he hid anything. He didn't have any abiding concern over a colored night watchman or the man's friend. There was an apprehensive look in his eyes as I left, turning to close the door behind me. It was a kind of fear based on uncertainty. A man like him only thrived in an environment he knew and could control.

Based on Lautenberg's description, it was easy to spot Randy Mason. He was a short guy; under five foot six I would guess. He had his hair cut close to the scalp, big cheekbones, and eyes that bugged out in anticipation of an attack at any moment. My calling out his name suddenly was a testament to his apprehension. It took me four long strides to get to him to allay his fears as quickly as possible.

"Althea sent me to look for Alonzo." It was as direct as possible.

"I don't know where he is." The response came too quick as though he had rehearsed it for several days. He was hoping it was to be his only piece of dialogue.

"Sure. But you know where he could be. Right?"

"Mister, that man could be any place far as I know. He could be back in Topeka."

I sensed a devoted friend who wasn't about to give out anything if he didn't feel it would do any good or if the one asking the questions posed a direct threat.

"Look, you talk to Mrs. Washington and see that I'm on the level. She just wants to know where he is. That's all." He nodded at me, eyes still showing great fear. "You know a guy named Johnnie Pajak?"

"That boy is crazy." He spun his head around as though the recitation of the name was like calling a demon from Sheol.

"Oh?"

"You need a strong-arm, he's the guy."

"Who does he work for?"

"Who doesn't he work for? Show him the green, that boy is mean."

"What'd he have to do with Alonzo?"

"Alonzo's just about as big as he is. Johnnie always had a need for a guy to work with, and I sure didn't fit the bill." Randy started looking around, swiveling his head as though it were about to pop off. "I can't be talking to you." Just like one of my cats, he skedaddled right off as I turned to look in the opposite direction. It made no sense to follow him.

I got the drift of what else the missing Mr. Washington might have been up to. It also dawned on me he could have gotten into more deadly trouble than he anticipated, figuring a double sawbuck wouldn't involve anything dangerous. It occurred to me I might have to eventually meet up with Mrs. Washington in the morgue, a decidedly unpleasant prospect.

It would have done my father a world of good to share Sabbath dinner with him. However, it was Thursday, and I knew my opportunities at the nightclubs would be greater on the weekend. Dropping a nickel in a phone booth at a drug store near Twenty-First Street and Broadway, I inquired if my presence that evening would be acceptable.

To the members of Hebrew Congregation of Wichita, Menachem Mendel Bergman was a passionate practitioner of Judaism, a *hazzan* whose voice had faded yet whose heart was strong. To the many customers who came to him for jewelry and watch repairs on his small shop on East Douglas, he was a dedicated and highly skilled craftsman. To me, for nearly thirty years, he was Pop, the man who nurtured my mind and taught me to question and seek my own answers.

He still lived in the same house on South Kansas Street, halfway between the temple and his shop. He preferred not to be too far away from either. The labor of his hands and the espousing of his faith fulfilled all his needs. He was the truest example of a *mensch,* a man of integrity and honor. I had never known him to lie to anyone or commit deceptive practices. All people were equal in his eyes. His greatest disappointment, so far as I knew, was my choice of profession, both prior to the war and now. But he never spoke openly about it.

I got to the house a little after six, well before sunset. As per my youth, I kissed the mezuzah before entering, removed my shoes, and took the yarmulke from the small table by the front door. He left it for me knowing full well I did not currently own one. He was lighting the candles as I came into the dining room. Everything remained exactly as it did after my mother passed away nearly four years ago. My father's explanation was one should not intrude upon perfection as everything she had ever done was complete unto itself.

With his head covered and wearing his prayer shawl, my father had the look of a scholarly man, one who should be studying the Talmud rather than straining his eyes to fix ladies watches. He had aged a bit since my mother's passing, trying desperately to hold onto whatever meaning he could in his life. His hopes for me were the crux of those.

Barukh atah Adonai Eloheinu, Melekh ha'olam, bo're minei m'zonot.

"Amen," I responded quietly.

I sat as he brought out a platter of baked fish, a bowl of steamed carrots, and a fresh loaf of challah. For the first five minutes or so, we served ourselves and sat in silence. I knew from the past it was up to my father to break the silence as it was his prerogative to break the bread.

"Are you working?"

"Yes."

"Tell me."

I recounted the events of the last two days, the house in Eastborough and the man who occupied it, and the pious woman who longed for her husband's safety. He prodded me for more details with minor questions designed to provoke detailed responses. I outlined what I learned and what I thought, enunciating the difference between the two. Speaking to him in this way gave me a sense of both comfort and relief. Unlike the detectives on film, I had no office and no secretary, nothing but my own skills and instincts. At times, it was easy to find one's self lost. The goal was to get back on the right path.

"Harold, you should not think so poorly of Mr. Whitman. His wealth is a curse as much as it is a blessing."

"I don't think poorly of his wealth, Pop. I'm concerned about the power it gives him to control his daughter. She is likely rebelling against his, I don't know, strict nature and lack of understanding."

"Perhaps she requires a firm hand. Did you not indicate you believe her mother has passed away?"

I could always count on my father being the Voice of Reason, as opposed to the Devil's Advocate. While he would have preferred I followed a different path in life, he was not going to interfere with the one I had chosen. If it were possible, he wished to offer a kind of guidance not found elsewhere in the day-to-day life of the city.

"I'll grant you a mother's influence over a young girl can be profound. It is likely Whitman allowed his wife to deal with the domestic aspect of their lives and now finds himself unprepared. However, beyond all of that, there is something that is just not right," I said. "It was more than youthful rebellion. I sense Caroline Whitman has gotten herself into a predicament she may have trouble getting out of."

"The same as Mr. Washington."

"Exactly."

"Be eager to acquire knowledge," my father responded from the Talmud, "for it does not come to thee by inheritance."

For my part, I thought in my mind of Proverbs 28:20. *"A faithful man shall abound with blessings: but he that maketh haste to be rich shall not be innocent."* Something wasn't right about the first case I accepted, but I did not know whether it was the father or the daughter.

I helped clean the dishes and sat with my father in the parlor. All discussions regarding my work ended at the dinner table. My father lit his favorite pipe and allowed the smoke to fill the small room. It reminded me of incense. There was always the feeling we were in temple together, which was good considering the last time I was there was for my bar mitzvah. I understood why people looked upon him favorably and yearned to be a man like him. The hug prior to my departure was the same every time, as though this might be the last time I would see him. It was not, as others assumed, to be a morbid thought. In our faith, we believe in the time we have together with family, dear friends, and just walking this earth, so we value it preciously.

I walked up to Douglas Street and hailed a cab, spending a few moments reminiscing about my youth. There was a time when all I read was the Old Testament, the Talmud, or Master Detective magazines. Even then, I found myself caught between the sacred and the profane. Feeling a bit whimsical, I told the cabbie to drop me off at Douglas and Market, deciding to walk the seven blocks on this pleasant spring evening.

The farther I walked north away from Douglas and downtown, the fewer street lights there were. It was nearing nine o'clock and the sun had already set. The main drag was behind me, and the soft breeze played like a single note on a violin. I first heard the footsteps past the U.S. Courthouse after crossing Third Street. They were regular and even and matched my pace precisely. The fact there was no speeding up or slowing down was what got my attention.

While Central was a broader intersection, there was hardly any traffic coming through. I picked up my pace to a jog to cross it. Even though I stayed on the west side of the street alongside the ornate Sedgwick County Courthouse, the regular pace of those footsteps continued, the faint echo now growing a bit louder. I crossed the street quickly, without warning, right at the house with the two white lions standing guard. This time the pace of the footsteps quickened and were about three to four feet behind me.

"Best keep your nose out of other people's business." It was the baritone voice of a colored man.

"But it is my business," I uttered. "A wife is looking for her husband. That's all."

"She be better off without him."

I stopped suddenly. He did as well. My shoulder started to twitch, turn inward toward the right.

"You don't want to be turning around. You got nothing to look at here."

I hadn't gotten a line on Alonzo Washington enough to judge whether he carried a gun or not. I stayed still out of an abundance of caution.

"I can help you." I didn't intend to sound as pleading as I did.

"Ain't nobody can help me, mister. I seen too much."

"Let me try."

There was no response. Was he thinking about the proposition or eliminating me as a possible threat? Two or three minutes went by. There was no breathing or movement. I turned around to find the emptiness of the night. No one else was in sight and the street was devoid of shadows. I continued for another block and a half until I got home. That was a place Alonzo Washington no longer had for the time being.

Chapter Five

I joined the Wichita Police Department in 1937 immediately after my graduation from Wichita University. At the time, my parents felt I wasted four years of higher education as they could not fathom what a policeman would require other than a badge and a gun. While my degree in Business Administration did not prove applicable, the first college graduate in the family was still a source of pride.

Instructors at the academy as well as my first supervisor, Sgt. Robert Schwarzlander, were impressed with my work ethic. My father could have told them that. Sgt. Schwarzlander gave me invaluable pointers what it was like to be a Jew in the police department and how, if I didn't want my career undermined, I would need skin as thick as shoe leather. These were lessons we had learned for over five thousand years.

It was in 1938 the department went through one of its toughest cases, the Wichita Ripper. I met an officer from the Arkansas City Police Department, Baron Witherspoon, brought in to consult on the case. He was a beat cop who had a special set of intuitive skills. While I was not personally involved, it was impressive to follow along the course of the investigation. I knew then I wanted to be a detective and go beyond my supervisor's level within the department. I applied myself using what I learned in college and proceeded in an almost academic fashion through all my work assignments. I took every assignment, worked overtime, and ensured I filed my reports meticulously and on time.

However, after Pearl Harbor, I put my own personal interests on the back burner in favor of what I had to do for my country. There was no second thought to the matter. When I came back from Europe, a lot of guys asked me if I was going to return to the department. It was the sensible thing to do but I couldn't bring myself to following any dogma, whether it was personal or professional. My greatest success as a soldier was staying alive. Medals for bravery were not the treasure I yearned for, even though they stood out nicely pinned to my dress uniform. It was the temperament of war itself that had me questioning the nature of humanity. I had to find out who I was all over again. I was Jacob traveling to Laban's house; alas, no dream could guide me, and the journey continued.

Nevertheless, my various friendships remained intact. There were many who were willing to lend a hand, pass on critical information, and do what they could for my small efforts. Floyd "Gunny" Gunsaullus rode one of the first radio-equipped motorcycles west of the Mississippi, rose to Division Commander, and finally promoted to Traffic Safety. A well-respected man nearly twenty years older than me, he acted more like a big brother always watching my back. I needed him once again.

"When I see you," he said with a smile, "I expect trouble."

"Who? Me?" Oh, for the days of vaudeville.

"What are you sniffing around for now?"

"The name Johnnie Pajak ring a bell?"

He let out a long whistle, not the kind of sound you made when an attractive gal walked by. More like one of exasperation with an oncoming headache.

"He's got a rap sheet, that's for sure. But it doesn't tell the whole story." I gave him a look to let him know I waited for him to continue. "Mostly Drunk & Disorderly. A fight here or there. You throw him in the can for twenty-four hours to cool off and send him on his way."

"But?"

"Word is he's muscle for hire. Doesn't choose sides. You need a big boy to back you up, hire Johnnie."

"Would he mix with the coloreds?"

"Like I said, he doesn't choose sides. Only color he's interested in is green."

"So I've heard."

Floyd gave me a description of a man who sounded more like a bear or a mythological demon. He was well over six-foot tall, wide shoulders and thick chest. He had a scruff of black hair and a knotted black beard. Maybe he was more of a pirate. I didn't think it would be difficult to find him but often men of this type didn't just stride down the middle of the street. The other problem was what to do when I eventually encountered him. My hand-to-hand combat training was woefully insufficient for the beast this man was made out to be.

There were abstract thoughts rattling around in my head. Alonzo told his wife he was going out to earn a little quick cash. Randy Mason was deathly afraid of Johnnie Pajak, a man described as a large brute. Alonzo Washington indicated he had seen something I couldn't protect him from until I figured out what it was. Finding Johnnie was the key to filling in the blanks.

A desk sergeant I knew who had been there since the founding of Wichita rattled off a few places where I could locate a mug like Pajak. He highly recommended I not bring a gun, as that would only make him mad and more inclined to hurt me. The sergeant's mischievous smile was the only send-off I got. My feet and back were already hurting in anticipation of this task.

I worked my way up to the King's X over on 1st and Broadway and took a seat at the counter. That was where I first encountered Jennie Palmer roughly six months earlier. Even though she recently graduated from North High School, her mind worked like a forty-year-old dame who had seen a thing or two. A wizened girl of the street who didn't have secretarial college in her future. Just as easily, she would fall back into sweet and innocent mode if it suited her. Her arms were in constant motion, whether it was wiping down the counter, pouring a cup of coffee, or scooping empty plates away from satisfied customers. Her mind worked as deftly and too often more quickly.

"Cheeseburger and coffee, Jennie."

"Good thing you ain't Kosher with that milk and meat thing." She was right. I thought about all the culinary delights I would have to give up if I followed my religion a little more strictly. That would include the delightful ham-and-Swiss on rye from the Old Mill. My attitude was the Lord was more concerned about following His laws than His menu. Maybe it was a rationalization. Since He hadn't struck me down thus far, I figured on following the dictates of my stomach.

The lunch crowd worked their way in and out of

the small café as I wiped meat grease off my chin and got a couple of refills of java. No one from the place begrudged me a spot after I smacked down an attempted robber last winter. I had a permanent reservation even though this wasn't the Ritz. Jennie finally came back and leaned her elbows on the counter, staring at me like a starry-eyed bobby-soxer.

"You know a lot of gals who hang out at the jazz clubs?" I asked casually.

"Oh sure. It feels daring and dangerous."

"And who doesn't like danger, right?"

"Oh, not me. I like gentle, mellow crooners. Give me Freddy Martin and Eddie Howard any day of the week."

Anyone listening to our conversation would have thought young Miss Palmer to be a shy and assuming maiden. However, as she decided not to attend college, she worked as often as she could, breakfast shifts, lunch shifts, or the late-night crowd. She saw things and heard things about parts of the city I did not have access to, while no one paid her any mind. Those qualities made her an invaluable resource for me. Her disarming smile opened doors a mug like me found closed.

"Maybe a few of these gals come in for an after-hours bite?"

"Maybe a few."

"High on hooch perhaps?"

She stood up straight, those starry eyes now clear as the sky after a summer rain.

"Or other things."

She walked on down the counter and refilled everyone's coffee. I gave it a considered thought before leaving. As always, I tipped her well.

I headed over to the cab stand at Douglas and Market and found both Richie and Charlie.

"Which one of you gentlemen is available for a little late-night carousing?" They understood all too well I did not intend to buy them drinks all night.

"I got to spend time with the wife and kids," Charlie responded. "Richie can take you if he's up for it."

"What time, Hirsch?"

Richie was to be at my place at eight o'clock. This time I was going to make my way toward to the north end of Broadway. Sadly, for me, I had similar clothing to the previous night's adventure. It was a testament to my lackluster sartorial interests. Any other guy my age with a more normal job in an uninspiring office with the pounding of typewriters and bland empty smiles would be spending his hard-earned pay on good clothes. Mine went toward paying bills and buying cat food.

We started at Swingland and then headed up to the Black Cat Inn. The bartender there indicated a young gal fitting Caroline Whitman's description had been in the prior Saturday evening accompanied by two colored gentlemen, one of whom he recognized as a local musician. He didn't know the gal's name but confirmed she had been in before on several occasions. I got the impression from Caroline's two college friends she enjoyed the company of the jazz musicians. To what extent I couldn't be certain.

I hit pay dirt at the Rustic Inn. She sat at a table to the side of the band in a recessed area, not quite a booth or hideaway. There was one colored man with her, drinks and cigarettes on the table, and certainly looking nothing like a college student but not quite a pro skirt.

She was more ambivalent than anything else, a stark contrast to the hep cat her friends made her out to be.

"Big House Walker? Is that you?" I had the look and sound of a slightly inebriated jazz fan. My intention was to be disarming. He presented an attitude of dismissiveness.

"Yeah?"

"I saw you play with Jay McShann at the Trocadero in, what was it?" I kept snapping my fingers in feigned remembrance, my gaze up toward the ceiling. "August of '40. Wasn't Bird playing alongside you?"

"I played one set with McShann. Bird was out in the back smoking tea. And you weren't there, man."

I sat down uninvited at their table, lowering my voice and making it sound more like a professor showing disdain for his student. My face went from slack to taut.

"You're right, Dale. I was on the Wichita police force cracking the heads of hopped-up musicians. Didn't make enough to afford nights out at swank clubs like this. Oh, but I listened to a lot of jazz on the radio. Good evening, Miss Whitman," I continued, turning my head away from Big House and straight at Caroline.

There was no surprising her. I didn't catch her off guard in the least.

"Dale, you want to bet this is an unimaginative snoop my father hired? How long did it take you to find me, snoop?"

"Bergman. Harold Bergman. And it was one evening down on South Broadway and half an evening on North Broadway. Not very long at all. I'm good at what I do."

"So what are you going to do now?" There was electricity in her voice, but I saw her hands clenching and a vein throb in her neck. She exuded toughness, perhaps because she was with a big colored jazz musician or because she thought I might be out of my element. Maybe she watched the same movies as her father. When I reached out my hand toward her, Walker's big paw came crashing down on the table in between us. I took it away quickly as though the table were on fire.

"Big House, huh?" I said looking at him without a hint of emotion. I breathed in deeply and exhaled slowly. "How about Dale Walker, formerly of the Colored Musical Settlement School before studying for a year at the Mannes Music School under the tutelage of David Mannes himself? The real hep cats would not take such a refined gentleman from New York seriously as a jazz musician. So that was where you added the moniker 'Big House' to give people the impression you did time for, what did you tell them? Oh, well. Never mind." I turned my attention back to Caroline with a greater amount of dismissiveness. "Here's how I look at it, little sister. Your dad pays the bills, one of which is college. You've run out on him. He wants to know why. What you do with your life," I said, turning a disgusted look toward Walker before returning to her, "is your own business. You can settle this with your father any way you like. But if I found you this easy, any gumshoe with less scruples will as well. And then where will you be?"

I impressed myself with my speech. It had enough strength to jolt her into seriousness with a hint of compassion to identify my honesty, integrity, and good nature. Dick Powell could learn a thing or two from me. Or maybe I learned it from him. Instead, she impressed me with qualities not often found in girls of her age.

"You've got it all wrong, Mr. Bergman. This isn't a wild fling or phase I'm going through. This is an escape."

"From what?"

She stared me dead in the face. Even with her musician paramour in a place her father would never set foot in, there was a profound fear in her eyes. It was as though she could be with a priest in church or a soldier in a garrison at Fort Scott and she would not feel safe.

"Don't follow me. Just let me be."

Dale Walker helped her out of her chair, and they scurried off toward the back behind the band. I decided not to follow them.

This was not what I expected to encounter. This wasn't flamboyant Temple Drake caught up with gangsters and bootleggers. It was easy to believe Caroline Whitman was running away. While many boys and girls are rebellious and fear the wrath of their parents, this was more profound.

I had taken a job based on simplicity. The fear in Caroline Whitman's eyes made it far more complex and, consequently, more dangerous.

Chapter Six

There was only one time a client was not as forthcoming as I expected. Last fall, a truck driver named Gene Spearman wanted me to "get the goods" on his wife. It was a typical divorce case, relatively easy to manage for a guy like me who was relatively new to the business and good for building a professional reputation. However, Spearman was a grubby little man lacking in anything resembling good taste. As a successful salesman, however, he had plenty of money and was gone a good deal of the time. I spent an entire week following Mrs. Spearman at a total cost of $200. She went grocery shopping once, had her hair done once, twice went to J.C. Penney's and ambled more than shopped, got together with three other ladies for lunch at the Innes Tea Room midweek, and mostly sat around in the evening listening to the radio. She had neither the time nor the inclination for anything resembling "the goods." Turned out old Gene was making time with a floozy in Hutchinson all along and simply wanted me to keep his wife away. With sheepish eyes like the kid whose mom caught him with his hand in the cookie jar, he handed me two C-notes. I did not want to be around for Mrs. Spearman's rebuttal. Unless, of course, she was interested in my services as well. Gene Spearman seriously disappointed me.

The point was I had to trust my clients to accept

work. To do otherwise would have set me back to a policeman's careful analysis of everything and conviction in nothing. Yet I couldn't help but think back to Caroline Whitman and Dale Walker desperately leaving the Rustic Inn. It was as though they receded into the shadows in hopes they would disappear completely. I had visions of Paul Muni in "I Am a Fugitive From a Chain Gang." The two of them chased by an unidentified evil spirit. While there was no reason not to believe Albert Whitman's story, I required a little bit more to make sure I was doing the right thing.

Whitson Import & Export was a sponsor at radio station KFH, located in Carey House Square. Al Buck was the station manager and the father of a guy I was in basic training with a million years ago. I had a hard time remembering myself back then compared to now. Al was a rare one to come in on a Saturday, primarily to check on things.

"Howdy, son. What brings you around?" I assumed the years working in country music had given Al an unnatural twang in his voice, given he was originally from St. Louis. He was a big man, not fat, just naturally large, and wore silk snap shirts in the style of a Texas dance hall dandy. With his girth, no one was inclined to comment. He rarely wore a ten-gallon hat. However, if he started chewing on tobacco, I would likely get a bit worried.

"Seems like I'm still walking a beat. How's Bill? Still up in Seattle with Boeing?"

"Yes siree. Although it costs a bit more to live up there, he's making good cabbage. He might be back before long though. If he gets home, I'll send him around."

"Do that. It'd be good to catch up."

"So what can I do you for?"

"What do you know about Whitson Import & Export?" I tugged on my ear out of habit before realizing I was doing it. It usually happened when I felt awkward about making an inquiry.

"They send a check over once a month, and we put about fifteen spots on for them. Like clockwork."

"Yeah, but what do they import and what do they export?"

"Darned if I know." The laugh was bigger than the expanse of the Rio Grande. "They got a warehouse over on Waterman near Washington. But the return address on the check is an office over in Delano." He dug up a recent envelope for a building right on the corner of Douglas and Handley that didn't ring a bell. I wished him well and said I'd be looking forward to chatting with Bill if he ever got around this way.

Snooping around a warehouse owned by my client was a bit unsettling. I thought it best to go to what I assumed was a business office and pass on a preliminary report. I waited until the following Monday when I knew an employee would be around. The place was across from the Dillons. I didn't have time for grocery shopping. There was no signage on the building on the northeast corner, nothing but a window on the upper floor simply stenciled WHITSON IMPORTS. I figured they might have another office for the exports. An unobtrusive entry was up from the corner entrance of the ground floor.

The frosted glass on the main office door had the same verbiage. I opened the unlocked door and entered without knocking. A woman in her mid-thirties sat behind a desk with a stack of folders on it and a four-drawer wooden filing cabinet behind her. There was a water cooler over to the side where a closed door without a window stood. There was no signage to identify the room it led into.

The woman wore her dark brown hair pulled into a tight bun without a single hair askew and was pleasantly appealing in pale red lipstick without much makeup around her emerald, green eyes. She wore tortoise shelled horn rimmed glasses that indicated a sense of elegance and class. Her fingers were devoid of any identifying jewelry. Rather than appearing startled or put off, she gazed at me with an inviting smile when I entered. Perhaps I didn't look like a warehouseman or a bill collector.

"May I help you?" Her voice carried a certain amount of professional courtesy but no other emotion.

"My name is Harold Bergman. I'm working—"

"Oh, yes, Mr. Bergman. Mr. Whitman has told me about your business arrangement."

My eyebrow rose unintentionally. Her awareness of me was a bit surprising. It was also a bit disconcerting considering I didn't even know her name.

"I would have thought that fell into the category of confidential."

A serious look, one blank and considerably more direct, replaced the warm welcome of her face.

"I'm Mr. Whitman's personal assistant. He confides in me on all matters, personal and professional."

"Congratulations. I hope it pays well." Her mouth remained agape. "I didn't catch you name, Miss…"

"Mooney. Saundra Mooney. And it's Mrs."

The lack of a wedding ring strained the commitment of my ultimate belief which apparently showed on my face.

"My husband died during the war."

"My condolences." I recognized I had been on edge coming into this situation and didn't mean to take it out on an employee. "Look, I'm sorry we got off to a bad start. I hoped to catch Mr. Whitman and provide him with a progress report."

"Mr. Whitman never comes to the downtown office. Occasionally, he'll check inventory at the warehouse. However, he is rarely involved in the daily operations. He has personnel for that very purpose. I'll make sure I forward him your report."

I described my visit with Caroline's friends at the college and my nightly visits to the clubs, without admitting I had come across the wayward daughter. This was where conflict arose in me. A cop follows the letter of the law: A man hires you to find his daughter, you find her and report it. Yet the words from the Talmud haunted me: *Just as you are obligated to speak when your words will be heeded, you must remain silent when you know your words will be ignored.* I wasn't sure on the latter part. I was only guessing.

I did not know the girl's story enough to determine she was not an innocent victim. Dale Walker or any of his associates might have manipulated her just as easily. At this point, I figured I could find her again or perhaps she might even reach out to me. It was the tipping point on the seesaw, weighing both my professional and moral responsibilities.

"Do you know the girl?" I asked Mrs. Mooney.

"Only in passing. I've encountered her once or

twice when I had to drop documents off at Mr. Whitman's home." Made me wonder what kind of encounters they were.

"Any impression of her?"

"None to speak of."

I nodded because that was all you can do when an interviewee is unwilling or unable to express themselves further. I waited for a continuance but found I had fallen off a cliff.

"What does Mr. Whitman import? Or export for that matter?"

"We don't really export anything. It looks better on the company letterhead. Mr. Whitman has connections all over the world and can bring in a stunning array of decorative artwork. Paintings, sculpture, bric-a-brac. He sells them to high-end dealers and interior decorators." Sounded like a tag line put together by the Marketing Department, assuming they had one.

"Nice. But the name always confused me. Whitson?"

"An amalgamation of the last name of the two founders. Albert Whitman and the late Helmut Sondergaard." Her answers sounded scripted by the ad agency who created their radio spots. She presented herself as the epitome of constrained professionalism and discretion. That is, until she asked, "So what exactly do you do when you're not investigating…things, Mr. Bergman?"

It was an innocent enough question. For such a sharp left turn in the conversation, I thought maybe her intentions might be flirtatious.

"Listen to the radio. Read."

"What shows do you listen to?"

"Lux Radio Theater. Fred Allen is good for a giggle."

"I suppose you read detective magazines."

"I used to. No need anymore. I see how things really are."

I nodded again and left. A war widow with a sense of curiosity was not my cup of tea. Then again, I wasn't sure what type of gal was.

I continued walking east until I could catch a cab outside of her possible view if she happened to look out the window. He dropped me off on the backside of Union Station on Waterman Street, half a block down from the Whitson Warehouse. It was a typical unassuming brick building, loading dock, side entrance to what was likely a small office, no windows, and only one door on the side nearest to me. Turning down Mosley Street, I passed open bays where trucks unloaded large and medium sized crates. They could have easily contained paintings and sculpture and bric-a-brac. Or about anything else my imagination could dredge up.

None of the trucks had a company logo or other identification. For that matter, neither were the crates marked in any fashion. Just plain unadorned wooden crates. I took quick looks as I passed each bay but on one occasion, my gaze lingered on a small crate with what looked like Asian writing on it. As it was the only item with lettering, it captured my attention. As best I could, I made a mental note of the configuration of what I assumed were letters.

Three guys were about to open it, all of them the size and shape of a marble sculpture as well, although far hairier and less refined. I didn't get the impression

they were comfortable with my gaze. There might have
been a slight movement in one guy's shoulder and a
turning of another guy's feet. I figured it best not to
determine those movements for sure, considering it
didn't appear a welcoming embrace was forthcoming. I
turned to the front and my gaze followed. My pace
quickened, but with my limp, I appeared a lot like
Quasimodo. Rapid movement exacerbated the pain and
caused the ankle to stiffen. I turned onto Dewey,
shuffling along for a spell, before settling into a small
diner at the corner of Dewey and Washington for a cup
of coffee. I buried my nose in the steam while the
throbbing in my ankle subsided. After about twenty
minutes with no one approaching, I whistled for a hack
speeding north on Washington, crossed the street, and
went home.

It was late afternoon when I got back. Upon
opening the pocket doors, Lady Mittens came out
immediately and rubbed up against my legs. Peeking
into the bedroom, I saw Sir Pounce curled up into a soft
orange ball on my bed. I had no desire to disturb him.

The Lady and I sat down on the sofa, me rubbing
her head and scratching her ears while she purred
affectionately. My mind wandered to the business
dealings of my client, Albert Whitman. It certainly
made sense to have a small administrative office to
reduce overhead. Based on the information provided by
Saundra Mooney, I could accept warehouse workers
being protective of extremely expensive merchandise.
All of it made sense, one way or the other. I was
creating ill-gotten theories out of legitimate dealings.

The image in my mind that struck me the most was
the face of his daughter. There was no mistaking it, no

way to perhaps assume she was afraid of a father who ruled with an iron fist, unable to bring affection to his role as parent after the passing of his wife. No, Caroline Whitman wasn't afraid of her father. She was afraid of a man with an incredible amount of power who was as likely to bring that iron fist down upon her.

There were two things to consider as deeply as possible. Was her fear well founded? And, if so, was it any of my business?

Chapter Seven

My regular place for dinner, or any meal as far as that was concerned, was the Pan-American Café, down the street from me at 150 North Market. With less than a fifteen-minute walk, I could develop quite an appetite. The aromas always overwhelmed me half a block away. King Mar owned the place nearly twenty years. An amazing accomplishment for a guy who made his way over from China with little more than the shirt on his back and half a dozen words of English at his disposal. A lot of folks thought I lost my head over the chop suey or lo mein, maybe the egg rolls. The truth was he had the best roast beef in the whole city. Even if there was a kitchen available to me in my apartment, I would never have been able to cook up a meal as good. My father often chided me about my culinary preferences.

King Mar had become more than a confidant to me. He was almost like a big brother, a guy who I could joke with and pass along my troubles. The irony was a Jew, and a Chinaman could bond so well despite vast differences. I guess food was the best thing to bring all types of people together.

I had fallen asleep on my settee. It was only the famished ravings of Sir Pounce after it grew dark that brought me back to life. Lady Mittens was quite content lying on my chest. After their evening meal, I realized I hadn't eaten anything all day and strolled down to the

Pan-American.

It was while I sopped up the last of the mashed potatoes and brown gravy I found myself accosted by a young patrolman. He came in, head swiveling as though looking for a specific person, until his gaze settled on me. With a certain degree of uncertainty, he stepped forward. It was likely I had the same look coming out of the police academy nine years before.

"You Harold Bergman?" he asked politely. Either he was too young to be mean or I wasn't in any kind of real trouble. I nodded, trying my best to hold back a smile. "Detective Mendenhall asked me to find you."

"Well, you have." He stared at me blankly. "Found me, that is." It wasn't my intention to be disarming but this raw recruit would have to learn how to get to the point a little quicker.

"Would you mind coming with me, sir?" I didn't think it wise to push the Burns and Allen skit much further. I dropped enough for the fare and a decent tip and motioned for the young man to allow me to follow him out. I glanced back. King Mar looked perplexed. My only response was to shrug my shoulders.

We drove up north on Market until we got to Twenty-First Street and then turned east. I got a bad feeling when we passed the Wichita Livestock Exchange. Two patrol cars with lights on and a coroner's wagon confirmed my feeling.

With his hat pushed back on his forehead was Detective Clarence Mendenhall of the newly created Night Detective Squad. If it weren't for the war, I likely would have been a member of his unit. Mendenhall pushed hard for my return to the force, wanting me to work alongside him. It would have been the promotion to Detective I previously thought to be my one true goal. Mendenhall never understood why it became more difficult for me to return. He respected my ambivalence, nevertheless. He currently stood over a rather large body covered in a white sheet.

"Don't tell me," I started. "You're trying to convince me of all the fun I'm missing by not joining your squad. Plus, these late hours are simply fabulous."

"Harold, you ought to be in vaudeville."

"Vaudeville's dead."

"Yeah? Well, so's this guy." He leaned down and pulled the sheet back halfway down the man's body. He was large, big shoulders and chest with an unkempt mop of black hair and a very large beard.

"Johnnie Pajak?"

"The one and only. Gunny said you had been asking around about him."

"So did he get caught in a stampede?"

"Not unless cattle know how to use a .38."

I noticed six bullets in his torso, two right around his heart.

"How do you figure it?" I asked.

"We don't. Pajak was involved in more dirty stuff than a garbage collector. Not that I'm all choked up about his passing, but I do have a job to do. This could have been from any one of several hoodlums, shylocks, shysters, or bootleggers."

"I thought Prohibition was repealed." He shrugged his shoulders. "The name Alonzo Washington ring a bell to you?"

"Nope. Should it?"

"The word is he went out on a job with Pajak here two Saturdays ago. I can only imagine what that means.

Apparently, Washington never came home." There was no point in revealing my encounter with Alonzo, at least not now.

"You think we're going to find him someplace like this?"

"I hope not. For his wife's sake. She's my client."

The patrolman dropped me off back at home. It would take the rest of the evening to get my mind wrapped around this as best I could. The problem when you didn't smoke and didn't regularly drink hard liquor is the evening dragged on a lot longer. The radio on in the background picked up a jazz station from Topeka. There was enough of a rhythm to keep my brain clicking.

I sat at my kitchenette table writing notes to myself as a way of figuring out the riddles. There were too many tic-tac-toe images and figure eights and not enough words that made sense.

I had Alonzo Washington pegged as a basically good guy trying to take care of he and his wife the best he could. A night watchman's pay wasn't enough to keep them out of poverty, and decent jobs for coloreds weren't available. A side gig a little shady here and there, adding to the nest egg. He kept his wife in the dark, so she wouldn't worry and get into trouble herself. Johnnie Pajak had the reputation as a brute who could take care of himself, but an unknown assailant emptied a revolver into him. Why? Did he see the same thing as Alonzo and was silenced because of it? Where could Alonzo go to get away from whoever killed Pajak?

Currently, there was only Althea Washington and Randy Mason who had any answers. I took a cab over to her home. A decently dressed white man in this dingy colored neighborhood drew looks but not too much attention. I knocked politely on her door. She was pleased to see me and also concerned.

"The police found Johnnie Pajak last night. He's dead. Killed."

She gasped desperately.

I decided right there to tell her of my encounter with Alonzo. "Something happened Saturday night," I continued, "that got your husband scared enough to run and his buddy to get rubbed out."

"Oh, my Lord." Tears formed in his eyes.

"Even Randy Mason seems too scared to tell me anything. Look, I need to know everything I can about your husband. People he knows, places he frequents."

"I really don't know anything, Mr. Bergman. He mostly keeps to himself except when we go to church. You can check out his dresser and his closet." With a wave of her hand, she directed me toward the sanctity of their bedroom and the secrecy therein.

It was disturbing going through a man's possessions while his wife looked on. Nevertheless, Washington was now a rabbit on the run. With limited resources, his wife could soon be planning a funeral.

Back deep in his closet, almost so far back I had to be a prospector, were two fancy pinstripe suits, the kind real cool hep cats wore to clubs. On the floor were two pair of shoes. One was a black-and-white saddle style and the other plain black with a spit shine polish enough to see a man's reflection. In the side pocket of one of the suits was a pack of matches stamped Green Gables. On the inside pocket of the other suit was a piece of paper with "Hollow Inn—Abyssinia" written on it. I showed them both to Althea.

"These mean anything to you?"

"Don't know nothing about Green Gables. But the Hollow Inn is a place for coloreds. It's over by Wichita Park."

"The cemetery. Yeah. What does 'Abyssinia' have to do with it?"

"Might be a password of some kind back when it was a speak."

If it was awkward coming into her neighborhood, going to this club might put me in a little more jeopardy. I'd be Daniel in the lion's den.

The next day, I waited outside Cudahy for Mason when he got out of work. If he saw me right away, he would likely run off. I stood right around the corner from the front gate, grabbed him by the lapels, and slammed him into the fence. It wasn't my intention to appear angry. He needed to know I was serious.

"Johnnie Pajak is dead." Mason's eyes lit up wide, ready to bust out of their sockets. "Shot six times and dumped over in the stockyards. Now, if Alonzo Washington is your friend, you've got to tell me where he is."

"I don't know." His desperation was evident in spit flying from his lips.

"Take a guess," I yelled. My frustration got the better of me, and I knew it. Two nightclubs were all I had to go on. Alonzo Washington had to be bunking somewhere every night, possibly scared, and trying to figure out a way to get out of the mess he found himself unintentionally drawn into with few resources and fewer friends. "Look, you talked with Mrs. Washington, right? She said I was on the up-and-up?"

He nodded feverishly. "Alonzo cannot get himself out of whatever he's in. He needs help."

"You?" he asked, almost incredulously.

"Yes." I was as definitive as I could be.

Randy looked up and back both ends of the sidewalk, and then again.

"They got a homeless shelter at the Southern Baptist Church."

"Over by Lawrence Stadium?"

"Yep. Alonzo, he's a big baseball fan."

"Does he think he's safe there?"

"If not there, where?" There was a pathetic sadness in his voice. He was right, though. That much was true. I couldn't answer his question. Maybe I didn't want to.

The building on the corner of Douglas and McLean was simple in nature, as the Southern Baptists had only recently come into Wichita. It had the look of a decent sized white house with a wraparound front porch, just without a steeple. A hand painted wooden sign out front identified it as a house of worship. I entered quietly and respectfully.

Walking toward me as I entered was a small and delicate looking man with an oval face and a receding hairline. His eyes were distressed at first. They became welcoming as we got closer. They were a brown with a hint of gold, perhaps a divine light shining through.

"I'm Reverend Orbie Clem. How may I be of service, friend?" His voice had a strength to it that did not match his angelic demeanor or slight appearance.

"My name is Harold Bergman." I emphasized my last name though I'm not certain why. "I understand you offer a shelter for the homeless."

He looked at me, not in judgment or condescension

but analytically.

"I must assume you are here to support our cause rather than avail yourself of it."

"Alonzo Washington." I figured by stating my intentions directly and clearly, we could get to the heart of the matter.

"Men in need come here anonymously. The Lord looks into their hearts and calls them all his children. He does not require a name."

There was no need for me to take a harsh stance with a man who was faithfully following his mission and his conscience. Nevertheless, I impressed upon him my honest intentions.

"His wife, Althea, asked me to find him. He has a home, and she wants him there." My eye caught movement coming from behind the altar, perhaps a door or passageway. "He asked me recently not to help him. But how can I merely walk away from a man in need? At some point, we are all servants of the Lord."

The movement became the form of a man, very tall, almost as broad shouldered as the late Johnnie Pajak. He took slight steps from where he had been to right in front of the altar. Reverend Clem turned his head toward him protectively and then back toward me.

"It would be a sin, Mr. Bergman," the reverend responded. I smiled and nodded politely. Spiritual beliefs aside, we could both come to agreement in this matter.

"Mr. Bergman, you can't help me," Alonzo said from a distance. Yet there was almost a pleading quality to his voice.

"Johnnie Pajak is dead," I blurted out.

"I know."

"What did you and he see that made you run and got him killed? Whatever it is, we can go to the police."

"We can't."

I squinted. While I could gather he was concerned about an accusation, I thought my reputation with the police department would carry a little weight. He wasn't making sense.

"Why?" I asked softly.

"It was the police."

Chapter Eight

Most women use the basement of their homes to store canned goods and supplies, perhaps the infant clothing of their older children, even the fine china if they do not have an adequate sideboard. The below ground room of the Southern Baptist Church was largely a storm shelter with about ten cots. It was safe and clean, providing the necessities for ten indigent men. Alonzo Washington had a good home with a wife and plenty to eat, far from impoverished. He was more desperate than anything else and found this to be his only refuge.

As it turned out, he immediately went to Randy Mason late on the ill-fated Saturday. It was Mason who suggested the church as he figured no one would consider a colored man hiding out in a white man's church. While the logic made sense, I still had to know how all this started.

"You know Glick Helbert? He runs Green Gables." I nodded. "A man with a truckload of bourbon was shaking him down for more money. Johnnie says we go and back up Glick. Says there was a C-note for each of us."

"What were you supposed to do?"

"Nothing. Just look mean and strong."

"Ok. Sounds simple."

"Except a man drives up to the meeting. Glick

knows him 'cause they shake hands, get close. They seem friendly, but who knows? Johnnie's eyes light up. He must know him, too. The man with the hooch says neither big boys like me and Johnnie nor coppers are going to push him around."

"Coppers?"

"That was what he said. Didn't know what it meant. Then the man pulls out a rod and shoots him dead right there." Alonzo choked down the spit he worked up from telling his tale. "Glick looks like he's shaking. This weren't supposed to be how it went. The man says no one at the station will think nothing of this. Tells Johnnie to drive the truck to this warehouse he mentions and for me and Glick to dump the body somewhere."

"You know where the warehouse is?"

He shook his head negatively.

"What about the body? Can you tell me where you left it?"

"Mr. Bergman, I done told you enough. There's a dirty cop out there who'd like nothing better than for me to go to my maker as soon as possible and make Althea a widow."

"If that were true, you'd already be there. Glick Helbert saw him, too."

"Yeah, but Glick'll do anything to keep his business going. And he's a white man. Me, I'm just a useless colored and they got plenty of them around. And then some." He was convulsing slightly as though shot with a jolt of electricity through his body. A heavy mop of sweat formed on his forehead.

I could appreciate his point. It would be nothing for a crooked cop to shoot a man, claim he was resisting arrest, especially if the cop was a decorated veteran. The first thing I needed to do was to bring the body out in the open, assuming it hadn't been found already. He might be more important, so to speak, than Johnnie Pajak. It might rattle a few cages. After that, it was important to figure out where this warehouse was. This was where I would dive into the world of roadhouses and privately owned colored clubs. It was certainly different than stalking jazz clubs for the daughters of rich businessmen. An old proverb teaches us "A little bit of light pushes away a lot of darkness." I would need all the strength of my forefathers to be such a light.

Reverend Clem concurred with me that, for the moment, it was safer for Alonzo to remain here. However, as soon as the parties in question were aware of my involvement, we would have to make other arrangements. I knew King Mar had a rooming house above the Pan-American Café, but it might have been too obvious given my regular dining habits. Nicholas Leonides was the ideal alternative. He ran a small grocery store on the corner of Douglas and Topeka and offered a few rooms to let above the store. This wasn't common knowledge. He had several family members and friends who were, shall we say, known to get into trouble now and again. Nothing that would mean a felony. Just enough to keep them out of commission for a short spell.

Nick and his wife and young sons emigrated from Greece back in the early '30s. He spoke loudly and used his hands a lot. I imagined him talking in his sleep. I never encountered him while on the force, never got a call for so much as a stolen apple, but I would go there frequently for the quality of the produce he had. His wife made the first baklava I ever had, and it was as sweet as she was. However, he never could get me to enjoy feta cheese or stuffed grape leaves. For the time being, Alonzo would remain in the church. There would be enough people praying for him to make it worthwhile.

Without checking it out first, I made an anonymous tip about a dead body in a field around North Arkansas and Thirty-Seventh Street after I convinced Alonzo to confide in me. Within twenty-four hours, I reached out to Gunny Gunsaullus to get the facts. He eyed me slyly at first before reading from an official report he kept close to the vest.

"Bootlegger named Timmy Barczak. Got a sheet dating back to the late '20s. Mostly for booze but also possession of stolen property and one violation of the Mann Act. Typically worked anywhere from Nebraska down to southern Oklahoma. Sometimes Missouri. Didn't venture anywhere into Texas and apparently didn't step on too many toes."

"Well, this time was different. Cause of death?"

"He had an allergy to lead." My face let him know his humor was outdated. "Two shots, close range, belly and heart. So how did you know about this?" Gunny tried his best to be serious and put my feet to the fire.

"An unconfirmed tip."

"From whom?" he pressed.

"Can't tell you right now. There's another angle to this that could put us all in hot water. I'm willing to take the heat for now. But I might need you to back me up eventually."

"I hope it's not too late by then." Right then, he

was completely serious.

Richie was ready for another go around at the clubs on the north side of town. It made sense to hit the Rustic Inn first off figuring I'd find Walker and the girl there. Unfortunately, I struck out like Charlie Keller during a tough doubleheader. It was a slow Wednesday night. We then drove up to the Black Cat Inn where I spent less than ten minutes roaming around. It was in the parking lot of the Forty Second Club, farther up north, an immaculately dressed colored man approached me. He was tall and slender without being skinny. Perhaps a center on a semi-pro basketball team. He was outwardly friendly with a disengaging smile. I suspected there was a gat tucked in his belt.

"You can tell your man you won't be needing him no more. You got a ride from now on for the rest of the night." I smiled and nodded, walked back over to Richie's hack, and advised him of the situation. I handed him a ten.

"Don't forget. I owe you a receipt," he said nervously.

"I'll be back for it later." I continued smiling if only to reassure Richie of my safety. Despite being younger than me, Richie had the impression he was my guardian angel. It was comforting someone thought that way about me other than my father.

I followed the man, bypassing the front door and heading toward a back parking lot. Unfortunately, a gun was not part of my arsenal. The typical jobs I took didn't require it. I had enough training in the military to fend for myself. Hand-to-hand fighting was one of the courses I passed. Even with my bum foot, I could still hold my own. Yet I was doubtful this was the big knockoff. Assuming this man was associated with Dale Walker, I didn't figure they would brush me off permanently.

Parked away from other cars was a brand new shiny black 1946 Ford Super Deluxe coupe. The light gray leather interior was plush. Had it been daytime, the sunlight would have blinded me bouncing off the chrome.

"That's beautiful," I commented, not realizing I was talking out loud.

"Yeah? Got it at Byron Stout on Douglas."

"They sell to coloreds?"

"They sell to anyone who's got the green, man." He smiled broadly, as proud of his car as he was of his bankroll. I wasn't about to ask where or how he got it. He nodded for me to get into the front passenger seat.

"No blindfold?" I asked.

"What you think this is?"

We got in and he drove north on Broadway. The low hum of the engine was all I could hear. He wasn't one for small talk or passing the time. The moon shone full until lingering clouds passed in front. Then it was just the headlights to show us the way. This was almost too pleasant.

After about fifteen minutes, we turned into a long driveway a scant half a mile farther north of the intersection of Fifty-Third Street. A small bungalow was out of sight behind a row of trees. While it wasn't completely in a state of disrepair, it could have used a coat of paint and a couple three nails on the railing of the porch. There were no lights on the outside.

"They waiting for you inside," the colored man said, leaning against his car and lighting a cigarette. It was a gracious invitation.

There was very little furniture in the front room. A small sofa, one chair, and an ugly coffee table with scratches and glass stains. The fireplace appeared unused. Not clean, per se, but free of burned ashes. Off to one side was a quaint dining area. Like my place, it contained a table with enough room for two chairs. Sitting in one was Caroline Whitman, a glass of amber liquid in front of her. She was voraciously smoking a cigarette, the ashtray already filled. Her gaze flitted here and there, never focusing on anything. Either she was high on dope or deathly afraid.

Standing behind her was Dale Walker, looking every inch like "Big House", the supposed mean ex-con who would do what it took to protect his lady. Whether I had any doubts before, I fully realized they were an item and he meant to take care of her any way possible. I had no idea what that might mean at this moment.

"What'll it take for you to back off this case?" he said softly and with perfect diction. "Tell Whitman you couldn't find her?"

"The truth."

There were countless folks who wondered why I, or anyone else, would take on the job of a private investigator. Several movies and books and magazine articles told fabulous overly romanticized stories of lone men with their own personal codes. Men with pasts impacted by a crime of one sort or another, maybe losing a close relative like a wife or sister. There were notions of cracking a big case and securing a huge windfall. Those were sob stories put on paper by pulp writers and guys acting tough. For me, it was all about finding myself again. I had plans and dreams once that a global conflict swallowed up. I killed men, the enemy, and watched men I was close to die needlessly. The words 'justice' and 'morality' no longer made sense, only caused confusion. The thing I was looking for most was the truth. Too few people knew what that meant anymore. It didn't mean I would stop looking.

The tale they told me was of a man who attained his wealth through largely illicit means. His late partner was an early advocate of Hitler, made secret business deals with him to supply machines for factories as well as weapons. Sondergaard was able to secure his departure from Denmark in 1939 and formed a partnership with Whitman which combined other resources Caroline was not aware of.

The most recent venture involved heroin smuggled out through Turkey. As Caroline became involved in the jazz scene, Albert Whitman encouraged his daughter to make connections for the purposes of establishing a foothold for drug trafficking in the Midwest. She went along out of fear until she met Dale Walker. Falling in love with him was not part of anyone's plan. Now it meant more than anything, perhaps even her life.

"So what are you going to do now?" I asked, as though I were the parent.

"I've got money and enough acquaintances in Chicago, Los Angeles, New Orleans, even New York. We can get out of here." Walker was determined and eager. The problem was he hadn't seen enough of the evil in the world.

"Whitman likely has connections there as well. A colored jazz musician and a young white woman will stand out just about anywhere you go." I didn't mean to be so blunt, but their story won me over resulting in a hard case of honesty. I was prepared to let them slide since I couldn't stick my neck out for them too far.

"We'll take our chances." He stood tall, shoulders thrown back, chest out. I nodded respectfully.

"I'll apologize to Mr. Whitman for my failure and wish you both a good night."

I turned back at the sound of a faint woman's voice.

"Thank you, Mr. Bergman."

She was completely different now. She looked real.

Chapter Nine

I was fortunate the cats allowed me to sleep in. Either their bellies were not rumbling, or they decided upon graciousness, neither one of which occurred to me upon waking. Unfortunately, it was well past nine o'clock and the better part of the morning slipped away. My job required me to be adept at any hour of the day, any day of the week. Late nights still didn't set well with me. I wondered if I was getting too old before my time, and I still wasn't even thirty. At this point, I imagined being my father's age.

I started putting on a pot of coffee when I noticed a telegram slid under the door. My guess was it arrived last night as I hadn't heard the insistent knock of the delivery guy. I couldn't help but wonder if he was annoyed not getting a tip.

PLEASE COME TO MY HOME EARLIEST POSSIBLE. STOP. WHITMAN.

I assumed he meant 'convenience'; then again, I couldn't imagine Albert Whitman concerning himself too much with anything that was convenient for me. I let the coffee go, showered, shaved, and fed the cats before walking down to the King's X. Jennie was only too happy to serve up a plate of two fried eggs, sunny up, on top of two pieces of buttered toast. She filled my coffee cup enough times to warrant brewing a fresh pot. She proffered a guess as to the cause of my late evening, coyly suggesting a rendezvous with an as-yet unidentified alluring female companion. My raised eyebrow ended the conversation. I started to come around and be forthright enough to tussle with Whitman. As he was still my client, I wiped the cobwebs of my opinion of him out of my mind. For the time being.

Richie had pulled up to his usual spot when I flagged him with my hand and nod of the head. The reminder was we needed a hefty receipt for the house in Eastborough. He smiled broadly.

It was a few minutes before noon when we arrived. There was no certainty I would not be interrupting Whitman's lunch. In any case it didn't matter much to me. If this was urgent to him, I was confident his midday repast could wait. I knew I would indicate my efforts were unsuccessful, see if I could push for a few more days to stretch out the job, and then beg off the case altogether. That was my plan. He surprised me with his directness before I even started. The envelope was light, but it was hefty inside. A check for five hundred dollars.

"This is far more than I've earned thus far, Mr. Whitman." Sadly, I caught myself sounding like a grateful lackey, perhaps one of his warehouse guys who always said 'sir' in his presence. Money has a way of turning a righteous man into a slave. I was back to making bricks for the pharaoh.

"The issue, Mr. Bergman, is I cannot control my daughter's actions forever. She will turn twenty-one shortly. At that point, she will have full legal authority as an adult. My hope was you would find her and make her see some sense."

"What changed your mind?" My tone shifted to one of a younger brother, everyone's favorite uncle who was the voice of reason. It was a role easier played than that of a buddy, assuming Albert Whitman got close to anyone, which I doubted. I made it appear as though I were disappointed rather than pleased to allow Caroline and Walker to run off. Acting is one of the necessary skills for a private investigator. I took my cues from Dick Powell.

"I've learned a few things." By saying so, I wasn't certain if he meant from a personal and spiritual standpoint or significant information. I almost stuttered but held it together. I waited for a continuation of his comment, a revelation of his enlightenment, the specifics of his epiphany. None of it was forthcoming. Albert Whitman was the kind of man who said what he said and no more.

"Thank you for your generosity."

My mood changed rapidly from the foyer of his home out to Richie's cab. At first, I was relieved. Then Skepticism quickly overtook Confusion. By the time I sat in the back seat, Fear and Apprehension sat alongside me. I pulled out a twenty-dollar bill and handed it over Richie's shoulder. He whistled in amazement.

"A double sawbuck? And no receipt?"

"This party's over, Richie." Then, in my mind, I added "For the time being." From a professional standpoint, that was the end of it. However, if anything Caroline said was true, I felt morally obligated somehow. I couldn't be sure exactly what to do nor was I able to decide how deeply to get involved.

Despite the differences in our beliefs, I had always

been able to reach out to my father for advice and guidance. It was the greatest bond between us. He challenged me in a Socratic way, even though he might not admit to it. All he ever needed was to ask questions. So when I told him I appreciated his counsel, he invited me to dinner. His home, the one I grew up in, was as close to a sanctuary as we could find between us.

He imbedded the roast with whole garlic cloves and covered it in rosemary sprigs. He quartered the potatoes and cut the carrots into thick rounds. He likely got home early from the shop to get it into the oven early enough to cook to a slow and tender consistency. Regardless of his insistence of my mother's grand culinary skills, my dad was quite a good cook. We ate in silence. The familiar blue smoke of the pipe filled the parlor after we cleared the dishes from the table.

"So is the case over?" he asked.

"The job is over because the client provided payment."

"Then the case is over."

"The payment was close to twice what it should have been, and the reason provided for ending the job did not have resonance to it. More of an excuse than an explanation. It sounded rehearsed and half-hearted."

"To whom? To you?" He had a point. My comments were based on my personal beliefs and the fact Caroline had been honest with me as far as I could tell. Then again, as she was the only one who was forthcoming, perhaps it was wrong to accept what she said was the truth.

"I can't let this go." Without the specifics described, my father understood my forthright attitude. I acted staunch and adamant, looking for him to be contradictory. Perhaps I didn't want to further my involvement. These rich people typically walked into their problems and bought their way out. My presence would not resolve anything of epic proportions. Yet I felt wronged, as though the lives and manipulations of Albert Whitman and his daughter were a personal affront to me.

"Then proceed. But remember, it is written: *Don't throw stones into the well from which you drank.*"

The worst thing I could do is go against a client who has paid me handsomely for my efforts. If I assumed Albert Whitman was the villain in this scenario simply because I resented his wealth and attitude, I might lose out on future jobs. To be righteous in my field had consequences. It was at these times I wished I worked with Clarence Mendenhall on the Night Detective Squad. There was only the law to consider. Better yet, if I were in the middle of preparing a Friday night Sabbath service I could speak of upright morality. To have life cut and dried would provide clarity. Then, I reminded myself of the clouds of turmoil that were everywhere. The world tended to be aberrant, and answers often led to further questions.

Out on Douglas, I waited until I could find a colored taxi driver. He was suspicious when I asked him to take me to the Hollow Inn. He kept shaking his head without saying anything, trying to figure out what a shabbily dressed white man would want there other than trouble. From his rearview mirror, he watched me rip a twenty-dollar bill in half, holding on to one piece and reaching out to him with the other.

"I need ten minutes inside and you get the other half."

"Mister, you get killed I get nothing."

"Well, let's see that doesn't happen." I was as reassuring as a coroner.

To me a cemetery is peaceful at night. The living don't disturb the dead as they rest. Memories can't impact their sleep. However, there was every possibility I might be in the neighborhood of my final resting spot if I weren't careful. I gave myself decent odds considering the Germans had done nothing more than shoot me up pretty good.

"I best go in with you," the driver said bravely after taking in a big deep breath.

"What's your name?"

"Cal Dutcher."

"Pleased to know you, Cal," I said, extending my hand. "I'm Harold Bergman." He nodded in affirmation.

Perhaps it was fortunate it was a weeknight and not too crowded. Music was playing on a jukebox as a piano sat empty on a small stage. There were a few tables with several couples, but a dozen folks, both men and women, crowded the bar. The bartender saw me first before noticing Cal.

"Boy," he called out to Cal, "what you bringing that cracker here for?"

I held a dollar bill up between two fingers.

"Think the two of us can get a drink?" I asked. "I mean, you do serve liquor. Right?"

The bartender took two shot glasses, practically slammed them on the bar, and filled them with whiskey. Cal and I walked over. The bartender snatched the bill from my fingers. I wasn't expecting any change. Cal swigged his drink fast and nervously to get those ten minutes to speed up a little bit. I sipped mine, noticing it tasted more like unfiltered tar oil. Manischewitz it was not.

"Alonzo Washington," I stated to the bartender, a simple declaration that wasn't quite a question.

He leaned slightly forward, trying his best mean look. His face was like a slab of concrete, sweat covering it with a nice sheen. "Never heard of him."

"I have. He's in trouble."

"If he is, it's from a white man," he said derisively.

"Yes. Likely Glick Helbert." The bartender maintained a cold stare, but the mean look faded a bit. He was surprised I either knew about Helbert or acknowledged he was the one responsible for Washington's troubles. "Alonzo works here on occasion, or so I'm told. I figured someone might know about Abyssinia." The bartender's eyes grew wide, almost scared. It was like putting a claw into a bear trap.

"Nobody knows nothing about nothing, mister."

The man who spoke was halfway down the bar. He stepped forward slowly. I barely caught him out of the corner of my eye. He wore a bowler and a brown pinstriped suit with pale yellow shirt and black and gold tie. There was a diamond stickpin, diamond cuff links, and diamond rings on one finger of each hand. He exuded wealth, class, and style, the kind that would be noticeable in both worlds. His bloodshot eyes and pronounced cheekbones indicated a sinister disposition. There was nothing on his face resembling any kind of emotion. He was likely saving that for a pal he cared about a whole lot more.

"That was what I thought," I responded blankly.

"Still, when a man's wife hires you to help her husband, you make the best effort you can. Wouldn't you agree, Mr. …?" I let it hang out there, hoping he'd fill in the blank.

"Jones." He uttered it blankly, with a solid thud.

"Thank you for your time, Mr. Jones."

I swigged the rest of my drink, making sure I didn't gag in front of them. Cal and I walked back out to the hack. I took a brief glance behind me as we got outside. Reaching forward, I handed Cal the other half of the bill.

"You earned it."

He smiled.

The shriek of a woman's voice stopped us before we got in the cab.

"Hey, mister." We both turned around. The woman standing at the front entrance wore a pale pink dress about fifteen years out of style. She was rather slender to the point of emaciated, with hair like straw covered in snow. What really caught my attention was the blank stare in her eyes. She didn't appear intoxicated. Then it finally dawned on me she was blind. "You really work for Althea?"

I walked back slowly toward her while Cal stood by the driver's side almost in awe. I got close enough where she could hear me breathing.

"Yes, ma'am. She's worried about Alonzo."

"Lots of folks are. Then again, lots of folks be looking for him, too."

"Yes, ma'am."

She reached out, touched my shoulders, and then worked her hands up to my face. She read me the best way she knew how.

"Describe yourself."

"I'm about five foot eight…"

Her hands went back to my shoulders.

"More like five foot nine."

I smiled.

"I have blue eyes the color of the sky after a rain. My hair is a light brown, kind of like a maple tree bark. Nothing special about my chin or nose which surprises people because they think all Jews have big noses."

She touched my nose and then laughed.

"Are you an honest man?"

"That was the way I was raised."

"We was all raised that way. Are you an honest man now?"

"Yes, ma'am."

Her hands dropped to her sides. Her facial expression went deadpan.

"What do you know about Abyssinia?"

"Other than an ancient African empire, I don't know what it means around here."

She might have been staring at me for all I knew.

"You won't find Alonzo at that church no more. We got him hid."

It wasn't clear who she meant by "we," and I didn't bother asking. She was a lady who knew things, and I didn't know who she was.

"I don't suppose I could see him." She shook her head. "Is that because you don't trust me?"

"No, sir. It's because I do." What she lacked in sight she made up for in vision. "You reach out to Mr. Helbert, put a little heat under his britches. He's in as much danger as Alonzo. You come see me if you need anything else."

"What's your name?"

"You can just call me Sibyl." And she laughed again.

Chapter Ten

When things got too difficult and I felt overly burdened, I went to Wichita Park and visited Dick Cowan. Richard Eller Cowan was a Medal of Honor winner who died bravely in December of '44 during the Battle of the Bulge near Krinkelter Wald. He graduated from North High in 1940; I graduated from East in 1934. I met him a few months prior to his passing. We chatted about growing up in Wichita, and he commented I was the first Jew he ever met and liked me just fine. It was a strange thing to say at first but I realized a lot of folks didn't have regular interactions with Jews in Wichita, despite our longstanding presence. At the time he said it, we were comrades in arms, indistinguishable by race or religion or economic standing. The equanimity he displayed was striking for a twenty-two-year-old.

As it turned out, I sustained my injuries the day after he died, a fact I didn't learn until many weeks later after a couple of surgeries couldn't heal my fractured foot to its original status. The doctors acted as though it were akin to an amputation, a permanent limp as an impediment to a fully functional life. I saw it as another obstacle to overcome. What was another one after fifty-seven hundred years?

Once I shipped home, Dick's parents asked me to accompany them to the White House for the medal ceremony. It was a somber affair yet profoundly moving. President Truman was a sincere and generous man who treated the Cowans like old friends from the neighborhood. I was in awe of his sincerity. Since then, I admired Dick's bravery and his courage. It means a lot when a citation states: *His heroic actions were entirely responsible for allowing the remaining men to retire successfully from the scene of their last-ditch stand.*

It takes a special person to do exactly what needs doing without considering the consequences. No one knows if they have those qualities. I don't think Dick did until he faced a King Tiger tank. I often wondered whether my choice to avoid both my professional and spiritual options was due to overly contemplating the ramifications of both. There are times when not making a choice is often more deadly yet far easier to do.

Nevertheless, there was a great deal of uncertainty within me upon returning from the horrors of war. While I did not consider myself a wanderer like Maugham's Larry Darrell, my mind drifted constantly. Perhaps the cases I accepted were as much a reflection of who I was or thought I was. In looking for lost and missing persons, I would find my own self out there among both the rich and destitute. This time, the reflection in the mirror was either a young wayward daughter or a troubled colored husband. Neither one looked too much like me. It didn't matter because I understood them both.

I stood at Dick's grave and marveled at his accomplishments. You couldn't help wonder how his life would have turned out had it gone beyond twenty-two brief years. I did my best to determine how mine would wind up. Like Richard Eller Cowan, I would continue until I faced the next challenge.

A quiet cab ride brought me to the Wichita Carnegie Library. Such an austere building did not know what to do with the likes of Carla Duggan. She recently turned forty and had red hair Rita Hayworth would be jealous of to go along with the personality and verbal acuity of Martha Raye. She dressed conservatively for the most part but certainly was not readily identifiable as a research librarian by many folks. She would have fit in perfectly on the Fred Allen Show. However, her knowledge on a wealth of subjects made her an invaluable resource to both executives and educators. I could never learn much about her background as she was an immaculate storyteller. Truth and fiction blended in a dizzying array of anecdotes, most of which had details out of whack whenever she retold them. It was as though she were continually editing the story of her life.

A broad Irish smile grew upon her face as I walked in. I was always concerned she would break the silence with a loud welcome even though she never did. She leaned on the counter as I approached acting like I was Frank Sinatra and she a star-struck fan.

"Greetings, Tribe of Judah," she said with great authority.

"Greetings, my Celtic imp."

"What brings you to the Halls of Wisdom?"

"Helmut Sondergaard." Usually, all it took was a name to set the conversation off like the Kentucky Derby.

"Danish. Emigrated a couple of years before the war. Went into business with Albert Whitman to form Whitson Import & Export. Died in 1943." She would have been a natural on *Winner Take All* or *Break the Bank.*

"Anything unusual about his death?"

"Nothing in the papers." I didn't know what I was

fishing for, but it was worth it to cast a line.

"And Whitman?"

"Until the business partnership, no mention of him in the *Eagle* or *Beacon.*"

It was disconcerting. Rich and successful people do not emerge like Athena from another's head or Aphrodite from a shell in the ocean. There were strange notions that popped in front of my eyes including the possibility of him being a completely different person before he was Albert Whitman. It certainly would have accounted for a shadowy background.

"You read a lot of newspapers, Carla?"

"As many as I can get my hands on." The smile was wider than the Cheshire Cat.

"Think you can find anything on these two prior to 1939?"

She took my inquiries in the past as worthwhile challenges. She was smarter than anyone I had ever known and had a strong need to prove it. Her disarming persona did not endear her to the intellectual cognoscenti. I was perfectly happy to allow her to demonstrate her academic capabilities. My greatest resources were friends with skills, knowledge, and intuition.

"If it's out there, I'll find it." Her smile faded into deep concern, almost maternal even though she had no children. "What gives, Harold? These are guys with money."

"I know."

"Big money."

"Yeah?"

"And money buys a lot of trouble."

"I know," I said nodding as I strolled off.

It was perhaps foolish to proceed with this inquiry, but I had a pebble in my shoe that stuck into me with each step I took. I closed files filled with cases of wayward husbands and wives, one older sister looking for a younger brother who may have been involved with an older dowager, and a sweet old lady in Riverside concerned about her next-door neighbor. Never had I encountered a daughter of privilege running away from a father of dubious business scruples. While I could accept Caroline Whitman having fallen in love with Dale Walker, the heroin story sounded more like a way to convince me her father was the evil one and she was pure as gold. That old line about a book and its cover spun around in my mind several times at a dizzying pace. The wheel hadn't stopped on any viable answer.

My father had a valid point regarding my pursuit of this. Whereas he would be the first to seek out the true answers to all things, he knew when it was best to let sleeping dogs lie. Jews, especially, understood which battles to pick and which to walk away from. Pitfalls lay everywhere. Most people were looking for a Jew to fail to validate their petty and ignorant beliefs. Yet the contradictions struck me enough to start down this path. After a bit, I had pretty much convinced myself it was wrong to reach out to Carla to dig deeply into Whitman's background when I saw him walk into the J.C. Penney store on North Broadway with his daughter. My curiosity got the better of me and I followed them inside.

There was a gaiety about them as he escorted her to the ladies clothing section. They acted as though they didn't care who might be watching them, which made me believe they knew I was doing just that. They compared various dresses while she tried on several pairs of shoes. Whitman himself exhibited tremendous encouragement. He was Donald Crisp in *National Velvet,* a sure candidate for Father of the Year. The smiles on their faces, however, were more like performances by Bette Davis and George Brent in the latest melodrama. I couldn't figure who the audience was supposed to be.

Caroline saw me first as I approached. It may have been my imagination, but I thought it was a gasp before it became a smile.

"Ah, Mr. Bergman. How nice to see you."

Whitman turned around at the sound of my name. He stood tall with a relaxed manner about him as though he no longer had a care in the world. He was acting like the owner of the store giving away the merchandise.

"Miss Whitman." I nodded at her and then turned toward her father. "Mr. Whitman." He extended a hand for a warm and firm greeting. It was not the death grip I was expecting. Instead, it was a confident hold of my hand. Perhaps he felt he had a complete hold over the rest of me.

"We've decided to throw Caroline an incredibly decadent birthday celebration, and I want her to be appropriately attired. She's allowed me to show off a bit."

"You do spoil me, Father."

The dialogue was campy, the kind you would hear from a B-picture at the 81 Drive-In. Unfortunately, the store did not offer popcorn, and I wasn't at all interested in staying around for the second show.

"Mr. Bergman, I do hope I didn't cause you too much trouble," Caroline continued, playing the part of the debutante immaculately. "It seems I was a bit reckless after a falling out with father and certainly didn't act like myself."

"Who did you act like? Joan Crawford in *Mildred Pierce*?" I smiled to let them know it was a joke as opposed to an exasperated utterance. My acting skills were still subject to debate. Considering the crowd, I don't believe I fared too badly.

"I'm certainly grateful for your effort and your professionalism, Bergman. I've brought your name up in conversation with several business acquaintances of renown. You may be hearing from them with additional offers. They would certainly appreciate your discretion. As I have." The smile was friendly even though I knew there were darts behind it.

"I am entirely grateful, sir." While not sounding subservient, I made sure not to show my suspicious nature. "And I hope everything is okay with Mr. Walker?" I added, returning my attention to Caroline.

"I'm sure he can take care of himself," she said with a tone of confidence.

Right then, I noticed a gleam in her eye, perhaps a tear starting to form, the slightest sign of regret and uncertainty. Maybe it was the only way she could tell me what she really thought and felt. Perhaps I wanted to see more than was there. The glitz and glamour were far too blinding for anything like the truth to appear. It stayed hidden in the heart.

As there was nothing more to say to either of them, I nodded and walked off politely. I headed up the block and hung around outside the Orpheum Theater. It was far enough away to be unnoticeable and close enough to spot them coming out. Apparently, it was a legitimate shopping outing because they did not emerge for another forty-five minutes. As though through prior arrangement, a car pulled up and they entered the back seat. I hailed a cab with instructions to follow but keep a good distance. The driver was eager as well as capable.

Whitman's car returned to his home in Eastborough. I had the driver go around the block once as unobtrusively as possible, slow down a bit as he went by the house, and start to bring me back home. I was deep in thought when he spoke up.

"Hey, you know, I been there before."

It was as though I snapped awake.

"You mean inside that house?"

"Me? Nah. Not inside. It was a fare. Good lookin' gal, too."

"Like, a college girl?"

"No way. More like a lady. Thirties maybe. Well dressed. Nicely made up. Professional gal. Hey, I don't mean like one of them kind…"

"I understand. Say, what's your name?"

"Billy Turgeon."

Billy was likely in his mid-fifties, maybe older. From his bulbous red nose, my guess was he was a boozehound.

"Bring her more than once?"

"Half a dozen times as I recall. First couple of times, I happened to be driving by."

"Driving by where?"

"Where she works. I guess. She was always standing outside the building."

"Which is where?"

"Over in Delano. After that, she'd tell me when she'd need me, and I'd pick her up. That kind of stuff don't happen too often in my business. You know, like I'm a chauffeur or livery driver. Regular fare and all. Good tipper."

The description he gave me sounded a lot like Saundra Mooney. While it didn't surprise me the personal assistant of a businessman would visit his home, it was important to connect an awful lot of puzzle pieces still lying around. If it weren't for the sad performance in the department store, I might have let it all go. At this point, I was eager to see what Carla Duggan had dug up. There was a small part of me that knew this was a mistake. I didn't know who might be in more jeopardy.

Chapter Eleven

The cabbie dropped me off at the West-Urn Grill over on East Douglas. On the way, I saw Richie parked at his usual spot and figured an early dinner would give me enough motivation to see Glick Helbert. As I stepped out of the hack, I pointed back across the river.

"The building across from the Dillons in Delano. Is that where you picked up the lady you took to the house in Eastborough?"

"Yeah, that was it."

"And you said she worked there?"

"Well, I suppose so. It was where she always had me pick her up."

I absentmindedly slipped him a fin. "Wow! Thanks, Mack. You need a driver, you call me." I smiled and nodded. Hated to tell the guy I was full up with drivers.

I had to acknowledge the fact there was the slightest chance it wasn't Saundra Mooney. Could have been a friend of Caroline's or an as-yet unidentified acquaintance of Whitman himself. The last one was doubtful. I didn't make him for the suave playboy type. It made the most sense it was Saundra visiting the Whitman household on a regular basis. I couldn't figure out the almost secretive aspect of the cab rides. It was straight out of an espionage thriller and as cheaply concocted.

I ambled into the West-Urn Grill and grabbed a stool at the counter. I stared at the menu for what felt like half an hour before settling on a grilled chicken sandwich with mayo, lettuce, and tomato on wheat toast. Their coffee wasn't as good as King's X, but the sandwich filled me up. On top of that, the green-eyed waitress smiled and winked at me, which was always good for an extra kick in the pants. I didn't think Jennie would be jealous considering this gal seemed to have been around the block a time or two. For the most part, I was lost in thought, eating without realizing it, trying to balance Saundra Mooney's actions with Alonzo Washington's connection with Glick Hilbert. It felt like I was playing chess with a deck of cards.

It was rather warm, so I walked down to where Richie parked.

"Hey, Richie, I need you tonight if you're up for it."

"Sure thing, Hirsch. Where to?"

"Green Gables." I looked at him in anticipation of a response.

"Okay." He shrugged.

"How's about eight o'clock at my place?"

He gave me a thumbs up.

While it didn't have the element of danger like going to the Hollow Inn, Green Gables was a notorious roadhouse. They had no designs to be pretty or offer exotic drinks. They had girls dancing seductively as a floorshow and a three- or four-piece combo to get toes tapping and arms in the mood for lifting and pouring booze into one's gullet. The place catered to most working men's basic urges. Helbert and his partners, Max Cohen and Jim Stiff, owned the Ringside Sports

Center. It was where all the glamour was, where bigwigs and celebrities could rub elbows with athletes and gangsters, get a thrill in doing so, and then go back to their supposedly clean and starched lives without breaking a sweat. This roadhouse was a place to blow off steam and make a few bucks. It likely served as a place to launder dirty money and cater to a more unsavory crowd. That was an infraction for the police to pay attention to. My interests lay elsewhere.

Until the story Alonzo told, my impression of Glick Helbert was a big-time operator with a couple of legitimate businesses. To learn he was basically bootlegging and unintentionally involved in murder courtesy of a crooked cop made him much more dangerous. Since I didn't know how deep the corruption ran, there might be several on the force I could be up against. In that case, my former profession wouldn't save me. It became a stark disappointment, especially considering the fact I had at once desperately wanted to work with the likes of Clarence Mendenhall. To accept the notion of a dirty cop made me feel soiled. Perhaps there was still a bit of naïveté the war had not completely squeezed out of me.

I got home in time to freshen up and figure out how I would handle the evening's adventure. Fortunately, Sir Pounce and Lady Mittens had no time for discussions of morality and were only interested in dinner and continuing their bathing. I did not disturb them on either point. Approaching eight, I left the apartment and caught myself looking at the doorframe. I wondered if I should have placed a mezuzah there. While becoming a full-fledged rabbi was an impractical option, I had never given up being a Jew. Maintaining the scruples and morals inherent in the religion was more important to me than lighting candles and avoiding *treif.* Though I was no longer on the police force, I still worked as a man seeking justice. There are those who might not have considered my early incarnation as an assistant to divorce proceedings to be so noble. However, the treatment proffered by one spouse upon another was at times almost sinful. I was not a completely righteous man. I had honor but allowed thoughts of iniquity to enter my mind. I was painfully aware how human I was. At times, walking in darkness clouded my judgment. Unfortunately, this is now where I spent most of my time. Eventually, I felt I would emerge into the light.

"You ready, Richie," I said as I hopped into his hack.

"This a job? 'Cause there're a lot swankier places to go." He saw me in his rear-view mirror holding a sawbuck between my two fingers. "I've got my receipt book."

"No need."

He straightened up in his seat, tugged on his collar, and straightened his tie. He was overly polished for a guy driving to a dive.

The place was out of town on Thirteenth Street. To me it was slightly more than a bungalow yet turned out to be deceptively bigger inside. I gave Richie the option of coming in to join me, but he declined.

Despite being a white man in a white establishment, I still got looks upon entering. They obviously had a cadre of regulars, so I stood out. I wasn't dressed as shabby as on those nights looking for Caroline Whitman. This time it was a gray suit, white shirt, solid maroon tie, and black loafers. To all appearances, a typical run-of-the-mill Joe looking for a drink and a good time. Then again, I might have been overdressed.

Every place has a preferred method of gaining the bartender's attention. I lifted an eyebrow and nodded my head. Both actions gave me the look of a man with a nervous twitch rather than an ideal of suave sophistication.

"Beer." The bottle was up on the counter and the cap off in less than ten seconds. I slapped a dollar bill on the counter and the change appeared magically, as though he anticipated my every move. "Is Mr. Helbert here tonight?" The bartender's eyes widened as though a demon had landed on my shoulder.

"They told me you'd be around." The voice behind me was a booming baritone. A shadow anticipated my moves. The man behind the voice was slightly taller than me and rather fit looking for a man I guessed to be in his early sixties. A full head of dark brown hair and completely clean-shaven with a ruddy complexion, he came across more like a schoolteacher than the owner of a roadhouse. I couldn't recall any teachers I had who might have fit the bill. "You must be Mr. Bergman." He extended his hand. We were close to playing tug of war when I grabbed it.

"Thank you for taking the time to visit with me." I spoke as though I made a doctor's appointment, and he fully knew what I required. He might have been surprised I never asked who 'they' were.

"I have a fondness for Alonzo. Just sorry to hear he's not around."

"Missing is more like it, Mr. Helbert. And his wife

is deeply concerned."

"As she should be," he stated matter-of-factly. Then, after a pause, "As all wives should worry about their husbands. Just look around here at all the missing spouses." I didn't respond to his attempt at humor. "Are you married, Mr. Bergman?"

"I haven't found the messiah nor a woman who can put up with my idiosyncrasies."

He laughed heartily. I had to wonder if he were Jewish as well.

"Come with me." It was not as much of a request by the tone of his voice.

He led me into his office, a room hardly bigger than a water closet that held only one small desk and two chairs. A brass lamp stood between us. I also noticed several drawers within arm's reach. There might have been papers, pencils, or a gun in them.

"How is it you're acquainted with Alonzo Washington?"

"He's a reliable man who has made himself available for various odd jobs. As you can imagine, it's rather difficult to support a wife on a night watchman's pay."

"What kind of odd jobs?"

"Related to my business."

"Which is?" It was a gentle game of Ping Pong, the words bouncing back and forth in slight clicking sounds, each one coming on the heels of the prior one. Eventually, the ball drops off the table and a player scores a point.

"Anything I'm involved in." He smiled broadly. He wouldn't say or admit to anything. Perhaps he, like Albert Whitman, knew a bit of my background. It was good policy to not say anything too revealing no matter who you were speaking to, especially as the owner of a roadhouse. He was like an impatient father feeding a cranky infant. He would give me enough to keep me quiet and allow him to be satisfied he did his job. "I assure you if I see him, I'll tell him his wife is deeply concerned."

"That's all I can ask," I responded politely. His smile faded like a snowflake in the wind. He sat up straight in his chair.

"You can ask for more, Mr. Bergman, but this is all you're going to get." The genial host returned from a brief hiatus after conveying the message. "Please have a drink and catch the show. The ladies are delightful. I doubt you'll find your messiah. On the other hand, you might find the next Mrs. Bergman." The smile was one of a satanic clown, a puppeteer pulling strings and getting everyone else to dance.

It was everything I could do to quell the nausea rising within me. I imagined cutting him down to size by revealing what I knew. For the moment, I kept it bottled up until I could figure out an angle of attack.

The original beer I ordered was nowhere around. I nodded in the direction of the bartender who very quickly opened another one, placed it on the bar, and walked off. Perhaps I had preferred status due to my acquaintance with Mr. Helbert. It could have been this was the "one for the road."

I wandered through the place casually like a cop to see if anyone looked familiar, all the while fully aware Helbert's goons watched meticulously. Sitting in the back gazing lasciviously at one of the dancers was Aaron Lautenberg. I strode quickly over to him and sat opposite, partially blocking his desired view.

"I didn't quite take you for this kind of joint." My tone was friendly, almost over the top. Initially he stared at me as though I were an intrusive stranger. He eventually realized I was just a man he met casually who was being intrusive.

"Doing you a favor and looking for Alonzo." It was what passed for humor with Mr. Lautenberg. Apparently, everyone in the joint had a sense of humor. Perhaps there was a burlesque show later in the evening.

"Let me buy you a drink as a token of my appreciation." I looked around for a waitress. A loud whistle on his part brought an overwhelmed young girl to the table. She was pretty, not enough to be dancing on the stage, and had the faintest resemblance to Cinderella.

"Has Mr. Washington come back to work?"

"No." He spoke bluntly and with a sense of finality even though I wasn't finished. I got the impression he was.

"Why would you look for a colored man here?"

"Look, buddy, I'm here for a couple of drinks and to look at these dames after a long day of work. Alonzo comes back or doesn't, delivery boys like him are a dime a dozen."

"Delivery boy? I thought he was a night watchman."

He stared at me blankly, no anger or concern. It was like a mechanic pulled a plug and a machine simply stopped. Suddenly, he got up and stormed off. I started to follow when a group of men, fondling one of the dancers and getting roughed up by a bouncer, slowed my progress.

When I eventually got outside, I jogged up to Richie's car and leaned in.

"Did you see a tall man with a reddish-brown goatee come out just now?"

He apologized for having his attention solely on his newspaper. There was no reason to be upset. I had more parts to assemble. My only hope was once I assembled the picture completely, Alonzo Washington would come back home.

Chapter Twelve

One of my jobs was officially over on account of receiving payment for it. That was the determination in my profession. A clear demarcation that is transactional in nature. A clearly defined *quid pro quo*. Yet I kept it rolling around in my mind as though a train had plowed me over in Union Station. I realized I should get back up and keep moving. I fully grasped the concept a good businessman would never have worked without the possibility of payment, but this Whitman issue was purely a moral dilemma. My other case was not the typical wayward husband scenario of divorce cases that had formerly been my bread and butter. It was an issue that threatened to turn me into Alice falling down a rabbit hole or Daniel in a cave filled with lions. I didn't like where I was going with either. In the end, I felt I had no choice.

There were times in my life when an unidentified compulsion pulled me or pushed me in a direction I believed contrary to my nature. When my gut moved me faster than my feet. The truth is I didn't fully understand my nature until these things happened. This is how epiphanies occur, in alleys or small deserted streets when no one else is looking.

I saw all the pieces like tarot cards on a velvet cloth. There was an interesting collection of folks involved with bootlegging and dive clubs that caused

Alonzo Washington to lay low. All of them apparently had their own reasons; none of them mattered to Alonzo. Glick Helbert and his associates had money and connections. Yet they were apparently under the thumb of a corrupt cop who murdered a bootlegger and seller of contraband named Timmy Barczak. With such a demeanor, he was not one to trifle with. Not being able to identify him made it tougher on me to use my old friends on the force. Any of them could have been involved; it was a disheartening thought. Aaron Lautenberg, a dull-headed supervisor of a meat packing plant, was likely a stooge for whoever ran this operation by providing low-level workers to earn "extra cash" and become expendable pawns if necessary. Perhaps he was smarter than he acted and more involved than I considered. I had to assume the cop and perhaps an unidentified person were the key figures to find. The person or persons I sought were likely hiding in plain sight. That would wind up making me an easy target as well.

I never made any assumptions the goodwill extended to me by my former co-workers would last forever. If I didn't abuse the privileges of inside information requests, I could at least stay in their good graces for a while. It was early on Saturday morning I sought out Floyd Gunsaullus at the police department on East William. I found him chatting up Mel Baumgartner who made detective in early 1941. For a few months back then, his promotion rankled me quite a bit largely because I was so determined to rise in the ranks and felt cheated. I had taken on extra work, had in-depth discussions with other detectives to learn the trade, and paid due respects to the appropriate officers.

Furthermore, I had been on the force longer, but Mel made detective before me. Of course, I couldn't make any excuses, as he was Jewish as well. It finally dawned on me he was more qualified at the time than I was. It is surprising what you see when you finally look in a mirror. An old Jewish proverb states "Better an honest slap in the face than an insincere kiss."

"Hello, gentlemen." I shook Mel's hand firmly not having encountered him since before the war. Mel smiled sincerely without returning a response. I turned my attention to Gunny. "Any updates on the Barczak murder?"

"Not to my knowledge. Marty Hoeg is heading up that one."

"I guess I can check with him." Gunny grabbed my arm as I darted off. He had the look of a father cautioning a son about to drive off with the family car.

"I wouldn't do that if I were you."

"Why not?" I said, genuinely surprised.

"He does not like you. At all." Mel had an agreeing smirk on his face.

"Says who?"

As Gunny moved closer, the three of us converged.

"Back in '42 after you enlisted, he said he was glad we were getting rid of 'that punk' and hoped you would end up a hero."

"You mean dead?"

"Exactly."

"I can ask for you, Harold," Mel offered. "Floyd's told me this relates to a case you're working on."

"It's pretty big. I'd say explosive." It wasn't my intention to be melodramatic but after my night at Green Gables, it was much more than I initially realized. My breath came out like the air out of a balloon. I hated to think the attitude of one cop might wind up stonewalling my case. However, it wouldn't be the first time.

Something didn't feel right. It was like ball bearings sloping back and forth from ear to ear. I had to let Baumgartner find out what he could and see where it would take me. In the meantime, I had second thoughts about my conversation with Dale Walker after the cab dropped me off back home. So I continued walking a block north up to the York Rite Temple. The ballroom there held dances featuring Gage Brewer and whatever name his current band's incarnation may have been. My favorite was Gage Brewer's Hawaiian Entertainers because of their exotic sound. Plus, I had a strong desire to visit Hawaii. Wichita, or just about anywhere in Kansas, did not have white sand beaches, blue water, or palm trees. I met Gage before I joined the police department and saw him at the old Shadowland Dance Pavilion before it burned down. By then, younger musicians were developing intricate chord progressions, which eventually became bebop, and I felt a freedom in music I had not known before. Regardless of the musical trend of the day, our friendship stayed strong. He had a round face, high forehead, and an amiable grin, except when he was playing his guitar. Then, it was total concentration and seriousness.

I knew he would be rehearsing with his group because he was a perfectionist. Despite living so close to one of his favorite venues, I hardly ever intruded upon him. He made a living as a musician, and his rehearsals were the closest thing to a religious service you could find. It was a quality of his character I easily respected. Fortunately, Gage called out—"All right, take ten"—right as I walked in. He greeted me with a warm smile and scrupulously avoided a handshake. The hands that played the first electric guitar in Wichita were like fine china. He could not abide chips and scratches.

"Harold Bergman, what brings you into a Masonic lodge, so far away from your Twelve Tribes?"

"Why, the melodic musings of Gage Brewer. What else?"

We were as opposite as could be. His music was reminiscent of warm breezes and gentle waves, but he played with a concrete determination. He always dressed immaculately, whether it was a radio gig, ballroom, or a plain old rehearsal. A dozen years older than me, he focused all his attention on his musicianship, similar to the way I sought the truth in all things I did. Perhaps our single-mindedness was the key to our friendship. After all, I couldn't carry a tune.

"What do you know about Dale Walker?" I asked.

"Big House? I think he did himself a disservice with that moniker."

"How so?"

"He's just about the gentlest man I know. Works diligently to find his sound although he still has a bit of Wardell Gray in him. Very fluid, very clean. Oh, there's nothing wrong with that but at some point, you've got to find your own voice. Eventually he will."

I nodded in understanding, both musically and personally. "Think he could be involved in anything?"

"Like?"

"Like something not musical and not good for his health."

"Uh-uh. The kid's clean. Good upbringing. Fine education. I can't see him wandering off down the yellow brick road."

"Many have taken the wrong fork along the way, Gage."

"Not this one. Say, why the interest?"

"He could be heading down a mistaken path unknowingly."

I tapped Gage on the shoulder as I headed out and went back home. There was no need to drag him into this mess any more than these simple questions. It was after noon and my stomach was rumbling, not enough to drown out the incessant droning of Sir Pounce. I filled the kibble bowl to satisfy his yearnings and then scoured the pantry for a snack to satisfy mine. A box of saltines and a jar of peanut butter would have to suffice.

Sitting at my kitchen table and spreading peanut butter on crackers, I had to agree with Gage's assessment of Dale Walker. While a nickname for jazz musicians or ball players was as much about creating a persona, the real person was often different. Whatever Caroline Whitman had gotten herself into, I truly believed Walker loved her and had a need to care for her to validate their relationship. There were enough distinctions due to race and social class as to drown love in a vat of reality. How he would wind up doing that I couldn't be certain.

However, after encountering her and her father out shopping and putting on the appearance of a perfect relationship, I had to wonder what Walker would do next. There was a chance he could respond violently or lapse into a drunken stupor. I intended to find out considering he was the only link to the truth.

My search started and ended at the Rustic Inn. He was at the same table where I first saw him and Caroline. His glass had a small swig remaining while the bottle was nearly empty, and the place had opened less than an hour before. His head teetered on his thick neck and threatened to simply fall off like King Kong plummeting from the Empire State Building. As I approached, I noticed fiery, blood red eyes and dry parched lips, with a bit of foamy spit at the corners of his mouth. He was halfway between Today and Forgetfulness.

"You'll never play in that condition," I said quietly as I sat in a chair close to him. He didn't react, didn't try to push me away.

"What do you know? Bird can blow mean on junk."

"You ain't Bird." The words were like ice water thrown in his face. Right then, it was as though he cleared out of his stupor, got straight, and was ready to go ten rounds for the championship. That was how fast his head swiveled. But a glaze covered his eyes, and there was nothing in his legs to lift him. Recognizing the futility, he poured the remnants of the bottle into the glass.

"He got her back."

"I know." He looked at me as he would a friend, realizing my understanding. "Tell me for what."

"We told you."

"If she knows it was wrong and she wants to leave with you, why would she go back? Unless—" I let the word hang there like a bell to ring him out of his stupor.

"Unless what?" His shoulders squared up, and he leaned partially forward in anticipation of my answer.

"Unless she doesn't want to go off with you. Unless she was just one of those young white gals that thinks it was cool to play around with a colored jazz man to make their daddies angry." His jaw was busy clenching his teeth hard, and his hands balled into fists he could hammer my face with. Now, he was getting ready to turn into Joe Louis. "I don't think so either. Then why? You've got to give me something."

"You work for him. I ain't giving you nothing." At this point, everyone was his enemy. Perhaps even Caroline.

"Worked for him," I said with emphasis. "There's a difference. He paid me off, said I was done and everything between the two of them was worked out. So if you don't accept my help, you can go back to playing nightclubs until you're famous or dead and just say goodbye to Caroline."

The comment was an absolute. It showed there was no other recourse than to fight for what was true and right, what he wanted. But it was up to him now, no one else. No one else could decide for him unless he retreated. He would have to go up against money and privilege. He would be an underdog to a powerful white man. He would likely lose but he would have no chance of winning unless he tried. I have read: *There is no pity for a man who moans about living in one town and does not move to another.*

In his condition, I knew there was nothing more I could get from him except a promise of sobriety the next time we met. I invited him to lunch at the Pan American Café which he was reluctant to accept. When I told him of my friendship with the owner and a promise of privacy, he acquiesced. I only hoped he would remember after trying so hard to drown out his memory and pain.

Chapter Thirteen

A knock at my door at seven the next morning startled me more so than the cats. It wasn't that it was too early, not when a hungry Sir Pounce was jumping on top of me with hungered moans and a couple of ill-placed claws. I expected and accepted the machinations of felines. It was more like I never got visitors at such an hour or on a Sunday for that matter. Not even prospective clients. I peeked out the front window and saw a black Ford parked out front. It had no markings yet it came across as official. It was far too unadorned to be anything else. Opening the door, I encountered the weary smile of Clarence Mendenhall. His eyes had a heaviness to them as though he saw more than he cared to of the darker side of the city. And this was the man who wanted me to join him on the same crusade, perhaps for nothing further than to lighten the load.

"This is a surprise," I commented. "You want some coffee?"

"Nah. Heading home after the end of my shift."

"Is this what I would have had to deal with?"

He smiled. Maybe it would still have been worthwhile. "What gives?" I coaxed.

"I was following up on the bootlegger killing. Timmy Barczak."

"And?" I was a dentist, pulling info like teeth. If a visitor disturbed my sleep on a Sunday morning, the least they could do was spill it fast.

Mendenhall scratched his head and frowned. He was uncomfortable, maybe partially confused. He was ready to give me the skinny on it but acted as though he didn't know how to start.

"Well, I can't rightly figure this out. According to Hoeg, he says he's got nothing so far. Doesn't even have much on the victim, Timmy Barczak. He sounded rather blasé about it, too. Like he didn't care much about it. Am I making any sense?"

"Well, it's still early in the investigation." I couldn't figure out what the big deal was to his uncertainty.

"Yeah, but I just had a brief chat with Captain Huckins over in Vice Division. He gave me a list of about half a dozen Known Associates, all a bunch of squirrely characters and all have had minor run ins with the law on a few occasions. Not to mention a couple of priors on Barczak down in Oklahoma and a last known address up in Newton."

"Ok. So?" This time, it felt like pulling wisdom teeth.

"Well, if I got all that in about five minutes, why doesn't Hoeg have anything?" Mendenhall held out his hands like Roy Partee waiting on a pitch from "Boo" Ferriss.

My first thought was Marty Hoeg was an arrogant, incompetent fool who was in way over his head. Yet a veteran cop, even one as lackadaisical as Hoeg, would have a wealth of resources to at least begin a proper investigation. I doubt he could have slid through all those years and not have a single clue what he was doing. There no reason to think anything else.

However, the Barczak murder was the key to the reason Alonzo Washington went into hiding and why his life was in danger. At this point, it was important to ingratiate myself into the case even if it meant getting close to Hoeg. While it was not an appealing prospect, it dawned on me it would be a necessary one.

It was awfully hard to squeeze blood from a stone. After Floyd Gunsaullus told me of Hoeg's comments it was apparent there was no love lost between us. I figured he would be as dismissive and rude as possible, holding me in a special kind of contempt, especially since I was a private investigator now. It would have been understandable if he were an anti-Semite. The fact he didn't like me was a conundrum I just couldn't figure.

Clarence was far too tired to continue figuring out something that wasn't even one of his cases. I thanked him for stopping by, and let him get a little much needed shut-eye.

After a couple of cups of coffee, a shower, and an ear scratching session with the cats, I walked down to the Carnegie Library to find out what Carla Duggan had dredged up. When I first entered, she was flitting between two elderly ladies like a ballerina, showing a delicacy she hid from her closest friends and acquaintances. Her belief was to be as honest and forthcoming with the latter. Everyone else got the silk rose.

"You won't believe this, but I only found two photos, one of each guy, Whitman and Sondergaard." She gasped in exasperation. Such a lack of success was abhorrent to her. She truly believed in her own intellectual omnipotence.

One photo was from the *Appleton Post-Crescent* of Sondergaard in early 1939. He was standing with a group of prominent German-American businessmen from all over Wisconsin, Michigan, and a couple from Chicago. They were welcoming him to the United States after he left Denmark. They might have been prominent in Appleton, but they were unrecognizable to me. I wasn't sure if it would be necessary to further identify them. I held off for the time being. In the *Los Angeles Times* Albert Whitman was smiling with producer Bryan Foy, a couple of attractive starlets, and a guy I recognized as John "Handsome Johnny" Roselli. The date on the photo was Tuesday, January 2, 1940. The headline proclaimed, "Hollywood's Fresh New Faces in the New Year." I wondered which of the faces it meant.

There was a vague lascivious smile on Whitman's face, one I couldn't imagine on the gentleman I conducted business with recently. Additionally, his current demeanor did not impress me as a womanizer comfortable in the Hollywood milieu. This was a scant six years prior. I wondered what, if anything, had changed.

The surprising thing was Carla could find nothing else since then. There were no articles or photographs for any other professional announcement, charitable event, or social occasion of these two enormously successful businessmen. Not even the obituary of his wife, which I could only assume was at a time further in the past and which not even Carla had located. If I hadn't met Albert Whitman myself, I couldn't be sure he even existed.

Perhaps I was working under the mistaken

impression a certain kind of affluence craved media attention. On the other hand, it was reasonable to allow for the fact extremely wealthy individuals might shy away from the spotlight, content to make their money and secure their power in private. Like the Wizard of Oz, those kinds worked best behind a curtain. It was also easy to assume a nefarious background lurking there that threatened to unravel a financial empire. A disgruntled daughter and her jealous boyfriend could either be making up stories or lighting a fuse that could become explosive. This lack of publicity was leading me in one definitive direction.

The silhouette of a big colored man filled the doorway to the Pan American Café. The blinding light of the mid-afternoon sun just disappeared. Until then, I did not truly have a feel for the girth and size of the sax player known as Big House. The name had more than one connotation.

Surprisingly, as he stepped forward allowing his eyes to adjust to the relative darkness of the interior, he acted more like a wayward child who found his way home. I could only hope he had. I waved my hand from a booth in the back. After a moment, he saw me and walked slowly in my direction. He slid into the booth opposite me. He held his hands crossed in front of him and his eyes examined the tabletop.

"King Mar has the best roast beef sandwich in town," I exclaimed with elation to break the ice. "I guarantee it."

"I'm not hungry," he responded politely albeit quietly.

"Suit yourself." With a nod of my head and a point of my finger, I placed my standard order with a waiter standing off toward the side. "You sober?"

"Yeah." He lifted his head with a hurt look in his eyes as though I thought of him in only the basest and stereotypical terms. That was not my intention. I shook my head lightly in the affirmative, letting him know I believed him. He would, however, need to convince me of the rest of his story.

The waiter brought out a sandwich so thick it could be a weapon. I picked up a half, took a big bite, and started chewing ravenously, making the same satisfied sounds I did as a kid, and for which my mother scolded me. Walker's eyes lit up.

"Too late to change my mind?" His voice was now light and almost pleading. I smiled and made a second motion to the waiter.

We ate our sandwiches like hungry men on a chain gang, enjoying the meal but feeling as though it could be our last. I often wondered what the disciples felt on that fateful Passover. The waiter cleared and wiped down the table. Two cups of coffee stood steaming hot before us. I was waiting for Dale Walker to get comfortable enough to speak on his own terms. Time could be as much of a friend as an enemy.

"Caroline started coming to the Rustic Inn, sitting up front, staring at me practically."

"That bother you?"

"Nah. Lots of white girls got their fantasies. It was when she started following me around other clubs I took notice. One night she caught up with me out back of a club on a break. We were smoking reefers and she asked for a puff. I thought she was being cool until I realized she could handle her stuff. Rest of the night she was in Bop City."

"Did you make her?"

The question embarrassed him. It finally dawned on me Dale "Big House" Walker was no stereotype. It shamed me I had treated him as so many others had done to me, having an opinion of Jews before I could get my mouth open to speak. What makes a person is an aspect beyond race or religion, a deeper facet that does not automatically appear on the surface. I vowed to do better in the future.

"I wasn't looking to. She talked about the music, rattled off the names of half a dozen local cats, knew where they played and what they were good at and what they weren't. Chords, melodies, stuff musicians talked about. She was aces. This was no bobby-soxer with a dream. Funny thing was she didn't tell me much about her and I didn't ask. Until one night we were sitting in my car, and she started crying. And then she blurted it all out."

"What?"

"Who her dad was. How he really made his money. What he wanted her to do."

"Which was what?"

"Find a stooge to help her sell the stuff."

"And you were the stooge."

His face and body language were a rainbow of emotions. His eyes got glassy as though he were on the verge of crying at the same time his fists balled up in hot-blooded anger. A volcano can't help but erupting; men have an option, but they must choose.

"It wasn't like that," he shot back through gritted teeth. "She couldn't go through with it. She said it wasn't right. She said--" He stopped. I knew the next words out of his mouth were a proclamation of love. He would profess it to the end of time. They made countless B movies with this same story. The problem was she was nowhere around to confirm it. Last time I saw Caroline Whitman, her daddy wowed her with his money in a clothing store. I began to think she played him for a sap.

"If everything you say is true, why hasn't she come back, gotten a message to you, something? It doesn't make sense. You've got to convince me, Dale."

"Why?"

"Because I only half believe you on my own. You've got to give me the other half."

He looked at me as his eyes cleared and his hands relaxed. He sat upright, shoulders firmly squared to the back of the booth. He understood.

He explained in whatever detail he could grasp what they had done to simply satisfy Albert Whitman at first. Walker knew a few junkies, musicians and otherwise. It was easy to push packets of dope onto a group of folks willing to throw out their hard-earned cash. It wasn't as though they were turning anyone on to the stuff. Until, that is, one of Caroline's friends begged her to try it for a kick. She went with Caroline and Walker at the house I visited, and they shot her up. It got her hooked. It was Annette, one of the girls I spoke with at the college. Junk soiled sweetness and purity. And created a new market. There were far more where she came from.

Apparently, this success pleased Whitman as he figured the existing dope fiends would die out or wind up in prison, taking away a viable resource. It was important to create new customers to replace the old. As Walker explained it, this turn of events sickened

Caroline. Her father threatened to cut off her lavish lifestyle. Eventually, she came to appreciate the real relationship she had with Dale and simply wanted out. Whatever it took. The problem was neither realized to what lengths Whitman would go to maintain his business.

Listening to him, it felt like a haunted version of a warped fairy tale. This was not the dream of immigrants like my parents but the perverse manipulations by a man of pure evil.

"And now?" I asked.

"I don't know, man. Either he's got her under his thumb, or she can't go it alone with me. I want to believe it's the first."

"But it could just as easily be the second."

He nodded in fearful understanding.

From my perspective, it wouldn't be easy to bring down such a business which likely had protection all the way around if Caroline would not act as a wedge against her father. I certainly was no Joshua fighting the Battle of Jericho. No shiny shields would blind the wealth and power of a ruthless man who used his own daughter to run a criminal organization. At this point, it would take a miracle.

Chapter Fourteen

My lack of belief in superstitions did not dissuade me from, at the very least, the consideration of an adverse happening on this April Fool's Day Monday. Allowing for any possibilities was a mark of preparedness, if not a touch of madness. It was a pleasant and sunny day, nearing the seventies, with not a drop of rain in sight. Nevertheless, the wind gusted and threatened to throw me off my path. A wind wagon would have been useful right then.

I had a limited circle of friends and acquaintances as much by both choice as opportunity. There were several policemen who were former colleagues for whom there was mutual respect. Marty Hoeg was most certainly nothing more than a cop I knew. We weren't close before the war and from what I gathered there would be nothing resembling a communion now. I was on good terms with many members of my father's temple. They did not share the same desire for me to join the rabbinate but an appearance at Shabbat services came up on occasion. There were no comments regarding my current profession in casual conversation. Several servicemen from Wichita and the surrounding area were ones I would run into now and again. A few were fond of reminiscing; others acted as though the past was in an iron box, sealed for eternity. I completely understood how memories could either strengthen or weaken a person's constitution. Of course, there were the local denizens like Richie and Charlie, Jennie, and King Mar. These were people living their everyday lives in the best way they knew how. I often considered them more like family.

There was one distinctive couple I met at a social function at the temple even though they were not affiliated with it. Bradley Wolrebinski was a Polish Jewish émigré who wrote lurid crime fiction under the name R.C. Donnelly. His wife, Svetlana Halonen, was a half-Russian half-Finnish artist who had an astounding greenhouse in the back of their opulent home on Park Place. I was never aware of them having gainful employment nor being involved in anything unsavory or illegal. Somehow they threw lavish parties, attended all manner of citywide events, and were both crazy as loons. It was possible the art world was more profitable than many others would have you believe. I was closer to them than to anyone other than my father.

Due to his avocation, Bradley's mind thought in criminal terms, the devious and nefarious being an explanation for just about anything, including why the Orlando, Florida Army Air Base lost last year's National Baseball Congress Championship. It was the unique quirk that allowed him to write his stories. I could never be sure if he genuinely had a criminal background or was associated with anyone who did. The uncertainty led an air of mystery to his gregarious persona. When it came to formulating a plan of attack, I chose to consult with him rather than Mendenhall or Gunsaullus. Unlike the movie detectives, I was not about to commit a breaking-and-entering to acquire information. Beyond the legal aspects, I could not bring myself to perpetrate a crime to catch a criminal. From Amos, it is said to hate evil, love good, and maintain justice. I wouldn't be able to do that from a jail cell.

The front door of their home was thick oak, impenetrable by a swift kick. A beveled glass allowed him to view visitors while a delicate lace curtain afforded the necessary privacy. I had no need to knock as the door opened magically upon my upraised hand. When it came to Bradley, I was dubious about miracles and more inclined to believe in surveillance.

"*Bubbeleh,*" he proclaimed, referring to me in Yiddish as he would his grandson. Bradley had a shock of white hair, mostly unkempt, and a huge gnarled white beard, almost as long as John Brown's. A white collarless shirt covered by a paisley vest and black pants gave him the look of a vagabond artist from 1920's Paris. An all-encompassing hug followed. It took me a moment to breathe again.

"Schnapps?" he offered. Whereas I did not drink much hard liquor, I could not bring myself to turn down his generosity. It was a different ambiance than a couple of patrolmen hitting a bar after their shift. This had all the elements of refined gentility. There were many evenings of chess until well past midnight, discussions about Kierkegaard and Schopenhauer intermingled with tales of awful crimes committed in one part of the country or another. He read every newspaper he could get his hands on and listened to both radio and shortwave to gather knowledge from around the world, even if it were only gossip or hearsay. For him, keeping informed meant staying one step ahead of everyone else. This was the secret to his literary success.

We sat in his parlor and sipped our schnapps while I described to him the Whitman case without divulging too many specific names. The idea was to determine how an operation of this magnitude would work. Given his reach into the international aspects of crime, I figured him to be able to enlighten me.

"Obviously, they need connections in countries where they grow and harvest poppy. The Asian writing on the one crate you saw was testament to this."

"But how can they bring it into the country? Aren't there inspectors?"

He waved his hand in a dismissive fashion.

"This country is so intent upon returning to economic normalcy much of the regulations are overlooked by fools happy to have a job. That, of course, and a little bribery goes a long way. The issue your man has is not acquiring the stuff but distributing it. Might I assume he is a man of affluence who does not frequent the lower circles of society?"

"Your assumption would be accurate." Bradley was no mind reader, just an astute writer.

Svetlana waltzed into the room, practically walking on air. Her extremely long jet-black hair was pulled into a mammoth bun on top of her head. She wore a smock covered in paint over a man's buttoned-down dress shirt and pair of corduroy pants. She was also barefoot. Whatever her wardrobe, she exuded an elegance few actresses in Hollywood could match.

"Ah, Harold." It was her traditional greeting, no matter the occasion. She grabbed the glass from Bradley's hand, finished his drink in one swallow, and placed the glass back into his hand. "You have come to visit this cretin and not me?"

"Alas, 'tis true."

She glided over to me, kissed me on top of my head, and left the room, lyrically reporting, "The canvas is calling."

"She's working on a landscape of the Arkansas River. Says it represents the wandering aspects of the city with a Freudian interpretation of growth from infancy to geriatrics." He shrugged in uncertainty. "Where were we?"

"Distribution."

"Yes. This must be why he is using his daughter. His only alternative is to seek out people he is not familiar with and trust them with his product. This would be unlikely, for any businessman. Not only is the loss of the investment at risk, so is the business itself, not to mention incarceration. So you see he has few other options. Unfortunately for him, the girl's rebellion has thrown a wrinkle in his plans, which forces him to place her subordinate. Barring some kind of *deus ex machina,* it's his only recourse."

"My thought was to drive a wedge between them, but it looks doubtful given my limited access. After all, the job, such that it was, is over."

"He cannot be running this operation by himself. There must be another aware of it all to manage things. Direct involvement would shine a spotlight on his activities. Such businesses have a dirty side and a clean one. They hardly ever mix except during monetary exchanges. Occasionally, there is another clean associate, one who is not noticed or suspected. Rather innocuous I would say."

It was then my mind raced to Saundra Mooney, the cabbie's regular fare. She had a spotless character being a war widow and would certainly be above suspicion. There was a possibility of turning her flirtations toward me to better use. While I did not relish the notion of using a woman in that fashion, I had to come to terms with the suspicion she could be as deeply involved, consequently placing Caroline in further jeopardy. If that were the case, perhaps it would absolve my guilt. What a shame it would take another's guilt or duplicity to allow me to clear my conscience. Maybe it was the cosmic balance I knew nothing about.

Richie helped me track down the cabbie who was a regular driver for Mrs. Mooney, the roughneck named Billy Turgeon. I had to assure Richie I was not considering using Turgeon's services on any kind of a regular basis. A fin helped loosen Billy Turgeon's tongue. I was able to determine her favorite places to shop and eat as well as the approximate times she went over to Whitman's house. It would be a simple matter to "run into her" at one of these locations and allow her to do the rest. I had no problem playing the role of the gullible dupe.

It was in the Ollie Moses East End Department Store she found me looking at ties. She sidled over to me, feigned surprise and then playful delight at the encounter. I was hoping a producer would get Jimmy Stewart to play me in the film version, although he was decidedly taller. Saundra coyly indicated she was shopping for a gift for a special man but didn't say whom.

"I didn't really think of you as the shopping type," she said demurely.

"All private detectives are not the grubby little men you see in the movies. I think it's important to make a clean presentation to a prospective employer." I kept my tone professional until I determined there was a need to drop it.

"So now you'll go home and listen to a radio show while dressed in your finest digs?" She was chiding me. I allowed her to do so.

"Why? Is there something else I should be doing?" Now I was halfway between a naïve schoolboy and a village idiot.

"Mr. Bergman, shame on you. There is an available young lady who is showing a little interest in you. How good of a detective are you anyway?" I smiled. "Are you familiar with the Blue Moon Night Club?"

"On South Oliver? Yeah, I know it."

"Shall we say eight this evening?"

"Mrs. Mooney, it's a weeknight. Would your employer approve?"

"Truth be told, I practically run the place." She winked at me and started to leave, then turned back suddenly. "By the way, you can call me Saundra. And, uh, wear the tie." Not since Baby taught Bogie how to whistle had there been a better offer.

I walked down to the hack stand and found Richie, telling him to pick me up at eight o'clock. He questioned why I shouldn't leave early to get there on time. I briefly explained I didn't want the lady to think she had me completely won over so soon. When I told him I didn't need him to pick me up later, he gave me a big cartoonish wink. I let him think what he wished .

I tended to the cats and then went to Mrs. Hanover's apartment to pay the rent. Unlike some of the tenants, I paid in cash. It made it easier for her to pay bills. Miss Elizabeth Smith from two-twelve was on her way out. She smiled affectionately. I didn't have the heart to tell her I thought of her more as a kid sister, given I was seven years older than she was. Mrs. Hanover handed me a plate with a chocolate zucchini bread figuring I didn't eat as well being a detective. She was the kind of considerate lady most people wished they had for a mother. In one regard, she filled in for my own.

There was a good deal of grooming, more so than typical for me. It was always my desire to look presentable, but I self-consciously went overboard to put on the Ritz. While she was an attractive woman, I had no feeling for Saundra Mooney. Even before indulging in this subterfuge, she seemed to me to be of two minds. The part that was appealing was the dutiful wife treasuring her late husband's memory. On the other hand, she could be the schemer a la Mary Astor from "The Maltese Falcon" knowing perfectly well what was going on the whole time and playing both ends against the middle. I felt as conflicted as Sam Spade, in control of everything even though I was oblivious to what was going on. Perhaps the cinematic private detectives had qualities in common with the real ones after all.

Such was the world I inhabited by choice. My jobs entailed unearthing information on behalf of a client. Often the answer to their question was more misery and frustration rather than revelation and salvation. I was not supposed to get emotionally involved, nor was I required to make a personal connection. By my upbringing, I had no other choice. My mother and father instilled in me a sense of compassion for my fellow human beings. I wasn't sure if those were the aspects of Judaism or the teachings of my parents. In any event, I found myself conflicted in considering Saundra Mooney.

For the time being, the only thing that meant anything was I had a date.

Chapter Fifteen

It was about quarter after eight when Richie dropped me off in the parking lot, enough away from the front entrance as to be unseen. I was hoping that might add an air of mystery to my arrival. A pale crescent moon hung casually in a very clear sky. There was a comfortable warmth enveloping me like a favorite jacket. It was the kind of evening lovers talked about and reveled in. I, however, had different thoughts on my mind, also filled with hope and promise.

I used a pomade to give my hair a slicked back look and left my hat at home feeling it made me look too professional. It was important I came across as a real human being outside of the realm of buttoned-down business types. I wore a dark charcoal gray pin striped suit, white shirt, black and maroon tie with a gold stickpin. I polished my shoes to the extent they would bounce the spotlights in all directions and blind the musicians on the bandstand. Most guys revel in this kind of outfit. I saw it in the same light as a police uniform or a tallit and yarmulke. Clothes didn't necessarily make the man; they unapologetically defined him. Tonight, I was playing the role of lothario, a kind of Jewish Valentino. Given my lack of experience in such a character, my concern would be my target would see right through me.

There was an air of ambivalence about me as I

entered, surreptitiously scanning in a sweeping arc across the room. I made sure not to show too much eagerness, just a basic reconnaissance and nothing more. Facing to the right, a sultry voice came from the left.

"You didn't impress me as a guy who would leave a lady waiting." Saundra Mooney had the exotic look of Hedy Lamarr, one eyebrow raised in seductive inquiry not necessarily expecting an answer, as she knew them all. She wore a strapless white lace gown with pearly white rhinestone embroidery. Perhaps it was too much for such a joint or maybe she was working extra hard to impress me. It was a sartorial quid pro quo. On the other hand, this could have been what she aspired to all along and had obviously succeeded. If I had to say so, I thought we made an attractive couple.

"Well, I was trying to appear impressive. You, on the other hand, have far outdone me."

She smiled.

I extended my arm. We turned to the maître d' who was waiting for her signal. He escorted us to a table for two in front of the dance floor. There were catty looks from several of the women and dumbfounded ones by many men. This was not a mere office girl or personal assistant I was with. Perhaps those lingering eyes knew that more than I did.

She ordered two champagne cocktails. I wasn't sure if that was a way to make an impact on me or if her true colors were coming out. Perhaps working for Whitman afforded her the kind of scratch necessary to live an enhanced lifestyle. As my desires leaned toward good strong coffee and a decent burger, my profession suited me well.

"Tell me more about yourself, Mr. Bergman," she asked after her first sip.

"What would you like to know?"

"Oh, anything that might interest me."

"I would have thought you knew about me completely by now considering I was briefly employed by your boss. I mean, doesn't he have a dossier on me?"

There was a small bat of her eyelashes and an almost embarrassed blush in her cheeks. She was less like Lamar and more like Clara Bow.

"Well, I do take care of all Mr. Whitman's business matters. This was a family issue and he preferred to handle it himself. Otherwise, I would have hired a detective for him."

"But you're not sorry with his choice?"

"Not at all." She gulped down her drink and ordered another one. She wanted to get down to business. As she was completely different from the flirtatious professional, I had a hard time figuring out her true intentions. Perhaps she was better at her job than I realized, and I was simply bait in Whitman's trap.

We talked for ten minutes about the war and my experiences. At one point, her eyes glazed over, likely in remembrance of her late husband, and I realized I was losing her. The memories rolled in like the fog in San Francisco on a blustery night. A misty-eyed gal might end the evening prematurely before I had a chance to make subversive inquiries.

"I sure wish I could afford the classy stuff you guys sell. Heck, I wish I had a house." I fell into a homespun Mark Twain-like lilt in my voice, decidedly opposite of who I really was. She might have assumed I had a certain level of intelligence or thought of me as a stereotypical gumshoe. I had to avoid appearing clever. At the same time, I did not want to come across as daft and turn her off completely. This was an element of being a private detective I had yet to master.

"Someday you will."

"So you import Asian stuff, too?"

"No, not that I'm aware of."

Her gaze was vapid, and she was casual in her reply before looking off toward the orchestra. I couldn't tell if the conversation bored her, or she was flat out lying. One thing was certain. She did not want to continue the conversation about work and invited me to dance. A slow version of "Tuxedo Junction" gave way to "Jersey Bounce" at which point my ankle was killing me. Walking around on city streets was enough for me. Too much dancing made me feel like an invalid.

Apologetically, I begged off from continuing. She was not overly disappointed considering my skills were far less than Gene Kelly. Grimacing in her ear was likely unappealing as well. She now turned her attention fully toward me. To mitigate my pain, she ordered two more rounds of champagne cocktails in a span of about ten minutes while she rambled on about high-end furniture and objet d'art, speaking with an air of sophistication and class I took as a cover for an empty life. She still didn't know how much I read and exactly what I knew about life beyond being a flatfoot. That was okay by me.

While I was making a concerted effort to sip my drinks, she was guzzling them with abandon as though they were ice water on a humid Fourth of July. Her speech started to slur, and her movements were sporadic. We had been there barely over an hour. She blurted out a comment to do with Burmese teak pedestal end tables and bamboo armoires from Thailand. Initially caught off guard, I gathered my surprise and smothered it. It dawned on me the writing I saw on the crate might not have been Chinese. It could have been Thai or Burmese or about anywhere else in the South Pacific. Even with that thought, I was no closer to determining whether Dale Walker's assertions were true or not. There was too much of a coincidental nature and not enough facts.

My evening companion was gliding past the realm of controlled seduction into unregulated indecency. When I suggested getting a cab, she perked up slyly based on assumptions. It took a bit of an effort to guide her into the hack and prop her so she wouldn't fall over. I gave her a peck on the cheek as I sent the driver off with a fiver. There was a pretty good certainty she had done this before and would be bright-eyed and bushy-tailed for work tomorrow. How this was possible was beyond me.

I was surprised to find Bradley Wolrebinski at the Carnegie Library the next day. He leaned over the counter, leering at Carla Duggan who was making googly eyes in return. Whatever they were saying was far too silent and cozy to be recognizable. I almost felt ashamed for intruding.

"Am I interrupting something?" I asked after a phony throat clearing.

"I was telling my little *fagele* here she was the inspiration for my latest." He showed me the cover of "The Red-Headed Temptress" with an amply endowed

Amazon in a sheer negligee walking out of a bedroom with a barely seen dead man on the bed behind her. The tinting of her hands came across like blood. Her ample figure detracted from this minor detail. I could only imagine Carla's glee at the comparison.

"He autographed it for me," Carla replied baring a huge smile. I smiled in return, deciding not to inform Carla this was Bradley's twelfth or thirteenth book, all with buxom dames on the cover with a wide variety of hair colors. He had a great deal of inspiration.

"You're just the man I wanted to see." Bradley was able to switch gears, emotions, and subjects in a split second. "Darling," he said, turning to Carla, "track down the *Beacon* March 21, 1943, Sunday edition as well as the *Milwaukee Journal* from November 2, 1940. And do be quick about it. This man has the world to save."

She maintained her smile considering she was the inspiration for a lurid book cover and ran off to the stacks for the requested items. I didn't need that kind of recognition by Bradley.

"What in the name of the Almighty is going on?"

"I thought about our discussion and made a few inquiries." I started to respond but he held up his hand. "Don't ask." I knew better than to pursue that line of questioning.

It took nearly fifteen minutes of fingers strumming on the counter and exasperated sighs until Carla returned, practically skipping like a young schoolgirl. She clutched the book and wandered off while we stood there with the newspapers. Half the patrons of the library would be aware of her status as a muse by lunch.

The Wisconsin newspaper's headline was a

proclamation of the end of the Battle of Britain thanks to the heroic efforts of the RAF. It was an article below the fold that indicated a new business venture through several prominent leaders. A photo of a Sidney Korshak, the lawyer who helped incorporate the partnership, also included an H. Sondergaard and A. Whitman. The photo was too blurry for clear identification. The *Beacon* identified Mr. Korshak in an article commenting on the need for resumption of international business relations even during the war. There was a reference to his having a possible connection to the recently deceased Frank Nitti, although it was merely a "rumor."

"Who is this Korshak?" I asked.

"Top of the line mouthpiece. Very high level. Big time. Very big time. Extremely connected. And sadly, a Member of the Tribe."

"So what do we have here?"

"Pretend you're writing a book, like me. Talk it out."

I read back and forth between the two newspaper articles. I held a timeline in my head. I imagined a map of the world. I let the ideas come out like water from a faucet.

"I've already got Whitman in Hollywood in early 1940 less than a year after Sondergaard arrived in the States. At that time, Whitman had already gotten possible mob connections."

"Which are now being firmed up by a mob lawyer in Wisconsin later in the year." Bradley was fond of the Socratic method but often filled in the gaps to keep the conversation lively.

"The same lawyer is encouraging resumption of

'international business relations' whatever that is supposed to mean," I added. "So between Sondergaard's European connections and Whitman's mob associates, they start bringing in opium right before the war."

"Actually, it's likely to be heroin. The opium dens went out with the Depression."

"What would Burma have to do with it?" My mind kept going back to the writing on the crate.

"My guess is it is being smuggled out through Burma. Tensions are high in China right now."

As though an eyelash were impeding his vision, Bradley blinked once or twice and stared down again at the photo of Whitman.

"Hmmm!"

"What?" I asked in total confusion.

"Off to the side, close to Korshak, is Anthony Lacey."

"Okay. And who is Anthony Lacey?"

"Ran a juke joint in Scottsbluff back in the late '30s. He was desperate to prove to the mob he had the makings of an accomplished gangster."

"And you know this how?" I didn't have to ask, even though I was curious.

"Research, dear boy. It was when my writing turned from Henry James to Dashiell Hammett." He looked quickly in Carla's direction, making eye contact and then waving his hand as if he was ordering another round of drinks. "Dearest," he said to her as she traipsed over. "Fetch me the *Beacon* from one week ago today."

I stood, looking perplexed. I did this as much for theatrical effect as anything else. When Carla returned,

Bradley knew immediately where to turn in the paper. An article identified the murder of one Anthony Lacey, a known associate of Charles Binaggio, reputed head of the Kansas City crime family. Mr. Lacey was shot multiple times, had a wire garrote wrapped around his neck, and his tongue was cut out. The latter, as explained to me by Bradley, was to designate a creep who talked too much.

My head was spinning. What started out as a request to retrieve a wayward daughter was revealing itself to be an international drug cartel, all of it based out of Eastborough. A man of great influence and wealth was controlling the life of his daughter to create a distribution chain, a significant piece of the business operation that was lacking, an anomaly for a man of his stature and likely a perturbance to the criminal groups who encouraged his efforts. What the local gangsters would do if they found out was even further speculation. A highly emotional jazz musician had little recourse outside of his anger. What was I alone to do? This was the dilemma I placed myself within. As a police detective given this information, there would be an investigation with the intention of bringing the guilty to justice. Were I a rabbi, I would minister to the spiritual needs of those afflicted by addiction or pain. I specifically chose neither path. I decried both entities in search of a deeper truth. Faced with great odds, perhaps greater than those of the war, I could only fall back upon one precept: *Whoever destroys a single life is considered by Scripture to have destroyed the whole world, and whoever saves a single life is considered by Scripture to have saved the whole world.* The answer was clear to me now.

Chapter Sixteen

It felt like an aimless evening. Perhaps it was better that way, allowing myself to be and let the world swirl around me. I digested all the info handed to me by Bradley, all his research and the newspaper articles, until I required a bicarbonate of soda. I paced, ran my fingers through my hair, and sat with my head in my hands vigorously rubbing my forehead to generate any ideas. I wound up with sore feet and a need for a comb as well as more pomade. These were the times I wished I were prone to drinking. Sir Pounce and Lady Mittens lay on the floor in front me, eyes wide and wondering, waiting for me to make a move, and hoping I wouldn't. The jury was still out on what I would do. They could only continue to wait as well.

There was no concern about being over my head, as it were. There were times a lot more harrowing over in Europe and far more life threatening. They both had a lot in common: an enemy intent on your destruction, often unseen until it was too late, and a need to repel them from the safety you had created. The thing was to rely on everything you had and everything you were. It would have been far too easy to convince myself I completed a job to the satisfaction of an employer who paid me handsomely. But I still had to look into my father's eyes, and would not allow the matter to drop.

With a nearly empty refrigerator once again, I

walked down to King's X. A couple of fried eggs, bacon, and wheat toast hit the spot. Breakfast was good any time of day, even at night. Jennie wasn't there to remind me of my non-Kosher consumption of a pig product. I was quite content until Detective Marty Hoeg ambled in. He had the lazy gait of a man who was never in a hurry to do anything and a face that was prepared to yawn on a moment's notice. He appeared perpetually bored as though there were no thrills left for him. There was all the time in the world, and he expected you to move at his speed because he would not move at yours. He was tall, over six foot two, with a mop of dark hair mostly uncombed and a chin that pointed at you like a snub-nosed revolver. He sat beside me, tilted his hat up off his high loping forehead, and wiggled a toothpick between his teeth. Overall, he was a very unappealing man. He knew it all too well and used it as a weapon.

"So, shamus, what's this I hear about your interest in my case?" By not using my name, he could continue to consider me as less than human, an unidentified non-entity. I finished sopping up my egg yolk with my toast before pulling a Gracie Allen on him, slowly turning in his direction with a surprised look on my face.

"Are you speaking to me, sir?"

"Give." His chin bobbed up once, the downward frown on his face plastered permanently with frustration and annoyance. It was better than considering it was on my account but that was just as likely.

"I asked about it and was told you were rather slack jawed about your approach."

The steam was invisible, but I could feel it pouring out of his ears.

"Who told you that?"

I had to decide. I could either placate him, convince him he was a worthwhile addition to the Wichita Police Department's Homicide Division, and ease what I could out of him. My other option was to keep stiff, stay at a distance, and let him tell me how significant he was. Unfortunately, I chose the former.

"Look, I know no one cares too much when a gangster gets knocked off. It's either now or later, right?" He half nodded in agreement. "The thing is this Barczak guy came up in a case I'm working on. You know, for a paying client. I planned to interview him before this, well, you know, unfortunate turn of events."

"Who's your client?"

I sighed heavily, a pathetic admission of the burdens I was under.

"Now, you know that's confidential, Detective Hoeg."

He turned toward the counter, ordered a cup of coffee, and sat sipping it, holding it with both hands as though trying to get warm. I guess a guy like that has got poor circulation. Probably had to do with his lack of incentive.

"We figure it to be a deal gone bad. Likely as not we'll close this as unsolved." He turned back toward me with a smirk. "After all, I've got a few upstanding citizens whose passing is far more of a loss to the community." He got up from the stool, standing over me like the Statue of Liberty. "Sorry this didn't pan out for you." He stared at me blankly, and then smirked again. "Thanks for the coffee." This time there was a little more pep in his step as he left.

I knew Hoeg didn't like me. That much was

certain. What I didn't figure was him going out of his way to rub my nose in this business. I had to wonder if this was nothing more than an attempt to get me off his case to prevent him from looking bad. Then again, I couldn't imagine anyone doing it better than him. More than likely, Marty was imposing his will and dictating the hierarchy between police and citizens. To him, I was even less than that.

There was a Marty Hoeg on about every police department. Guys who were lucky to get a good job for the city or county who figured they could go on an easy ride for twenty and grab a pension. Or maybe he was the guy knocked around as a kid, now getting payback for all the times he'd had his face in the mud. The ones that were dangerous were those playing both ends against the middle.

At this point, it was prudent to visit with Althea Washington. There was doubt forming in my mind as to how much she claimed she didn't know. She was savvy enough to manage a household practically by herself for her to have so little knowledge of her husband's affairs and acquaintances. Perhaps it was the uncertainties of the Whitman case that made my mind walk in this direction. It wasn't fair but it was a reality for the moment.

I was fortunate enough to find Cal Dutcher at the usual hack stand on Douglas and figured it would be better if he drove me over. It took him a minute to recognize me, then his eyes burst wide. Out of the blue, he started treating me like a swell, opening the door for me and adjusting his collar. I gave him the address.

We turned up Market and then the first right onto First Street before he turned north on Broadway. I didn't think much of it until he pulled the cab over at the corner of Broadway and Central, right in front of St. Mary's Cathedral. A tall lanky colored man, maybe no more than twenty-five jumped in to the back seat with me. He leveled his gun, a six-inch Smith & Wesson 1905, at my ribs. From his inside coat pocket, he pulled out a black hood and threw it on my lap.

"Put it on," he said coldly yet softly. I nodded and complied.

"What's the matter, Cal?" I said slightly muffled. "Upset with the tip I gave you the last time?"

"Man says if I see you again bring you to him."

"Shut up." The lanky man spat a very firm response to Cal. I was going to a surprise party in silence.

We drove a long way, finally crossing a particularly busy intersection, before a train rolled past alongside us. I marked us as north of Twenty-First Street. The ride continued before we turned right over train tracks. At first, I thought we might have been on Twenty-Ninth Street. When we turned almost immediately left, I was guessing we initially turned on Thirty-Seventh Street, and then sharply onto Old Lawrence Road. My hope was to get Richie to retrace this route later, assuming I was still alive to do so.

After less than two minutes, we turned right onto a gravel road down what felt like a curvy driveway. The cab stopped suddenly. The passenger door opened, and my chaperone backed out, then grabbed my arm and guided me. The driver's door didn't open at all.

The damp smell of must and decay was too powerful to have been coming from the canvas bag. Whatever the building was, it did not have regular occupants. When my tall friend removed the hood, my eyes took a moment to settle into normalcy. There was one rickety wooden table, one old rocking chair, and a lot of dust and memories. There was no sense of a future found anywhere. Whatever past there had been was now vague and uncertain.

"At least your sight returns." It was the blind woman from the Hollow Inn.

"Why, Sibyl. Thank you for the kind invitation." It was perhaps foolish to project a snide sarcasm, considering they hadn't manhandled me. But I was inclined to let them know this kind of meeting was not to my preference.

"It was for your own protection," she said in an almost scolding manner.

"Oh? How so?"

She stepped forward, practically breathing upon me, as though she were starting right in my face.

"You have no idea how many sets of eyes are upon you."

"You say." Perhaps I meant to be defiant even though it didn't start that way.

"You was talkin' to that cop in the diner." Tall and lanky was defiant as well, but more in a protective mode. I turned toward him suddenly then back to her. A broad smile of victory greeted me.

"My boy, Jason." I wasn't about to inquire as to the whereabouts of the Argonauts.

"I'm a former cop. I know other cops. What was the big deal?"

"He was supposedly investigating the murder."

"What do you mean supposedly?" My head was about to spin around like a top until a deep baritone voice, like one I'd heard before, came from the shadows of this shack.

"It was him." Alonzo Washington stepped forward. Despite being in the relative protection of friends, he still had frightened eyes and a sweaty brow. He relished the shadows, the cover of darkness. It was as though he would disappear into it, perhaps for the rest of his life.

"Who do you mean, Alonzo?"

"The one that killed the bootlegger."

There was no love lost between Marty Hoeg and myself. It didn't mean I considered him to be crooked. My opinion was he was sliding his way toward an early retirement, doing as little as possible to get himself noticed or in trouble. But it was when you start thinking back to various encounters and meaningless comments a new light shines on that person. Only then do other possibilities manifest themselves.

Was it possible Hoeg knew Althea Washington hired me and was also looking for Alonzo to tie up loose ends? Mendenhall mentioned how careless Hoeg had been in the Barczak investigation. I got the feeling any good detective would have half a dozen leads by now. It must have been the lackadaisical laziness was hiding a deeper and darker character.

"How can you be sure?"

"We was out in the car, me and Jason, when he come out of the diner. I recognized him then. Jason went to the window and saw you in there."

Now we were at a point where Alonzo, in a deeply fearful state, wasn't sure who to trust anymore. Even though his wife hired me, he likely thought her wrong, and I was just another white man looking to jump on his back. This was not the time for war stories and camaraderie among all men, the trust we had in each other, the conviction to fight for one another. This was the concrete jungle where men of all kinds stuck with those that had a shared heritage because it was the most comfortable place to be. I couldn't deny, despite my occasional doubts, I was a Jew and understood them better than any other religious group. If I were Alonzo, I might not trust me.

"It's going to take a lot to bring him down." I was hoping I sounded affirmative, helpful, and honest.

"Ain't be nothin' to take him down," Jason replied, Smith & Wesson firmly gripped in his hand.

I whipped my head around, facing his mother.

"He does that, and he brings the whole police department down on whatever shady business you've got going. I'm not here to make judgment on what you do, ma'am. But a woman hired me to find her husband. It's up to him if he wants to be found."

Sibyl stared out, her vacant gaze going over my head. There was absolute silence. I couldn't even hear the wind outside.

"Put that thing away," she said to her son without moving her head.

"Alonzo, what's Abyssinia?"

"Password for a warehouse where they got hijacked booze."

"Where's it at?"

"Supposed to go that night. Didn't. Johnny went. Hoeg and me took the bootlegger out of town and dumped him. Hoeg dropped me off near my home. Must have killed Johnny and dumped him out near the Livestock Exchange best as I can figure it."

I turned back toward Sibyl, or whatever her name

really was. I looked directly into her eyes because I knew in a strange way, she could see me. I wanted her to hear my words and see them as well.

"This man is not a policeman. Not the way I think of one. He has no concern for the well-being of the community, white or colored. He is not a crusader or a man on a moral mission. He is worse than a thief. He insults my sense of righteousness. But he must face justice." She stared straight ahead. I imagined she was looking at me, through me. "Will you let me do that?" I pleaded.

The room was quiet again. My words were swirling in the air and finally settled into place, scattered like a gentle rain on a sunflower field. To this point in my young career, I never felt as though my work or efforts would hold lasting meaning to anyone other than those who hired me. This was different. This would take a strength I might not have.

"You go," the blind lady stated, not as a means of discarding me, more as an imperative, a commission, and a scared duty. I nodded with a slight smile at Alonzo. Jason held up the hood.

"No need," I said smugly. "I already know where we are."

Chapter Seventeen

Up until this point in my life, there were only three men to who I gave my complete trust and faith. One, of course, was my father. He was basically an impoverished peasant when he emigrated from Latvia at the age of twenty-five bringing along my mother, an eighteen-year-old who had more fire and strength than men did twice her age. She did not have the book learning afforded to my father, but she knew things of life merely by observation and introspection. She understood where others struggled simply to define. My father worked hard, remained diligent, and maintained an equilibrium between the Laws of Heaven and Earth. He was devout and resolute, quiet yet not afraid to use his words with strength of voice. There was a quiet majesty to him I was in awe of and respected. He was the truest definition of success in more ways than Albert Whitman could ever be.

Despite the brutal honesty and hard-nosed discipline of Sgt. Robert Schwarzlander, my first supervisor on the force, it was Floyd Gunsaullus I truly admired. Gunny was a man of impeccable integrity and professional commitment. He instilled those qualities in all the fellow officers he encountered, whether they were under his command or simply in passing. He could be dismissive if you called him a brave man, figuring the job we had done required it as an innate prerequisite. To him, all policemen were brave. I wouldn't have said he saw things through rose-colored glasses. It was more as though he had a vision, a belief in the way things ought to be and did whatever it took to make it a reality.

It would be easy to refer to Rabbi Daniel Saperstein as venerable. The chief rabbi at Hebrew Congregation of Wichita, Saperstein was in his mid-eighties and looked nearly a hundred. His hair was pure white, not wiry but smooth, and unmanaged. Sydney Guilaroff would have had a field day with the rabbi were he in an MGM flick. Rabbi Saperstein's beard had a similar texture to his hair and was long enough to cover his heart. He reminded me of Sam Jaffe from "Lost Horizon" both in appearance and in demeanor. The Russians viciously killed his father during the January Uprising in Poland. His mother brought him and his two older brothers across Europe enduring unimaginable hardships until they eventually were able to sail to America. He had known nothing but deprivation and still dedicated his life in service of the Jewish community. To give back, to give everything, made him the equivalent of a saint. In all my life, I never knew of him to ask for anything in return. This was a mitzvah.

While I rejected my father's requests to become a rabbi, I did often look upon Rabbi Saperstein for guidance to determine what the Old Testament and the Talmud would say in well-defined situations. I strove to honor my faith as honestly as I knew how, albeit without intensive involvement and absolute commitment. This had become more commonplace upon my return from the war. Being a policeman trained me to understand and follow rules, regulations, and laws. In battle, those things do not exist. For me to ensure my soul was safe after straying from legal institutions, I found it necessary to turn toward the *Halakha,* the collective body of Jewish religious laws from both the oral and written traditions. Rabbi Saperstein was my entrance to this knowledge, a Virgil to my Dante.

"I have come face to face with evil in two incarnations," I started solemnly, respectful of the adversaries I was facing. "Both pass themselves off as pillars of the community. Their sin impacts not merely other evildoers but the innocent as well. They are towers, like that of Babel. I have need to bring them down. Perhaps it is more like coming up against the walls of Jericho." Rabbi Saperstein was not acquainted with the legal aspects of my former profession, nor would he need to be. He saw things from the perspective of the Tanakh and the Talmud, the laws passed down from the Most High to Moses and written about and discussed for centuries. This description was all I required. He would understand in terms palatable to his way of thinking.

"The battle of Good against Evil is written about throughout our readings. Proverbs 4:16, *For they cannot rest until they do evil; they are robbed of sleep till they make someone stumble.* Psalms 34:13-15, *Keep your tongue from evil and your lips from telling lies. Turn from evil and do good; seek peace and pursue it. The eyes of the LORD are on the righteous, and his ears are attentive to their cry.* And from Rav Huna, *Once a person has sinned and repeated the sin, he treats it as if it has become permitted.*"

He stopped for a moment as though winded from a race, which this aforementioned battle had been for generation upon generation. Then I saw him pulling in another thought, and a light shined upon his brow. "However, I have always been mindful of Isaiah 5:20, *Woe unto them that call evil good, and good evil; that put darkness for light, and light for darkness; that put bitter for sweet, and sweet for bitter!*"

"What bothers you about that?"

"From the Void, the Almighty created all things. Those in communion and those things in conflict. Remember: *And He divided the light from the darkness.* Light is a part of darkness, Harold. Good is a part of Evil. The reason the battle goes on and will continue to do so is because they are inexorably entwined. Good exists simply and solely to combat Evil. Good alone is Paradise, and well, we know what happened to that." He smiled with a touch of melancholy. "There is also a striking line from *For Whom the Bell Tolls.*"

The reference to Hemingway caught me off guard. The tales of armed conflict were more akin to an inveterate reader like me. Then again, Rabbi Saperstein always could surprise me with both popular and obscure allusions.

"Yes?" My eagerness was all too apparent.

"The world is a fine place and worth fighting for."

My gaze wandered around the synagogue. I saw the bema where I took my bar mitzvah, the pride of my father and his older brother, my Uncle Irving, as I read sacred words recited by a multitude of thirteen-year-old boys for many years and decades before me. I imagined this was where the services for my mother took place while I was over in Europe with family and friends reciting Kaddish and sitting shiva. My superiors offered me leave to come home but I declined because I was fighting a greater evil. My need to be on the field of battle at that moment was greater than my grief. Though my mother opposed my enlistment, she understood my sense of duty to our country, a place which accepted her and my father and afforded them a life under their terms. This, however, was different. You could point to the paperhanger with the funny moustache as the key to conflict and the perpetrator of great affliction. Yet you would have a much harder time convincing anyone a prosperous businessman and a decorated veteran police officer were the devils of your city. They were not comic figures. They were not sniveling caricatures from a cheap crime film. They were the ones highlighted in the newspaper, held up as pillars of our community. They were the heroes of our American Dream.

"Rebbe, I have known for some time it is my sacred duty to combat the evil in my presence. I have been a police officer and a soldier. I understand the path I walk upon. But bringing down these institutions is like bringing down a great tower."

He smiled as though he were an old vaudevillian.

"Well, you could confound their language. Or march around them and then blow your horn. Or blind them with your polished shield." His humor showed the impracticality of a Biblical solution. He truly understood this was a dilemma firmly entrenched in the firmament of reality and life as it existed today. "You have all the tools you need, Harold. You have always had them. You come to me not for any answer but for validation. *Avodah b'gashmiut.* Your work is here, in this world. I know your father wishes you to be like me."

"I could never. I don't have—"

He held up his hand to prevent me from continued praise on him or extreme deference that would embarrass both of us.

"From the time you were a boy, you were to books what a fish was to water. Your eyes, as told to me by your father, moved over pages like a gazelle on the plains. You embraced knowledge. All that was missing was understanding."

"What do you mean?"

"I can describe the taste of garlic and why it tastes the way it does. That is knowledge. Eating it," he said, raising a clarifying hand, "is understanding."

Being a policeman and fighting in the war was my way of understanding human nature. They were hard and painful lessons, fraught with fear and danger, yet necessary. Even if I were to become a banker or a ball player, to know what it means to be human is everything. Unfortunately, I had the misfortune of rummaging around in the darker side of mankind with but a bright light to ward off the evil within.

He grabbed both my hands, bowed his head, and uttered a silent benediction. He left me with instruction to read Psalm 10:2-12. I thanked him and left quickly, not wishing to take up any more of his valuable time. I was grateful he did not mention Shabbat services the following evening. I left with a lightness in my step as though my soul were miraculously refreshed.

Part of me wished I had the desire to spend more time in shul. The mysteries of my religion often confounded me and admittedly made me too scared to remain. There was a certain degree of comfort in fighting an enemy that was human, regardless of the strengths they possessed. Invariably, the flesh is weak. We learned the lesson from Samson.

Thoughts of Whitman and Hoeg and Alonzo and Caroline, Mrs. Washington, and Dale Walker intoxicated me. Two jobs were to find people who were missing. I determined they were hiding and had to figure out if they needed guidance back into the light. Moreover, if I were the one to provide that guidance.

When I got home, I was dizzy with thought. It was as though my talk with Rabbi Saperstein were akin to confronting the burning bush. His lessons provided a sense of balance, an understanding of the battle I was fighting.

I made a pot of coffee which served as a dinner. I had no need of food, but I was hungry for another kind of sustenance. The verse Rabbi Saperstein referenced was sticking in me like a dagger in the back. I grabbed the bible from my bedside table, the one given to me upon my bar mitzvah nearly sixteen years ago. I located Psalm 10:2-12.

2 The wicked in his pride doth persecute the poor: let them be taken in the devices that they have imagined. 3 For the wicked boasteth of his heart's desire, and blesseth the covetous, whom the Lord abhorreth. 4 The wicked, through the pride of his countenance, will not seek after God: God is not in all his thoughts. 5 His ways are always grievous; thy judgments are far above out of his sight: as for all his enemies, he puffeth at them. 6 He hath said in his heart, I shall not be moved: for I shall never be in adversity. 7 His mouth is full of cursing and deceit and fraud: under

*his tongue is mischief and vanity. 8 He sitteth in the
lurking places of the villages: in the secret places doth
he murder the innocent: his eyes are privily set against
the poor. 9 He lieth in wait secretly as a lion in his den:
he lieth in wait to catch the poor: he doth catch the
poor, when he draweth him into his net. 10 He
croucheth, and humbleth himself, that the poor may fall
by his strong ones. 11 He hath said in his heart, God
hath forgotten: he hideth his face; he will never see it.
12 Arise, O Lord; O God, lift up thine hand: forget not
the humble.*

I understood whose side I was on and what I
needed to do.

Chapter Eighteen

A word, a verse, a chapter. The smallest things can set your feet on the ground and your shoulders in the right direction. The profession I had chosen would not make me rich. However, it might help me understand the world with greater clarity. With that knowledge, I could go forward with purpose.

It was time to determine if Marty Hoeg was incompetent or corrupt. While I had solid and respectable acquaintances on the force, I approached this from the outside. It wasn't necessarily a trust issue. If it were me, I might hedge my commentary on a fellow officer in casual conversation. An internal investigation was another matter, but I wouldn't be privy to one. The true picture of what happened or what was going to happen would not wind up being clearer by simply passing around gossip and anecdotes. I had to witness everything Hoeg did and determine for myself the reasons behind his actions, given I had four years on the force to go by. Then, and only then, I might be able to decide if he were a stooge or a conniver. What to do afterward was still a little way down the road and perhaps beyond the scope of my abilities or influence.

This would take more than a single day, considering I had no idea how long Hoeg had his paws in the cookie jar, if that was what occurred. I started with Richie, offering him a double sawbuck to follow

Detective Hoeg around for the better part of a day. Then, when Hoeg was working a night shift, I made the same offer to Charlie Argento. While I knew they would eventually talk to each other, I had to ensure no one was following me too closely, although I figured Cal Dutcher might be tracking me for his friends. It was the unknown associates to consider. They might spring up on me at a moment's notice. And that might slow down the process.

Richie jumped on my offer for breakfast at King's X. Jennie and I stared at him while he shoveled biscuits and gravy into his mouth faster than Wilbur Shaw sped around a racetrack. I would have thought as fast as he was eating his lungs might collapse. Not being a trained physician, this was my impression of asthma. I never considered how difficult his life was, even as well as I knew him. He kept to himself on the personal side but went out of his way to help a friend. A decent meal was the least I could do to repay him for all the courtesies he offered me. I had to hope he wouldn't wind up with indigestion and require a Bromo-Seltzer.

We started out parked on the southwest corner of Market and William around the corner from the police station. Unfortunately, an unidentified plain-clothes detective picked Hoeg up a bit after seven a.m. If Hoeg were dirty, he would be playing it safe if this driver were legit. There was no way of telling who was involved. I couldn't ask Gunny or Mendenhall. They might have suspected a crooked cop but without any proof, I could be ruining a decent cop's career simply by an implication. Nevertheless, this was the course I started on and had to continue regardless. With anything viable, I could bring him down through the proper authorities. Evidence was the only cure for corruption.

The first stop they made was a residence on Grove beyond North Nineteenth Street. It was a plain white house in need of a paint job and a new roof. It wasn't as well maintained as the other homes nearby. While the other detective stood a few steps away, averting his eyes and kicking the pavement, Hoeg was verbally harassing the colored woman who answered the door. There was a lot of finger-pointing directly at the spot between her eyes while the woman cringed in fear. It wasn't entirely chilly out, but I thought I saw her shiver. It might have been questioning into an open investigation for all I knew. The scene further indicated Hoeg's style was less about brains and more about brawn, forceful scare tactics over quiet inquiry. She stared at them until they finally got in their car and drove off. She then closed her door as though she were locking herself inside a castle, one that didn't include a moat.

There were several other similar instances throughout the day and lunch at a burger stand on Mosley and seventeenth they didn't pay for. However, they kept driving up and down North Arkansas anywhere from West Twenty-Ninth Street to West Thirty-Seventh Street. They drove that stretch at least five different times, heading either north or south. There didn't appear to be any slowing down at a particular location or pulling over to the side of the road. This stretch took on a significance, but I couldn't figure out what.

The driver dropped Hoeg off at the station before three in the afternoon. I instructed Richie to drive the same stretch of road, going slowly one direction and then in the other. We came across a handful of single-family homes most in a state of disrepair, some perhaps even abandoned. It wasn't a respectable part of town for whites, colored, or Latinos. There was a filling station before West Thirtieth Street and an auto repair business right next to Mr. Bud's Burgers around West Thirty-Fourth Street. Nothing else had the appearance of being important or significant.

Beyond those two businesses on the east side of the road stood a rectangular brick building with a boarded-up front door, no windows, and no signage on the east side of the road. Half a block farther on the west side there was a chain link fence with a padlocked gate. The dirt road behind it led to a small row of tall trees. I could barely see a corrugated metal building on the other side. Again, no signs indicated the nature of the place and, for the life of me, I couldn't recall having seen it or been aware of it before.

"You know what either of these two buildings are, Richie?"

"I don't make my way up here an awful lot, Hirsch. If you know what I mean."

I continued making notations in my notebook. If I couldn't find anyone who knew the area well, I would have to use the city clerk's office and visit the Registrar of Deeds. Dealing with the city would take half of a day and open myself up to a lot of pointless questions.

Richie declined an offer of dinner, preferring instead to call it a day. The excessive amount of driving had gotten to him. I let him know with absolute certainty how much I appreciated his efforts. You can't thank your friends enough especially when they go out of their way for you.

The following night it was Charlie's turn to do the following around. It was a Saturday night and I realized I was pulling him away from more fares. I promised to make it worth his while, and he accepted my word on faith. While I didn't let him know who we were tailing, he figured it was important when we started at the police station. This time, however, Hoeg was driving himself. There was an imperceptible gasp when Charlie noticed him. He didn't say anything, and I didn't ask.

From roughly a little after eight p.m. until close to midnight, Hoeg made stops at just about every nightclub, juke joint, and dive up and down Broadway. Rock Castle. The Black Cat Inn. Forty Second Club. Rustic Inn. Swingland. He parked out in front of each and didn't bother to hide his car or park somewhere unobtrusively. He walked in as though he owned all the places, spent anywhere from fifteen minutes to almost an hour at each, and came out with a self-satisfied smirk on his face. It wasn't the look of a police officer contented with the efforts of his labor. It was closer to a devilish imp finding himself in an enviable position and figuring he was too high up to be dragged down.

Even though these stops should have been a straight path up and down Broadway, he continuously drove the five or six blocks over to North Arkansas, perusing the same stretch of road he went over yesterday. I could only surmise he was looking for something or looking out for something. While those two buildings came to mind, he never slowed down or pulled over to any one place. It left me with a great deal of uncertainty.

"Charlie, you've had fares before to these clubs,

right?"

"Oh, yeah. Sure thing Mr. Bergman. A few Fridays. Just about every Saturday."

"What's over on North Arkansas that was so interesting?" He took a peek at the rearview mirror once or twice but stayed quiet. He had a look as if he swallowed a bug. Paying close attention to the traffic and being a responsible driver was his way of avoiding an answer. "Come on, Charlie. Give."

He pulled the hack into the parking lot at Savute's, toward the back corner in the dark under a spreading elm tree. He turned toward me, his arm resting uncomfortably on the seat, a small bead of sweat trailing down the right side of his face. He was scared in a way I had never known before.

"Mr. Bergman, you gotta understand. I got the wife and daughters to take care of. You know? I can't get by on just driving a hack. You don't make so much."

"Charlie"—I interrupted—"as long as you haven't murdered anyone or are planning to murder anyone, it's okay by me. I don't judge anyone."

He got out and then came around to the back to sit next to me. The notion of answering difficult questions while separated by a seat was not worthy of a man with honor. If nothing, Charlie Argento had that.

"I know a guy who says he was willing to buy stolen merchandise."

"What kind of merchandise?"

"Any kind. A small-time hood robs a house. A gang of thieves hijacks a truck. If I hear anything, he says, send them to him. He takes the stuff off their hands, and I get what you call, you know, a finder's fee. A lot of times it was more than I take in on a weekend night driving the hack."

It started to make sense. Perhaps it was Hoeg, and he was getting paranoid checking on his storage facility. It would fit in with Alonzo Washington's story. Was this the place Johnny Pajak was heading to?

"The guy we were following tonight, did you get a good look at him?"

"That cop? Yeah, I saw him good."

"Was he the guy?" I asked hopefully.

"Nah. I seen that cop around before and he's bad news. No one likes him much. Throws his weight around like he was Charlie Potatoes. No, this guy buying up the stolen goods ain't no cop."

"So who is he?"

"Name is Barczak. Timmy Barczak."

There it was. The dead bootlegger was running a fencing operation. Now I had to determine whether he was running it with a partner and if that partner, likely the guy who killed him, took it over. The brick building would be easy to surveil. I could walk around it during the daytime and ask the few homeowners in the area what they knew. The difficulty would be the fenced property. It was the unknown commodity in this equation. I also had to consider this was potentially a large operation and determine if the main operator worked alone or with others and how many I could expect to encounter. If it was Hoeg, were his confederates gangsters or other cops? This one new door opened into a dark room. I still hadn't shined a light on anything. That made me a blind man on an unknown journey.

It was getting close to midnight, and a long night's rest beckoned. Despite the lateness of the evening,

Broadway was still busy with traffic. I let my head fall back while we waited for several lights to change. When I raised my head, I discovered we had only gone a couple of blocks, so I had Charlie drive down St. Francis so he could cut across to Market. We had approached St. Francis Hospital when I noticed a car pulling away rather recklessly from the emergency entrance. Caroline Whitman was in the passenger seat with an unidentified colored man driving. As we drove past, a group of orderlies and nurses was rushing out to gather a body lying there in a crumpled heap. A security guard yelled after the car then returned to help the medical staff. Whatever trouble she was in, Caroline Whitman would likely turn to her father where his claws would dig in deeper.

Chapter Nineteen

Eileen Horowitz and I dated a couple of times in high school. It was practically expected given we were both smart, well read, what a few called daring, and, well, Jewish. We were cute together but there was nothing to indicate we would follow in the footsteps of other Jewish kids in terms of matrimony and a stable family life. Had I let my mind wander enough back then, I might have given in to her charms. Her parents, however, were hoping she would meet and marry a doctor. A lawyer would be just as nice. Anything nine-to-five that made a good living. A patrol cop bucking for detective did not fit into their social plans. They liked me, called me brave, asked if I could fix a parking ticket. It was simply they couldn't picture me as a future son-in-law. At that point, neither could I.

Eileen had wavy brown hair and big blue eyes that looked like no lake I had ever seen. Certainly, no lake in Kansas. She was what genteel ladies referred to as buxom. To me, she was eye-catching and fetching. She was also one of the first people to visit me upon my return home, making sure I was acclimated to life back in the Plains. Maybe she was still taken with me, but she didn't push the issue. She had been working at the switchboard at the *Beacon* for a little over ten years. Unlike the tough guys in the movies, I did not have any friends who were reporters largely due to my noncommittal responses to them when I was a cop. Eileen was my only newspaper contact, always claiming she couldn't share anything with me and then turning around and doing it anyway.

I dialed the main switchboard and asked for them to connect me to her. Most of the other girls heard my voice numerous times. She let them think there was a flirtation going on between us. It made coffee breaks more interesting for her.

"I didn't think I'd catch you on a Sunday." I couldn't hide the surprise in my voice.

"Picked up a shift for Stacey Medeiros. Her water broke. So you calling to kibbitz or do you need me again, Bergman?"

"You're going to make someone a fine baleboste someday."

"Feh! You should be so lucky." Her spunk was one of the many things to admire about her. I doubted any man would be worthy of her. "What now?"

"Will you guys be running a story about a mysterious patient dropped off at St. Francis last night?"

There was a heaviness in the silence preceding her answer.

"We'll be running a story about an overdosed college student who was mysteriously dropped off at St. Francis." I could practically hear her heart pounding over the phone and thought I caught what sounded like a lump in her throat.

My eyes glazed over. A layer of sweat magically appeared on my forehead. The world of pushing drugs wasn't real to most people until a friend or acquaintance died from it. The same thing was true about war. The ugliness of life was best suited for most folks in lurid magazines or B movies.

"Got a name?"

There was another silence, but I could hear papers shuffling.

"Annette Copeland. You want I should find out more about her?"

"Not necessary. I know her." I detected a slight gasp in response. A litany of images ran through my head like a newsreel. It was unlikely this would have happened if Caroline Whitman had not been plying her father's trade. "Hey, I owe you a dinner. At least."

"Harold, please. Anything, just not the Pan American. Okay?"

I hoofed it down to King's X hoping to catch Jennie Palmer. I didn't need a meal and didn't want to have a hush-hush talk at a counter. When I entered, she was pouring coffee refills. As I stood at the door, our eyes met. The blank look on my face let her know this wasn't a social visit. She casually held up her hand, spreading her fingers wide. She would meet me out back in five minutes.

"I've never seen you look this way before, Mr. Bergman." She was likely referring to my darting eyes and sweat covered face. Maybe I acted like an addict now.

"How popular is junk with the young crowd?"

"Starting to get big. Booze was fun until the kids realized their mommies and daddies drank. Reefer was something rebellious but grew boring. Junk is moving past the jazz musicians to the kids following them."

"How are they getting it?"

"Not sure exactly. I don't run with that kind of

crowd. Who knows? Maybe from the musicians who are turning them on to it."

"What about one of their own?"

She had a glazed look as she mulled over the notion.

"It's a possibility." I shook my head almost in defeat and started to walk away. "Mr. Bergman, it's not the kids you have to worry about. It's the big guys selling it."

Young Miss Jennie Palmer didn't know how right she was.

I figured Dale Walker and Caroline Whitman might be too spooked out about this recent turn of events to put their trust in me even though I thought I had proven myself to them. Albert Whitman could toy with me like a cat with a ball of yarn unless I had relevant evidence hanging over his head. My only option now was to determine how vulnerable Saundra Mooney might be.

There would have been a tendency for me to double-time it down to the Whitson Imports office down in Delano. But it was a Sunday, and I would have to put my eagerness to rest. I was feeling like a soldier who needed to take an objective over an enemy. It wasn't a heavy pack that burdened me. It was the weight of moral responsibility, the kind very few are prepared to shoulder but was necessary all the same. It felt like the war all over again except there were no bombs or tanks or machine guns going off around us. Just the same, a combatant was out there, clearly attempting to subvert whatever laws one held dearest to them. In this case, I easily envisioned Albert Whitman as an abomination to both sets of laws. Both sides of me became his adversary.

Early on Monday morning, there was a lightness in my step as though I were Dick Powell in a Warner Brothers musical. The smile on my face was clean and clear and bright. The goal was to dazzle my prey, blind her like Joshua with my polished shield.

"Mr. Bergman, I thought it would be doomsday by the time I heard from you again." She dropped all pretense of being professional, not caring if the reason for my visit was for information, and acted like a lioness stalking what she thought was a weaker prey. It was convenient for me to allow that impression. The tide would turn eventually.

"I was terribly disappointed with the way our encounter ended the other night." I oozed cinematic charm.

"I would say that was a perfect expression. For it to be a true date, it would have had to end, well, much better than it did. Certainly, much different. Wouldn't you say so?"

The pastime I preferred was chess, having played it with my father as a young boy. It taught me to analyze, defend, and attack. My knowledge came in very useful now.

"I'd be willing to throw my hat into the ring again," I said coyly. It didn't occur to me at the time it was almost a military expression.

"Your hat? Oh, I'll need much more than a fedora."

Each of us was playing his and her own game. I had the upper hand only because I knew it. She thought this was a throwback to the burlesque days before the Hays Code made everyone respectable. There would be a little risqué banter between two people who each knew what they wanted. However, when a young college girl dies form an overdose of drugs because a wealthy man wants more money and more power, I understood the need to delve deep into a world that would make me feel soiled to fight the evil within. Then, I had to hope to come out clean on the other side.

We made similar arrangements as before, this time at the Brae Burn Pleasure Club way out on East Central. I was surprised at her suggestion as it was a private club to which she responded she "knew people." I could only imagine. She offered to pick me up but again I told her it was my intention to make a spectacular entrance for her. The truth was I wanted to get her back to her place for the privacy of an in-depth conversation.

For this occasion, I determined being fashionably late would only limit the time to give her a proper third degree. It occurred to me she might be strong enough to withstand it, my efforts would fail, and the drug trade in the city would expand beyond my ability to do anything. However, I needed to try. After all, David had only a sling and a stone. And a great deal of faith.

The front entrance was blocked by a man in a tuxedo, a would-be maître d' with a trifling of an accent somewhere between Boston and London. He had the face of George Raft and the manners to boot.

"I'm a guest here," I repeated.

"I don't know you. I don't recognize you."

"And that's important?" I replied glibly.

"It's the difference between an entrée into our establishment to experience our exquisite hospitality and being slammed by two nasty and brutish employees onto the parking lot. So, yeah. I'd say it was very important."

"I see." The smirk was to show him he didn't faze me in the least. There was a tense bit of silence and staring for about fifteen seconds before my rescuer came in the form of Saundra Mooney.

"It's quite all right, Peter. The gentleman is with me."

Her very appearance must have carried weight because Peter instantly deflated like a day-old balloon, bowing subserviently as though he were a coolie in New Delhi, and she were a Brahmin.

She brought us over to the semi-covered booth off the dance floor. This was decidedly more secluded than our first meeting at the Blue Moon. She intended to have fun and dance. The motivations had changed since then. For each of us.

The waiter arrived as soon as we sat, and she ordered two champagne cocktails. She presented a shiny gold cigarette case in my direction. I declined. I did offer her a light, albeit with a pack of matches from the Pan American. There was no hiding the fact I traveled in lesser circles yet still had charm and panache.

"The last time we were out," I said, having moved in closer to her, "we ordered too many rounds."

"I was perfectly fine the next morning." She sounded like a petulant teenage daughter claiming she could do her homework and still play with her friends.

"Yes, but it was not the following morning I was concerned about."

"Oh?"

"It was that evening."

She had the pleasantly surprised look, raised

eyebrows and all, of Claire Trevor in about any movie you could watch. She nearly choked on a puff of smoke before gathering herself. The lioness appeared slightly thrown off by the quiet roar of the lion. When she gathered herself, she advised me her car was just outside. We got up, she dropped a fin on the table for the waiter's trouble, and we were off.

She had a small bungalow on Rutan, south of the Hillcrest Apartments. That made me concerned about raising our voices or her screaming and yelling if things got out of control. The immaculate decor was not surprising given her employer and yet there was a coldness to it. It was not as sterile as a hospital room but there was no sense of character to it. The objet d'art had no personal meaning or connection to the occupant. They were merely things to be placed at specific and ideal locations throughout to give a sense of life. Anyone's life. Unfortunately, the person who lived there had no character and likely no soul.

She poured whiskey into two square cut glass tumblers, splashed a little soda in them, and handed me one of the glasses. I dove in right after the first sip.

"You familiar with Annette Copeland?"

"No. Should I be?"

"She's a friend of Caroline Whitman." Now, instead of the eyebrows, it was Claire Trevor's laugh.

"Dear boy, I can't possibly keep track of all of young Miss Whitman's flock." There was a gasp of exasperation. "Why are we even discussing this? Who is this girl? College friend?"

"She was."

"Was?"

"She's dead." The words fell from my lips like a

weightlifter dropping a barbell with a thousand pounds attached. "Drug overdose. Last night. St. Francis Hospital." The staccato rhythms were like jabs from Joe Louis. Her jaw dropped far enough for her mouth to form a small unmoving circle. The ice in the glass tinkled as her hand shook. Realizing this, she downed the remainder in a gulp and set the glass down on the coffee table.

"Why are you—?"

"I think you know why I'm asking. I think this Annette Copeland got hooked on heroin after Miss Whitman turned her onto the stuff. At the behest of her father." Saundra shook her head negatively with only slight movements. "I think Albert Whitman smuggles in drugs from Asia using various connections he made in both Germany with the Nazis and the mob out in California. I think there is a concerted effort to generate a demand here in the Midwest and to create a supply chain from the east coast to the west. The only thing I don't know is how actively you're involved with all of this."

Her head was now swiveling violently back and forth. If I didn't watch out, her pretty head might snap right off her neck. She was a whirling dervish, out of control. The words almost choked her throat.

"No. No." It was a blank and empty word.

"No what? No, I'm all wrong? Or no, you're not involved?"

"It can't be. Mr. Whitman wouldn't—"

"Why did he hire me? Caroline wasn't missing. She wanted to stop pushing for him. Isn't that right?" I had suddenly become aware of the angered tones of my own voice. It was fortunate she hadn't matched my volume. I knew I had to remain in control and not let this discussion seep outside where a neighbor might mistake it for something else. With cops intruding upon a "domestic disturbance", the game would be over.

"I don't know anything about smuggling drugs." Each word came out through clenched teeth, specifically and individually. There was no anger to her tone. She was doing her best to stay within herself, to keep from exploding emotionally and losing all hold on reality.

"But you suspected."

It was as though she could breathe again. She gulped air a couple of times, batted her eyelashes to clear her vision, and stood up slowly, turning toward me with a passive hesitancy.

"Yes. I suspected. Something."

I walked toward her too fast for her to back away. Holding her by the shoulders, I turned her to face me, this time showing her the compassion necessary to get her to cooperate.

"She's in danger. You realize that don't you?" She nodded. "Either she'll go along with her father and wind up getting in trouble if she gets into the wrong crowd. Or she'll reject him. What is he capable of if she winds up doing that?"

Her eyes were clear now. She stopped shaking even though what she was about to admit would scare all of us.

"He lives for power and wealth. Nothing else matters. Nothing. Not even his own flesh and blood. If she won't cooperate, he'll squash her like a fly."

Next to the war, this was the worst kind of evil I ever encountered.

Chapter Twenty

It was almost like watching a subject who was hypnotized the way she stood up, went over to the sideboard with delicate child-like steps, placed a few ice cubes in the glass one at a time, never bothered by the loud clinking, added the whiskey and a splash of soda in a great burst, and then downed it like a drowning man in a desert. They were well orchestrated intricate movements followed by a decisive action. For those brief few moments, she wasn't aware of me or the world beyond, perhaps even herself. There was nothing real and yet it was all too scary to be anything else. She finally turned toward me, her face a grayish white, eyes fixed and watery, a bit of spittle in the corner of her mouth. She was so much less than human. I couldn't tell what.

"I honestly didn't know anything about drug smuggling. You must believe me. I could never have suspected that." Her voice didn't carry the sound of desperation, only defeat. It was like saying goodbye and knowing she was never coming back. She was already dead and just going through the motions. I had to give her a reason to savor her life.

"What do you know?" My voice was soft and smooth, relaxing and coaxing. It was necessary to bring her back to the real world but slowly and with caution. It was too scary of a place to be in for her at this moment. It was, however, where I needed her most.

She sat back down on the sofa, away from me, looking down as she spoke. Whether she was embarrassed or ashamed, I couldn't tell because I didn't know her all that well. If I had to guess, it would be she used the luxury and glamour of her position to cover her sorrow at the loss of her husband. It might have been giving her too much credit. For all I knew, she was a conniving gold-digger. Right now, none of that mattered.

"I bring all the invoices from anywhere in Asia and other specific countries to Mr. Whitman in a sealed leather pouch on a weekly basis. Same night of the week. Same time. I never open them in the office. I don't even so much as look too closely at the envelopes themselves, just recognize their point of origin, and remove them from the others. The workers place the items they reference in a separate location of the warehouse. There is a kind of made-up room, like a prison cell, built out of wood and chicken wire that surrounds it. Everyone knows it is off limits even though there aren't any signs designating it so. Only about four, maybe five men are on the crew. Those men are not on the payroll. I don't even know their names."

"Why?"

"I asked once. Mr. Whitman said they are contract laborers, and he doesn't want them on the roster on account of payroll taxes. It made sense at the time." She shook her head in disgust with herself at having accepted that nonsense. "I've been such a fool."

"Go on."

She looked up at me blankly. The words had come out of her mouth directly and with little to no emotion. I saw what was likely the referenced crew when I passed by the warehouse. Men who were tough and strong but hardly the hard-working types who went home to adoring wives at the end of the day. They were alarmed at my presence, so everything she said made sense. Yet I was still no closer to the truth. I would need a lot more to bring this crashing down.

"You've got to help me." I couldn't tell if I was the one sounding desperate now.

"I can't," she said breathlessly. "If he wouldn't hesitate to make a lesson of his daughter, what do you think he would do to me?"

"You should have thought of that before." It was not my style to sound tough or hard-boiled. Anger was welling up inside of me because of the manipulation and destruction of so many people's lives over nothing more than greed and power. A cold electricity flowed through me right then. It was the same thing I felt before each battle or skirmish. This time it wasn't the Nazis, but it might as well have been. Despite being a soldier of the United States Armed Forces, I was my father's son. Now, as then, I kept repeating one line of scripture that guided me and pushed me forward.

Proverbs 24:20, *For there shall be no reward to the evil man; the candle of the wicked shall be put out.* It was righteousness and vengeance and the will of the Lord. I didn't need the Torah to teach me that, then or now. This rose so far above any of the laws of a city, state, or country.

I picked her up from her caved-in clump on the sofa. I held her softly yet firmly by the shoulders and stared directly into her eyes, speaking slowly and methodically, my words clear and precise.

"You are going to help me. You are going to provide me all the information about these invoices. You don't have to open them or delay their delivery to Whitman. Then you are going to give me a tour of the warehouse, introducing me as your new boyfriend, implying you are trying to get me a job there and vouch for me."

"I can't."

"You can and you will. Otherwise, I'm going to have my friends in the police department tear your life apart. If they find so much as a traffic violation, they'll haul you in. And then, just as quickly, they'll release you without charging you with anything. After that, we can leave it up to Whitman to figure out why. Only he won't have to because it will be obvious to him. He won't take any chances from that point on. Am I making myself clear, Saundra?"

"You wouldn't do that." She was defiant, pushing out the words with a hiss. It sounded more like a last gasp.

"A young girl, a college girl, a friend of Caroline Whitman, died of a heroin overdose. Your boss is bringing in the stuff from Asia and having his daughter sell it to these stupid unsuspecting gullible kids. A whole new market. And I guarantee you there will be more overdoses, more deaths. Do you honestly want those deaths on your conscience?" I asked, assuming she had one. There was a desperate need to tap into her humanity if, as she stated, Albert Whitman was a heartless soulless beast intent only upon power. Guilt was one way to bring her back to her human self. That moral complexity is what separated us from the animals.

"What do you want me to do?" she finally responded, sounding like a tire slowly losing air.

The first thing I determined was the day of the week she would collect the invoices and visit to gather further information about them. I also wanted to know if Whitman ever went anywhere socially. The idea was to 'accidentally' run into him with Saundra to reinsert myself back into his circle in a way that wouldn't arouse suspicion. If he caught me once again while he was with Caroline, it would be hard to claim it as a coincidence. While I would try to reach out to Big House Walker, my guess was he would be overprotective of Caroline and not allow himself to recognize I was the only one who could help them. That was okay with me. It would be ideal if he could keep her from doing anything to give me away.

As it turned out, Saundra would have a packet ready to go tomorrow. I indicated I would stop by the office at an unexpected time. There was still a gleam in her eyes indicating she wanted out from beneath all of this and might skip town altogether. I hoped I was wrong.

When I got back home, Althea Washington was waiting for me as she had before. This time, however, her eyes were those of one who had seen a ghost. I invited her in quickly and apologized for the incessant mewing.

"Alonzo got word to me that man come see him."

"Which man?"

"The policeman."

"And?"

"Told Alonzo he better help him move some stuff if he don't want to go to jail."

179

Detective Hoeg had panicked and forced the hand of an even more desperate sucker who happened to be my client. What bothered me even more was Sibyl and her group was obviously not very good at keeping Alonzo out of trouble. Until now, I was willing to let them tend to their own. Considering I was still under the employ of Mrs. Washington, it was time for me to take over, regretful I had delegated that responsibility elsewhere.

I walked down to the hack stand on Douglas and found Cal Dutcher. I jumped into the back seat of his car and slammed the door, which caused him to nearly jump through the roof.

"Take me to him," I demanded.

"I don't know what you're talking about, man."

"The next phone call I make is to my friends in the police department. I'm going to have them pull your file and see if we can't get your medallion revoked. From there, I'm sure they'll dig up more dirt on you. Is that want you want, Cal? Because I am so tired of getting the runaround. Do you hear me?"

The look he gave me in the rearview mirror was one of a rat caught in a maze, so close to the cheese but even closer to the trap. He pulled away from the curb with a little bit of anger in his foot.

The route he took was like the one when they had me blindfolded. He didn't realize this was what the Army trained you for, to be aware of your surroundings in the dark. As had happened before, I was back in the war.

Jason, the tall lanky colored guy, was there with Alonzo. Sibyl was not around. I felt like Jason's dad, castigating him for doing a poor job.

"You want to tell me how the cop got to Alonzo?"

"It was my fault, Mr. Bergman," Alonzo interjected, almost mournfully. "I kinda snuck out to see Randy, let him know I was okay." He sounded like half a dozen guys I knew in the war, hemmed in by a foxhole and feeling it more to be like a grave. I understood now why he felt more comfortable hiding out in a church. There was an honesty and compassion about this man who wanted nothing more than to take care of his wife in any way he knew how. Too often, the dark side of the world tended to gobble up the good and hide the light.

"Well, I've got a place neither the cop nor your friends know about. And he makes real good food." Alonzo and I headed toward the door when Jason reached out, not quite a threatening gesture, more as if he felt lost.

"What about Sibyl?" he asked desperately.

"Tell her I'll get in touch with her." This time, she would have to look for me.

We got into Cal's cab but seeing as how I didn't trust him as far as I could throw a stone, I had him drop us off outside the Orpheum. I watched as he drove away and motioned for Alonzo to follow me east on First Street toward Topeka. I tried to make sure no one was tailing us, whether it was Sibyl's group or Marty Hoeg. It was a matter of starting from nothing, getting Alonzo Washington to realize I was in this up to my ears just like him, and recognizing he knew nothing about who his real enemy was.

As we got to the grocery store owned by Nicholas Leonides past the corner of Topeka and Douglas, Alonzo gasped.

"The police station's down the street."

"Yeah." I smiled. "You'll be right under their noses. Rather funny, huh?"

I made eye contact with Nicholas' son, Gilbert, who gently nodded for me to head to the stairs at the back of the store. Alonzo and I moved quickly to the alley and went to the second floor. Gilbert and I hugged, and then he reached out his hand to Alonzo who hesitantly reached back.

"Any friend of Harold Bergman is family to us." While Gilbert didn't have his father's accent, he retained the strong values brought to this country by him. Gilbert recited the same litany about this safe room as he had done many times before: the radio for entertainment; fresh linens daily; a buzzer would go off in the downstairs office only in the event of an emergency; and the time each meal would be brought up to him.

Suddenly, Nicholas walked in. Gilbert knew to leave then. Another hug, this one more profoundly tight, greeted me. Greeks born and raised in the mountains know of no other way.

"How long this time?" he asked plainly.

"Three days. A week at most." Nicholas nodded. "Dirty cop," I said blankly.

"Worst kind." Nicholas turned directly toward Alonzo. "You're safe here."

Alonzo Washington finally exhaled, his shoulders dropped, and he nodded lightly. Nicholas left us as he wanted to know as little about the situation as possible. That would keep him as clean as he could be.

"Hey, man," he asked breathlessly, "why you doing this?"

"Your wife hired me is why."

"Uh-uh. We can't afford no gumshoe."

I felt my eyes scrunch up in deep thought. The trouble was how to explain a moral imperative to a man who lived by sweat and breaking his back.

"The Jewish people have a saying from the Talmud. 'Live well. It is the greatest revenge.' I want both of us to have the chance."

"Who you need revenge against?"

I patted him on the shoulder and left by the back stairs. It was too long of a story, and we didn't have the time. Hopefully, I would tell it later.

Chapter Twenty-One

Considering our last late-night outing, I counted on Saundra to be as fresh as a daisy. She had that ability. But it wasn't the booze that wiped her out on the most recent encounter. It was the unmitigated truth and paralyzing realization of her own mortality. The stark understanding the music would stop, and the dancers would walk away, leaving an empty ballroom. Whatever her views on life after the passing of her husband had been, now everything centered and focused on her and her alone. This was a tough pill to swallow. Real life was around the corner. Perhaps even closer.

I stopped by the Dillons on the opposite side of the street from the Whitson Imports office and had them fix me up a couple of corned beef on rye sandwiches and a kosher dill apiece. Regrettably, Wichita did not have a reputation for its delicatessens, so this resulted in a poor substitute. It may not have been as fancy as what she usually had but it was enough to impress anyone looking at us as a possible couple. Looking cute and smitten like a cat was another character I played, one I learned all too well at home.

I gave Saundra a peck on the cheek when I entered the office. She had a distant look on her face and didn't even blush. For all she knew, I had forgotten about my job and was truly interested in a relationship with her. If that is what would get her through this it would be okay with me. Perhaps, after a while, I could pay her back with gratitude and generosity. As she sat down at her desk and began eating her lunch, I rummaged through the envelopes containing the invoices and began writing down the return addresses in my notebook. At times, the foreign handwriting was indistinguishable, but I wouldn't have an opportunity to consult with Bradley. I tried not to drip pickle juice on any of them.

When I was done, I sat on the opposite side of the desk and enjoyed my lunch. The rye was too seedy and the corned beef rather dry. The last thing I wanted to do was kvetch in front of her, explaining the ins and outs of Jewish cuisine. At times, the subject even bored me. We passed smiles between each other while eating, being courteous not to speak with our mouths full. I gingerly dabbed the corner of her mouth to wipe away a small glob of mustard. If anyone walked in right then, they could have sworn I was a love-struck puppy dog. Mickey Rooney and Judy Garland.

"He's going out to the Blue Moon on Friday night," she offered without any coercion or emotion.

"With anyone?"

"He didn't say."

"Looks like we've got a date Friday night." I smiled broadly to entice her and make her feel less like it was an espionage mission which, in essence, it was. She was less frightened than she had been. "Listen, we'll go someplace later. Believe me, I don't feel any more comfortable about this than you do. I want to, well, do right by you." I realized that sounded a little open ended but, in all honesty, I didn't want her to be simply a pawn in this. From Proverbs 10:9, *He that walketh uprightly walketh surely: but he that perverteth his ways shall beknown.* While I had no illusions of matrimony, I at least wanted to be the strong arm for her to hold onto during this time of fear and apprehension. Whatever my opinion of her had been, it should take no great effort to be a gentleman.

When I left, I felt reasonably assured she trusted me enough to be her guardian. A patrol car slowed down as I walked down Douglas, practically in a daze. A young officer beeped his horn and reached over to roll down his passenger's window.

"You, Bergman?"

"Yeah."

"Mendenhall wants to see you."

I hopped in the front seat and received an escort to the police station. There was the nervous possibility of running into Hoeg. I'd have to deal with the prospect if it occurred, which it eventually would. The officer escorted me to Clarence Mendenhall's office, knocked and waited for a response, and then left after I entered. He finally looked up from a file, perhaps getting ready to talk about this case. "Come on. Give," he said in exasperation.

"What?"

"Aaron Lautenberg."

"Yeah. Questioned him about an employee of his."

"Who?" He was short with me, then went back to the file.

"Alonzo Washington."

His eyes shifted back and forth as though an intruder might have been able to get into the office by another method than the only door.

"This is between us." I raised one eyebrow as a

kind of acknowledgment. "You know a Chris Peterson?" There was a slight hesitancy in my face, a lack of eagerness to jump into the fire. I shook my head.

Mendenhall returned to the file, flipped a couple of pages, and then looked back at me.

"He's dead. They're calling it a workplace injury."

"What? At Cudahy?"

Mendenhall described a situation in which a forklift driver lost control and dropped nearly five hundred pounds of crates on Peterson. He was dead within minutes, his head crushed like a grape. The supervisor on the scene, Aaron Lautenberg, had called in the report.

"The thing is," Mendenhall continued, "Peterson was covering for a Randy Mason who was close with this Washington guy. And now Mason is nowhere to be found. Imagine that."

I hung my head, not quite in defeat, but in the sadness of knowing a man died because he was simply in the wrong place at the wrong time. Instead of being the tough guy and holding onto my case as if it was a precious gem, I explained how Althea Washington had hired me to find Alonzo and a few of the other items I had come across. I did not mention anything about the Barczak murder or Hoeg's possible involvement. I didn't have to.

"And you rousted this Lautenberg at Green Gables?"

"Rousted? No, Clarence. I'm not a cop anymore." He was perturbed at my middling attempt at humor. "He wasn't interested in cooperating with my investigation. Seemed dismissive. Initially I thought it was his nature. But now, I don't know. Especially after this."

"Could that be because Alonzo Washington is a suspect in the Barczak murder?"

"Says who?"

"Hoeg."

I laughed out loud. I didn't mean to. It let Clarence Mendenhall know for sure I doubted Marty Hoeg's integrity. I'm sure I wasn't the only one. Then again, there wouldn't be a poll taken at the station.

"Now, I'll say this," I continued, "and it's all I'll say. I've got Alonzo Washington holed up safely."

"I'm okay with that. Just don't try to go up against Hoeg. He doesn't like you. At all. Plus, he's got a gun and a badge. You've got your bible, a bad sense of humor, and a big mouth."

"And to think those were the attributes you wanted on your Night Detective Squad." He raised an eyebrow. "Well, I've got more," I said, but wasn't sure what I meant.

"Did I mention he doesn't like you?" He pushed his hat up on his forehead and gave a smirk that passed for a smile. "You sure you ain't interested in coming back?"

I raised an eyebrow. Then my face went slack, as though all the blood drained.

"I read in the paper a young girl named Juanita Morales was killed the other night. She appeared to be a pretty girl from the photo. Dark black hair and striking eyes. Really colorful dress. They found the body dumped in an alley behind the Nomar Theater. Stabbed like fifteen, sixteen times. Bruises all over her face."

"It was eleven and all she had was a black eye.

Stan Finster over at the *Eagle* likes to, shall we say, embellish the facts. Makes for good copy. The guy knows less about writing than Al Capp." Mendenhall sighed. His thoughts and his heart were spinning away from the press and back toward this tough case. "Talk was she was a roundheels."

"Does it matter?" Maybe I sounded a bit perturbed.

"No. I suppose not. On top of that, her case closely follows that of a Karina Garcia. No stab wounds in her case. She just had her throat slit from ear to ear and her tongue cut out. Early morning workers at El Centro Mercado found her in a dumpster behind the store. It was something they won't forget for a long time."

"Any connection?"

"Maybe. Maybe not. Both working girls. It was tough getting a handle on these types of cases. Nobody was willing to talk to the white cops. We're as much the enemy as the perpetrator."

"Well, dead colored factory workers and Latino girls who work the streets seem to wind up getting forgotten by everyone except their families. You think you'll find their killer?"

"We've got a couple of leads," Mendenhall replied in a kind of embarrassed tone. I understood the comment. It was a sad admission of a case that would eventually grow cold and wind up in a file in a cabinet in the basement.

"Yeah? Good luck with it."

"We'll need it."

By now, we both knew where we stood. I was to work my side of the street and Detective Mendenhall and the Wichita Police Department would work theirs. The goal was to meet in the middle. In that event, we might wind up crushing Detective Marty Hoeg. The notion didn't bother me in the least, although I had to keep it from being my primary motivation.

Althea Washington had indicated Hoeg desperately tried to squeeze Alonzo into a job moving merchandise. It would likely mean at the warehouse or building he had it stashed, just off North Arkansas. Whatever the place was, I certainly wouldn't use Alonzo as bait to draw out Hoeg. He'd just as soon kill Alonzo as let him talk and who knew what else. I had twenty-four hours before my date with Saundra to listen if the crickets were chirping around the area.

A quick jog over to the hack stand turned up Charlie Argento. My destination was two suspicious buildings on North Arkansas. We drove to the furthest one first, the building barely noticeable behind the trees surrounded by a chain link fence. Charlie stopped the cab, and I got out to look, staring at a mostly blank emptiness for nearly three minutes to get my brain to see things my eyes couldn't. It suddenly dawned on me there were deep tire marks straight along the dirt road. It could easily be surmised big trucks carrying a lot of weight made them. My guess was this was the likely place, but it would take perfect timing to be here when a truck came by again. It was unlikely they kept regularly scheduled hours. Then again, with the right inquiries, I could determine when Hoeg checked in and out for duty and deduce from there.

The unobtrusive brick building a little way down the street did have a faded painted sign indicating a former tool fabrication shop. I took down the name, Avcon Industries, R Verbeck, prop. but doubted I would find anything in the building codes to give me an idea who R. Verbeck was or if he even existed. My first thought was he was a straw man. I circled around to the front door where there was a notice from the city of a closure due to code violations. I thought it might give me further information about owners and inspections even though it was rather small to be holding stolen merchandise. If anything, it was an office. There was a slight hope some paperwork or other documents remained. I couldn't imagine Hoeg being stupid enough to leave concrete evidence behind that would tie him in directly.

If I could tail Hoeg, I could determine where he was going and what he had planned. Doing so in a taxi would be a dead giveaway. I had one idea. There had only been one other time when I asked Mrs. Hanover to borrow her car, the one she used primarily on Sunday to go to church and Wednesday to go to the market. Back then, it was to drive my father to Kansas City for the funeral of his cousin. Owning a car never appealed to me. There was maintenance and insurance and paperwork. I was rather surprised when she acquiesced for a job assignment.

The other reason I didn't drive was it put too much pressure on my foot, the one that was slightly shorter which forced a limp in my gait. I could manage walking with a minimum amount of pain, although long distance running was out of the question as well as ballroom dancing. The pushing down on the gas pedal or brake took a little extra pressure. There was always a concern whether my foot might give out and cause me to miss the brake completely, not to mention the shooting pain running up my leg. I figured someday it would be as useless as a wet towel. For now, it got me where I needed to go. When all else failed, there was always a hack around to accommodate me.

There were many times I attempted to determine if my pain was a reminder of the sufferings of many I encountered during the war or the acknowledgement of how painfully human I truly was. Everything we get is a blessing even if we are unable to understand it fully. The sudden stabbing pain came at uncertain times like excessive walking, running, or dancing. Certainly, if I drove a car. The cabbies in town, primarily Richie and Charlie, were considerate of my condition but benefitted from it, nevertheless.

I hardly ever thought about it, the shooting to my foot and calf, the long period of time before medics could tend to me and bring me out, the waiting and wondering if it would turn gangrene and require amputation, and the long rehabilitation before they sent me home. Now, it was only after a day had ended and the night emerged in which there was only myself and the cats who demanded my attention, the twinge of pain came on and all the past played out like a cheap B movie. I wanted to move forward and find the kind of salvation neither the Old Testament nor the statutes of the State of Kansas could provide. I didn't know where or how but I kept on looking, bad foot and all.

Too often recently, I thought if I could save Caroline Whitman or Althea and Alonzo Washington, I would find favor with the Almighty. It was the perseverance of Sir Pounce, with demands for his ears to be rubbed, there was a reminder everything in Life persisted. Cats would demand attention. Young girls would get hooked on drugs. Crooked cops would subvert desperate men. No matter what occurred or how, no matter the outcome, each day passed into the next. Perhaps this was not part of the greater cosmic plan. This was the thing I had to do. I alone could appreciate the rewards, whatever they would be.

Chapter Twenty-Two

There was much to do and precious little time to do it. It was the way things worked these days. I started with the brick building on North Arkansas, Avcon Industries, which, despite its name, was in a largely residential neighborhood. I checked out the supposed city sign affixed to the front door regarding the building as condemned per some unidentified ordinances and trespassing would be punishable by another ordinance. All rather official sounding. Numbers and letters and a dot and a dash here and there. At first glance, it had the appearance of legitimacy. I hadn't encountered many inspectors who wrote such violations and didn't have much experience with these types of ordinances. However, upon further review, the thing that made it look dubious was the handwritten nature of it. It wasn't the typical signage, pre-printed, with specifics filled in by hand on appropriate lines. There was a lot of pseudo legal jargon designed to give it the impression of formality to any rube passing by. It was an effort to dupe any curious parties who weren't prone to deep thinking. In this neighborhood, it would be the majority.

I peered in past the hastily taped newspaper around the windows. Whoever used the building had gone to great effort to maintain its anonymity. I had my hands cupped around my eyes to block out the sun to sneak a peek through a half-inch space in the tape job. With my hands the way they were, like blinders on a racehorse, a loud throat clearing caught my attention.

"Looking for something, mister?" The man was in his mid to late sixties, unshaven and wrinkled like a prune. He had on a worn-out pair of thick canvas pants held up by suspenders over a shabby flannel shirt. A pair of unshined and heavily scuffed brown shoes flopped around on his feet. There were sharp lines around his mouth, a clear indication of a lifelong smoker. That and his breath when he spoke were a dead giveaway. I couldn't be sure if the bloodshot eyes were from age, fatigue, or hooch. Perhaps a bit of all three.

"Yeah. A load of stolen merchandise." My tone was sarcastic. The words were true and honest. They fell on deaf ears, literally or figuratively.

"Police said to watch for anyone snooping around. You snooping?"

"If I ain't, it was a bad imitation." I hoped to push him into giving up anything he might know or just go away. He was hesitant to do either. "What police?"

"The Wichita police. Are you crazy, pal?"

"All of them or anyone in particular?"

"Tall guy. Name of Hogg. Funny name, huh?" It wasn't funny to me.

"I know him. He's a bad operator. I don't want to be messing with him. So what did he say was in here?"

"Evidence."

"Of what?"

"Beats me." He got bored either with the conversation or with me. "Say, you a cop?"

"Private."

"So you know this Hogg fella?"

"Yep. Sure do."

This was likely the most communication he had with any other human being all day, perhaps longer for all I knew. However, there was no reason for me to hang around any further. The old guy in the suspenders told me all I needed. It was unlikely this small building contained anywhere near the booze and stolen merchandise of an operation the likes of which Alonzo Washington described. Whatever was in there was a decoy made even more so by Hoeg letting on to the locals the building was of importance. It was an old magician's trick of deception. There might have been papers the District Attorney could use in a court case, but I doubted Marty Hoeg was much into proper record keeping.

I stopped in for lunch at the Pan American and got an opened faced hot turkey sandwich smothered with brown gravy. I promised myself once again I would someday order the lo mein because, well, the owner was from China. King Mar always suggested an alternative. A sullen dark figure stood in the doorway blocking out the sun while I was halfway through lunch. It was 'Big House' Walker. He stumbled over to my table after looking around for me, acting as though he had been on a drunk for several days. It wasn't easy to tell if he was still that way or badly shaken up.

"Mr. Bergman, I got a problem." He gulped hard. I wasn't sure if he was swallowing his pride.

"Oh?"

"This friend of Caroline's. She, well, she died."

"Sorry to hear."

"She didn't just, well, die. She—"

"Yeah. I know." His eyes grew large as though he

was on Mount Sinai, and I was the burning bush. "I saw you two drop her off at St. Francis." I waved my hand toward the seat in the booth opposite me. "You want to tell me what happened?"

"It wasn't Caroline's fault. You got to believe me."

I reached across the table, gently placing my hand upon his in an act of absolution as though I had any authority to do so.

"Tell me."

"Annette was at a house with a bunch of girls. One of their parents was away on vacation. Annette was trying to show these girls how to get it on. You know?"

"Where was Caroline?"

"She was supposed to be there to help them all out. Get them strung up on the stuff. It was what her father wanted."

"Yeah. I know." It was my turn to gulp thinking how utterly sick and depraved the notion was. "What went down?"

"Annette, she was out of control, shot herself up a couple of times, probably forgetting what she had done. The other girls were all gone, man. Just gone. Caroline shows up and Annette, she was out of it. Caroline got upset and called me at the club."

"That was when you took her to St. Francis?"

"Yeah."

"But you didn't know she was dead."

"No. Not then, no."

"What did Caroline say?"

"Ain't said nothing. Can't get a hold of her. Don't know where she is."

"She's out on a boat in the middle of nowhere." Dale Walker looked at me as though I was the one who was long gone. "Albert Whitman will pull his daughter so far away from this it'll be nothing more than a dream. The only one left is you, Dale. A colored jazz musician. You make the perfect schlemiel. If you're not careful, you'll wind up in the real big house. And Albert Whitman will make sure they throw away the key."

I didn't want to tell it so harsh. Unfortunately this thing had blown up bigger than Hiroshima. Whitman was too big for me or the police or anyone of this world to stop. Dale needed to hear it from someone who halfway cared.

"I can't stay away from her. I love her."

There it was. Like a moth to a flame, these two were the modern Romeo and Juliet, too filled with stars in their eyes to see there was a bigger machine all ready to roll over them and squash them like insignificant bugs. Then again, how could you argue with love? Maybe it truly had enough power to withstand all.

"Listen, I've got an idea of what Whitman's organization is all about. For now, he's not going to let anything happen to Caroline. He can't afford to. She's in trouble and she has her father. She's safe for the time being. Me, well, I can take care of myself. But the odds are stacked against you right now. You need to back off and give me space to take care of this."

"I can't do that, man."

"You must. Face it. You cannot get into their world. For better or worse, I can. Let me be the one to bring this house of cards down."

Dale Walker sat there shaking his head lightly, perhaps out of nervousness or an attempt at convincing himself I could do the job. His heart was clouding his judgment. I sat there with him, allowing my lunch to get cold and waiting long enough to make sure he wouldn't explode. I didn't like knowing I couldn't be sure if he would listen to me, pay attention to me, or trust me. When he left, I convinced myself I bought a little time.

Meanwhile, I found out surreptitiously Marty Hoeg ended his shift at three p.m. that afternoon and scheduled back again Saturday at five p.m. It would give him two full days plus a little more to make a move. He wasn't the sitting around at home type. Sure enough, when he came out of the city building a little past three, he drove his car up on north on Broadway and made his was to Cudahy. Standing in the parking lot by a big truck with him was Aaron Lautenberg and the always-scared Randy Mason, standing as if he had to use a rest room and rather nervously bouncing from one foot to the other. His eyes were not as wide as I had seen them before. It was almost as though he were dead inside, capitulating to greater forces.

Lautenberg was friendly and at ease with Hoeg as though they were drinking buddies or perhaps enjoyed watching those lovely dancers. Mason appeared as though he would collapse on the ground at a moment's notice if given the chance. Lautenberg glanced at his watch and checked a clipboard he was holding, giving instructions to Hoeg who waved him off with a dismissive hand. Randy got into the truck and followed Marty Hoeg as he drove off. My guess was they were heading up to a fenced-in property on North Arkansas. You would have thought I worked in a carnival considering these two went exactly where I anticipated.

Hoeg undid the lock on the fence, waved the kid

through with the truck, and followed him, locking the gate behind them. I parked about a half block down the street in front of a house with no porch lights on, ducking down in the front seat as much as I could. I was prepared to wait for as long as it took.

A good police detective would learn surveillance. I was able to study for my exam. Gunny had given me some schooling on it by way of Humphrey Bogart and *The Maltese Falcon.* He took me to see it at the Crest Theater shortly before Halloween of 1941. Instead of sitting back and enjoying the flick, he made constant commentary regarding the actors playing the police detectives.

"Sorry but I'm not buying it. Barton MacLane is too grumpy, and Ward Bond is too nice. The only grumpy guys I know are the ones close to retirement because they can't wait to get out. And you can't afford to be nice when investigating a murder on account of anyone could be a suspect, even a close friend." There were annoyed pleas for quiet, which Gunsaullus waved off. "Most of detective work involves your feet and your backside. You're either going everywhere looking for answers or sitting and waiting for them. If they come at all."

Pearl Harbor was less than two months later. I never got to take the exam.

If I told Gunny about my falling asleep while on a stakeout, he would likely have further commentary and dressed me down thoroughly, even without my still being on the force. The headlights of the truck jarred me awake as it headed south on Arkansas. I never determined where Hoeg's car went. My wristwatch indicated it was a little over two hours from the time they first got there. By the time I got my wits about me, I lost track of the truck as well. Over all, it had been a wasted opportunity. I was back to square one.

In a strange twist of fate, it was Floyd Gunsaullus who showed up at my door the following morning. After an hour of driving around in the general vicinity the night before attempting to make up for my snafu, I wound up getting home late and didn't even bother to stop by King's X or even the Pan American. My face felt numb, and my eyes burned. Gunny would typically have smirked at my appearance. This time he was somber.

"You know a guy named Randy Mason?" I stared blankly, afraid to hear any more words. "Worked over at Cudahy."

"Worked?" The word practically croaked out of my mouth.

"He was found on an Eby construction site up on North Fifty-Fifth Street. Beaten to a pulp." My eyes grew wide, and my legs nearly gave out on me. Sir Pounce meowing at my feet kept me from collapsing right there. "What's going on, Harold?"

Despite the deep fear welling inside of me, I knew time was of the essence. I poured myself a glass of orange juice I had made up the day before, gulped it down, and then poured another quickly. It wasn't the best substitute for coffee. For now, it would have to do.

I gave him the lowdown on my case with Alonzo Washington but didn't tell him where I had him stashed. Gunny nodded in understanding at every reference to Marty Hoeg. It was as though he was fluent in the language I was speaking. As I worked my way through it and said all the words aloud, I didn't hear myself indicating any solid evidence, any proof on any crime having been committed. Alonzo's identification of Hoeg as the killer of Timmy Barczak would not stand up under cross-examination by a wily mouthpiece. Gunny didn't have to say any of this. He had trained me well enough. All I told him was a fanciful story no cop would be interested in.

Chapter Twenty-Three

For the life of me, I never understood how those designated military officers carried out their tasks of advising family members their loved ones had died in combat. It was not an enviable job assignment. Did they simply state the facts and exhibit empathy before continuing? Did they shed a tear either in front of the family or back in their car? I couldn't imagine them being soulless men who faked their concern. I accepted the fact it was about time I let Alonzo know about Randy Mason seeing as they were almost family. Like a scared young brother, Mason looked to Alonzo as he showed greater strength, perhaps due to his faith or the love of his wife, Randy could not fathom. In either case, my client's husband was slowly becoming an abandoned cog in a corrupt wheel. He needed a friend now. I was all that remained.

The expression on my face was a dead giveaway of an unimaginable fear. It wasn't my intent to allow him to think any ill will had come to his wife but correcting it by the actual circumstances was hardly any better. There would be time for grieving. Right now, I had to find justice.

"I've got to know if Randy got caught in the clutches of Lautenberg and Hoeg. If so, how? What was going on there?" There was a tone of desperation in my voice because it felt like everything was slipping through my fingers, mostly the soul of Alonzo Washington.

"Lautenberg ain't what he appears. Hoeg got him his job there. Vouched for him. He done time somewhere in Oklahoma."

"For what?"

"Don't know. Not murder or nothing. Definitely something where you could do a stretch though."

"Why would Hoeg do that, get him set up like that?"

"Put him in a position he owed Hoeg. He needed cheap labor for his business, and we was it." Alonzo shrugged his shoulders, a sign he, too, had about given up. I completely underestimated Marty Hoeg's influence both in the criminal world and with legitimate businesses. It didn't make him smart, just devious.

"Okay, help me understand this. Lautenberg gets low-level workers like yourself and Mason to do, let's say, a special job, driving a truck or loading and unloading merchandise. You wind up making extra dough. He checks trucks out of the packing plant, so it looks legit. No one says anything and everything is Jake. Hoeg runs the operation, the trucks and the drivers get returned, and no one is the wiser."

"That's about it, I guess" he nodded in agreement.

"You know a Chris Peterson?"

"Heard of him. I think. Maybe a forklift driver?" My face remained blank. My lack or words spoke volumes. "Him too?"

I continued without needing to affirm the inquiry. "I found a padlocked gate up on North Arkansas. Gravel road with deep ruts. A building sat behind a deep clump of trees."

"Old plant, small business, used to make airplane parts during the war. Gone belly up before the war ended. Government didn't want it no more."

"Hoeg storing stolen goods there?" Alonzo shrugged. "The question is why would he move it all out now." It was strictly rhetorical. Alonzo Washington was a driver who saw too much and wound up rattling Hoeg's cage. It meant there was still a loose end out there now that Randy Mason and Chris Peterson were out of the picture.

A couple of cups of coffee wouldn't get me in a good frame of mind considering my date that evening with Saundra Mooney. Time was of the essence if I wanted to put a little bit of heat on Glick Helbert and his partners.

Ringside Sports Center was not quite a gym for boxers but too rugged to be a fitness center for middle-aged businessmen who wanted to impress their wives or mistresses. At best, one could call it "rustic." To me, it was like a warehouse that tried to be a sports palace it didn't have the character to be. There wasn't the pervasive stench of sweat and corruption, rather the vague aroma of bootlegged booze and contraband merchandise. Rumor was a good deal of it passed through here on its way to Green Gables.

A young towel boy slapped the older man standing next to him when I walked in. They were watching a dark-skinned colored fighter going through a series of combinations on a sparring partner. The kid had quick hands and a good jab, but his hook was loping, opening him to a jawbreaker. The older man upon seeing me immediately turned aggrieved. We met each other halfway from where we stood.

"Glick Helbert here?" I asked.

"Who's asking?" A pause and an attitude separated the two words.

"You know who I am."

"Glick ain't here."

"You're Max Cohen?"

"So now we know who we are, chum. You think we got something in common because you're a Jew? Hey, Passover starts next week. I'll invite you to my Seder." He laughed uproariously and started davening as though the holiday was supposed to be humorous. If this were ancient times, he would have been closer to being a Pharisee.

It started to annoy me how so many people used my religion as the basis of who they thought I was without ever really trying to get to know me. Maybe that was true of most people when it came to anyone whose skin color or religion didn't match theirs. To be perfectly honest, I never gave Mr. Cohen's spiritual beliefs, or lack thereof, a minor thought nor did I concern myself with his business dealings. Until it involved Alonzo Washington and Detective Marty Hoeg. Then I felt as though I carried Aaron's rod.

"You gentlemen are carrying an albatross around your neck. A dead weight in the form of a corrupt cop who is heading for a long stay behind stone walls and iron bars. Now, before you try to make any sense of my literary analogies take my advice and cut your ties with that creep."

"I got no idea what you're talking about, pal." He practically yawned as he spoke.

"I'll bet you don't."

Max didn't back down or flinch. There was a

tremor in his eyes indicating he heard me, understood, and possibly cared. Nevertheless, he didn't try to continue the conversation.

I was taking a big chance to challenge the owners of one of the shadier clubs and facilities in town. I was going on the assumption Hoeg's badge had Helbert, Cohen, and Stiff more scared than anything, considering there were a lot of cops they likely paid off. Letting on what I knew was in the hope they might push back, but not necessarily on me. It didn't take long to find out.

There were two of them, wearing ill-fitting suits and overcoats when they should have been wearing boxing gear. One had a nose that must have been broken half a dozen times. It had two sharp curves, and the cartilage was almost protruding through the skin. He was the better looking of the two. The other hardly had any eyebrows and a mouth shaped like a twisted oval. Both had guns stuck in my ribs.

Their style didn't involve any fancy talk. Somehow Bogart as Sam Spade popped in my head right there. "The cheaper the crook, the gaudier the patter." I let out a little laugh as they got me into the alley. They obviously didn't take too kindly to my lack of respect for their girth. Broken Nose hit me twice in the gut. When a person talked about having the wind knocked out of them, it was not a euphemism. At that point, I was empty inside. It felt like No Eyebrows used both fists as a club on my back in between my shoulder blades. It echoed in my ears as a dull thump. Between the shot to the belly doubling me over and the haymaker on my back knocking me down, the whole thing took all of five seconds. They said nothing as they walked away. After all, actions speak louder than words. Unfortunately, I was incapable of speech and even less capable of any kind of action.

My first thought was a hope I would not be too uncomfortable for my social obligation that evening. Then it occurred to me how desperate an act this was so soon after visiting Max Cohen and so close to his establishment. At this point, I could only imagine how Marty Hoeg would respond.

Rather than collapsing in the back of a taxi, I walked home. It was the best way I could think of to work out the pain and stiffness inflicted upon me by two non-contenders who still had a lot to prove. There was a distinct possibility I might have appeared soused in the manner I tried to put one foot in front of the other in an attempt to remain upright. Fortunately, there were no passing patrol cars to question my state of supposed inebriation.

Arriving at my apartment, I plopped down on my favorite chair, then immediately had to get up when two sets of felines expressed their disgruntlement verbally. As soon as I opened the pocket doors, I experienced a more pleasant assault than earlier in the day. Lady Mittens jumped into my lap while Sir Pounce continued performing circles around my legs. It wasn't a couple of aspirin and a hot water bottle, but it sufficed for the time being.

While recuperating in a hot bath, I did my best to make sense of Hoeg's involvement with the boys from Green Gables and the senseless deaths of Randy Mason and Chris Peterson. Peterson's death could have been an accident considering the report as written had only employees as witnesses. I doubted it and had to accept the possibility. However, the manner of Mason's death spoke volumes he now could not. Getting shot would have been an outright execution. I imagined Hoeg's desperate attempts to determine where Alonzo Washington was hiding. Alonzo was the only one outside of Glick Helbert who could identify Hoeg as a killer. Helbert would not bring his illegal operations down by acknowledging it. That left Alonzo Washington as a missing target. It finally dawned on me his wife, Althea, could be in his sights as well.

There was nothing I could do about it now. It was late in the afternoon and the recovery from my abusive encounter was not going as expediently as I hoped. I dressed casually and headed down to the Pan American. King Mar pulled me aside as soon as I entered.

"If you're not more careful," he said in mock desperation, "I'm going to have to close down my restaurant."

"What do you mean?"

"That sax player was here again. Said he was looking for you to help him find his girlfriend. If you're doing lost women cases now, I had this one gal back in 1922—"

"What else?"

"Big cop. Bad attitude. Says to give you a message."

"What's that?"

"It's Friday night. You better go to temple and pray."

Hoeg's response was not near as direct as the two muscular associates of Max Cohen, but it was as effective. King put together a quick chicken salad sandwich for me. I sat in the kitchen and suggested it might be better for me to avoid eating in his establishment for the time being.

"No way, man. I've been in U.S. thirty-two years. Still waiting to bring my wife over from China. I see you more than her. You like family. Family don't run away. Right?"

He had a point. Giving in to the bad guys and all the evil out there meant the serpent would wind up taking over the Garden of Eden. I had enough friends, my father, even Rabbi Saperstein, to provide me with the moral strength necessary to come out ahead of the dust storm kicked up by those who chose to hide. This was not the time to cower.

I looked decidedly better than I felt. With that in mind, I figured a smile and sly remark might get me through this evening. Still in possession of Mrs. Hanover's car, I picked up Saundra at a reasonable time. She was as lovely as before but didn't exhibit the vibrant demeanor she had worn as snuggly as her dress. I held the door open for her and acted as much of a gracious gentleman as I could.

"We won't stay long, I promise you. And I'd certainly like to take you somewhere for dinner. Maybe dancing?"

"No." The word was absolute, spoken about as quickly as a sneeze. "I just want this to be over with." I didn't really need her to change her mind. It would have been more pleasant if she had. Then again, this was only a business relationship, and my present physical condition precluded any Fred Astaire moves. We both expected this to end as soon as possible. If not sooner.

Chapter Twenty-Four

A Friday night in spring is perfect for the bigwigs to be out. They get the opportunity to flaunt their wealth and power, and generally assert their dominion over the working-class Joe. It might be in the form of a tip or a recognition the waiter or bartender was not expecting. In Wichita, a man like Albert Whitman was akin to a Hollywood star. He never came off in that fashion. The mystery and uncertainty of Whitman was his celebrity.

There might have been families habituating the Blue Moon occasionally. When the weekend rolled around it was strictly an adult affair. It was a place where "behind closed doors" was a guarantee to those who required privacy. The Johnny 'Scat' Davis Orchestra played there in the summer of 1940 shortly before Clyde McCoy and His Sugar Blues Orchestra. If those walls could talk, the cops would have closed the place by now. I wondered how much it cost to buy silence. Then again, I was no longer on the force so I could keep my mind focused on the matter at hand.

I was interested to see whom Albert Whitman, a notoriously private person, would socialize with at such an establishment. While his name was well known, his habits were not. I imagined wide-eyed hatcheck girls, debutantes ready to be defiled, show girls looking for the next big break and willing to accommodate Mr.

Whitman's indiscretions. To my surprise, he sat gleefully at a large table with only his daughter Caroline comfortably by his side, albeit a tad noncommittal. The empty chairs around gave him the appearance of royalty, a kind of satin rope or imaginary barrier to ward off the riffraff.

While I was expecting a gape jawed look and shifty eyes, Whitman surprised me with a warm and inviting smile as he stood and extended his hand. It grasped mine firmly and with bravado and had the cold caress of a pair of handcuffs. My level of comfort flew out the door at his greeting.

"Why, Mr. Bergman. I half expected you to be in temple about now." As was typical, he threw a jab at my religion and Jews in general. That was fair enough considering my unimpressed opinion of men of wealth.

"Not when I can be here hobnobbing with the likes of you," I shot back. The generosity of our respective smiles and the glaring white of our teeth were shallow facades. We both knew it. There was no invitation to join him. He remained standing and staring while Caroline remained distant as though she were anesthetized while she sipped her champagne cocktail as though it were formula.

"Mrs. Mooney never let on you two were... Exactly what are you two?" There was a dismissive tone in his voice. I couldn't quite gather whether he was less enthused about his former employee or his current one.

"I could ask the same question." I grabbed Saundra and walked off toward a table in the back that was in view of Whitman and his daughter. Admittedly, I was distracted by the encounter and was noticeably absent in my attention toward my companion. There was still a need to make an appearance of social propriety while at the same time not getting caught in a verbal spider web.

The waiter came over, very prim and proper.

"Two champagne cocktails," Saundra blurted out. I noticed what appeared to be a smile. I nodded at the waiter.

"We might make an evening out of this still." She looked down and then up again after a brief pause. Her teeth were baring down slightly on her lower lip.

"Mr. Bergman—"

"Harold. Please."

"Harold, you are probably right about all of this. I guess I'm being too selfish."

"You're simply looking out for your own safety and there's nothing wrong with that." I sounded vaguely like Rabbi Saperstein. The tone did not have any sway over my professional goals.

She took a moment to gather herself. What she was about to say might not fit in with the gaiety of the setting and a bit of courage had to be dredged up from within.

"My husband gave his life for this country. He believed in something and so should I."

It wasn't the blubbering recitation of a dyed-in-the-wool patriot but merely the realization of a woman who lost everything that was important to her and wound up taking the easy way out. She found her way back even though she had to walk through a conflagration to do so. I put a soft hand on her shoulder and smiled.

We had a couple of cocktails, danced closely so she could make comments in my ear, and felt the tension melt in each other. For the time being, there was a sense of decency between us. It felt good to be gallant in the fashion I had been raised. There was never a thought of taking advantage of her. It was necessary to convince her this was the right thing to do. None of that prevented my foot from being in extreme pain but this was all worth the sacrifice.

I had to surreptitiously make notations in my notebook as Saundra identified various men that came to visit Whitman's table. It was like a king receiving visitors in his court, the appearance of fealty akin to that of a medieval lord. There were, for the most part, smiles and handshakes, a couple of whispered comments, and at one point, the awkward passing of an unidentified object between Whitman and a Latin looking gentleman in a white tuxedo jacket.

"Right there! Oswaldo Acevedo," she said, a bit of spite in her voice. She spoke like a woman violated by an insufferable trauma.

"What do you know about him?"

"No one actually knows anything about him. But there are a lot of rumors."

"Such as?"

"Gambling. Prostitution. Drugs. Protection. He'll pull in a dollar any way he can. And yet the police can't get any line on him."

"Any legit businesses?"

"Sol y Luna Design. It means Sun and Moon. He supposedly does interior design for very rich people although he has the taste of a gutter rat."

"Let me guess. He gets a lot of high-end furniture and décor from Whitson Import." She smiled and nodded. "It could be he realized trying to sell to the colored jazz musicians was too dangerous. I'll bet there are a lot of those Eastborough and College Hill folks who secretly indulge." Saundra was looking somewhere between tired and bored, perhaps worn down by all these sudden declarations of criminality within her sphere, notions she had little experience in and less strength to deal with. I grabbed her by the arm, threw enough bills on the table to cover our tab, and left, giving a final glance and nod toward Albert Whitman. The serpent smiled back, daring me to eat of the forbidden fruit.

Saundra had a look of anticipation during the drive from the far south end of town all the way on North Broadway. The Rustic Inn didn't have the glamour or clientele of the Blue Moon, but it was a lot livelier. The look on her face had the slightest sting of disappointment. As we approached the entrance, her shoulders relaxed, and a light of relief made her face glow.

A sawbuck got me a good table close to the bandstand where Big House Walker was blowing a tune fast and furious on his alto sax. I recognized it as "Koko" and for a moment, I could have sworn Bird was back in Wichita. The trumpet player was having a hard time keeping up with Dale's riff, his eyes ablaze in desperation while his cheeks puffed like Dizzy. A smile of joy swept over my face. For me, these were the moments when the hand of Adonai was reaching down among us to bless one individual who would anoint us all. Whoever said the music of the Lord wasn't be-bop?

I figured the rye here would be a little harsher than Saundra would care for, so I ordered a couple of Manhattans, heavy on the sweet vermouth. She drank it as though it were iced tea on a hot summer day. Her smile made me even more comfortable. My eyes made contact with Dale who was a bit brighter in spirits than he had been of late.

"Mr. Bergman."

"Dale, this is my friend, Saundra Mooney."

"Pleasure to meet you, ma'am." Dale did not extend a hand toward her, she being a white woman. Everyone was on his or her best behavior. They had to be.

"Mrs. Mooney is the personal assistant to Albert Whitman."

"Caroline's father?" He was both shocked and surprised.

Immediately, Saundra's eyes grew as wide as half dollars. She understood this wasn't an extension of our evening, rather my intention to make her fully and completely grasp the repercussions of Whitman's operations.

"We just saw them at the Blue Moon." Saundra's tone was casual, almost indifferent.

"How was she?" Dale, on the other hand, had desperation oozing out of each word as his head turned back and forth between us, finally focusing on Saundra. "I mean, was she okay."

"She looked bored." I couldn't figure out if Saundra tried to get a rise out of him or expressed the absolute truth.

"She didn't look like she wanted to be there." It was time I had to become the diplomat. "I don't think they played her kind of music. You know?"

Then, suddenly, Saundra became maternal, for lack of a better expression. She reached out and touched Dale's hand in a comforting fashion. For his part, he didn't attempt to pull it back.

"Mr. Walker, you must understand Caroline's father is very influential. Extremely wealthy with connections to who knows what kind of criminal element. A colored jazz musician, a Jewish private investigator, and a white secretary don't have what it takes to fight him. He's too powerful." For the briefest moment, Big House was like a small child whose mother told him his pet goldfish died. "Let her go."

I understood what she attempted to do but I disagreed largely because I knew what Dale and Caroline meant to one another.

"No." I intended the word to be a dagger. "We can't let men like him win. Imagine if I felt the same thing during the war. No. We fight." Right then I saw a renewed strength that encouraged me. Dale Walker was back to his angry self. Saundra acquiesced though I felt she didn't entirely trust me. The resolve had returned even though we were still no better off than before.

I drove Saundra home in silence. It had been a long evening in terms of revelations and truths, a velvet curtain pulled back to reveal the stench of the gutter. Perhaps she was aware of them and was in denial. I wanted to believe she was just naïve. It gave me the feeling of hope.

I walked her to the front door of her house and watched her unlock the door. She turned suddenly, a tear in one of her eyes.

"Kiss me."

It caught me off guard. There was never anything of late to imply a romantic connection or any interest in one.

"Why?"

"I need to be reminded of a time before all of this, when there weren't any wars or criminals or evil floating around everywhere."

There was no point in telling her of history's conflicts or the constant prevalence of the unlawful and evil. Instead, I took her by the shoulders and drew her close to me, kissing her more passionately than I ever had done with Eileen Horowitz. For the time it took me to kiss her, I forgot about crime and evil and all the sins that had been unleashed on the world. I let everything that was bad and wrong disappear so I could embrace what was good.

When the kiss ended, she gently raised her head and looked at me. There was a kind of validation in her eyes. I knew at once she trusted me to do what was right. I couldn't be sure if she had the strength to get through all of this.

I parked Mrs. Hanover's car in the back garage, wiped it down with a rag to get the dust of the road off it. The car had seen things the owner could never dream of. It was my intention to keep the dear lady free from such knowledge.

The cats were already fast asleep so there was no point in disturbing them. I changed into pajamas and reclined with my hands behind my head. Making bold statements was often my way of hiding fear or uncertainty. I assured a lovesick musician and a scared widow I could help them defeat a dragon. It would take every bit of strength from every source I had to live up to the task.

Chapter Twenty-Five

There was a lot of tossing and turning throughout the remainder of the night. Uncertainty plagued me, not in the form of dreams but in a restlessness bordering on insomnia. My thoughts were plentiful though unconnected. It was like throwing a whole bunch of darts at a dartboard at the same time and hoping one of them would stick, Even the cats made no effort to jump up on the bed, afraid their tranquility would be constantly disturbed. Saundra Mooney placed a great trust in me, yet doubt was creeping in.

I awoke famished and decided it would be nice to take my dad out for breakfast. The chances were he might be at the shop puttering on a Saturday morning, but I knew as he was getting older, he tired easily and would just as likely sit at home reading from the Torah or the Talmud to honor the Sabbath. To him, the *Wichita Beacon* offered no hope of salvation. There was too much grounded in Today and not enough in Eternity.

He opened the door with a surprised look on his face. I also recognized the pursed lips indicated a slightly aggrieved state of mind. This was certainly not the way I would have preferred to start out my day.

"Didn't you get my message?" he asked plainly.

"What message?" My eyes were wide in a mix of fear and apprehension, a carryover from my youth.

"I spoke to your landlady last night. About five in the evening."

"I got back home late. I was on a case."

"You forgot our dinner plans?"

My hand literally slapped my forehead like a cliché. I could only imagine how much leftover roast or chicken there was not to mention scalloped potatoes. The one thing I learned growing up was the concept of waste, how limited the world's resources were, and how abundant was the love of the Lord. Yet in my experience, the U.S. Army had sufficient resources, but the enemy had no love.

After proclaiming the benefit of not needing to cook for a couple of days, my father halted my umpteenth apology as we sat in a booth at King's X over on Hillside. Despite his preference for Kosher food, he did enjoy a couple of fried eggs and wheat toast from a good diner. He did, however, stay away from the bacon. I did as well but solely as a respectful courtesy.

I provided him with further details about both cases I was on, bemoaning the fact I was now working, in essence, on my own time. Albert Whitman had requested I locate his daughter. I did. He paid me. Althea Washington wanted me to find her husband and determine if he was okay. I did and was now hiding him from the clutches of a corrupt cop. I never expected a significant payment from her. Now both cases had taken on a life of their own. While a few people were aware of the enormity of the crimes involved, I felt as though I were the only one capable of bringing them both to a resolution. This was not an admirable character trait in my opinion. It was a flaw.

From Proverbs 3:5-6 it is said, *"Trust in the Lord will all thine heart; and lean not unto thine own understanding. In all thy ways acknowledge him, and he shall direct thy paths."* While being a police officer or a soldier required following protocols and hierarchies, there was a sense of positive action. You needed to follow your instincts if it meant apprehending a suspect or avoiding death by an enemy. I was neither of those now, nor did I feel I could give in when so many lives were at stake.

My father interlaced his fingers and gathered them in a tight bond. He rested his chin upon them, eyes closed in contemplation, and remained in absolute silence. This was a scene I encountered countless times in my life. My father was as wise as any rabbi and so self-deprecating, he felt the need to consider his words deeply before commenting or responding. I tried hard to adopt this attitude. I was never entirely successful. Perhaps one day.

"Rabbi Tarfon used to say: It is not your duty to finish the work, but neither are you at liberty to neglect it." I recognized the words from Pirkei Avot. "You have always been an honest and upright man, Harold. Always reaching out a hand to help anyone in need. You must finish this work. It is your calling." His fingers untangled from each other, and he reached forward to hold mine. "Just know the Lord is on your side."

More than ever before, I felt choked up. Despite not following my father's desire that I become a rabbi, he wanted me to follow my own path as truthfully, nobly, and justly as I could. As I told Dale Walker, living a good life was the best revenge. In my case, it was against the cries of "Christ killer" by unknowing goyim in my youth, the boys from the deep south in boot camp who didn't think Jews could be good soldiers, and the general looks and comments by men of wealth and power. Men like Albert Whitman. These would not go away. Perhaps they were the fire in which my soul was forged.

The things I was able to accomplish in the war, my achievements previously in the police department, all felt as though a higher power were guiding me. Uneducated comments fell off me like water from a duck's back. Nevertheless, being aware of these things did not fully protect me from them. At the very least, I felt the fight was in my hands.

It was far too early to visit Green Gables but that was exactly where I went. Charlie drove me because Richie was having one of his episodes. They were less frequent but still of great concern. What was most frustrating was I had no ability to mitigate his suffering. I instructed Charlie to park at a distance from the entrance. I wasn't expecting a mad dash for a getaway. I just wanted to be prepared.

The front door was unlocked. The place was as silent as a crypt. Glick Helbert sat in his office. The two former pugilists turned upon hearing me, their faces impassive while their fists clenched.

"It's okay, boys. You can let him in." I walked past them and sat in a chair in front of his desk. After a moment, the two goons left, closing the door behind them. "I've been expecting you," Helbert said, almost apologetically. "Would you care to elaborate on your comments to my partner?"

"Your other business associate, Detective Marty

Hoeg, is on the hot seat. I wouldn't be sitting with him unless you want to fry in the same chair as well."

"I suppose it would be useless to tell you I have no idea what you're talking about."

"Stolen goods and stolen hooch are one thing. Hoeg is a murderer, and you know it. I've got a witness that places you at the scene of the Timmy Barczak killing." He opened his mouth to counter. I kept on talking. "I don't care about you or your partners and the illegal booze or whatever else it is you buy. I don't care about your business or the underage girls you have floating around for entertainment. I want Hoeg. That's all."

His mouth closed. He was aware it was not the time for rash commentary. While he was not as deeply in thought as my father had been, he still deliberated on his response.

"What do you want from me?"

I leaned forward getting as close as the big desk would allow. I wanted him to see my eyes and feel the heat of my breath.

"Hoeg is going to try to dump some goods on you. Sooner than later if my guess is correct."

"So?"

"Decline."

"What?" A burst of hot air pushed out of his mouth. It was rank with the foulness of corruption.

"Tell him no. Advise him to peddle his stuff elsewhere. If you take those goods off his hands, you've given him an out as well as making you an accessory to murder. You and Cohen and Still. It makes no difference to me. The State will send all of you to Lansing to swing."

"He'll kill me if I refuse." His emphasis on the word 'me' gave me to believe he didn't care about the deaths of Barczak or Randy Mason or Chris Peterson or any other lowlife that wasn't important to him. Perhaps he temporarily forgot his partners as well. I stared at him with nothing on my face to show I was concerned about him.

We sat in silence for a bit, my face like one of those on Mount Rushmore. The sweat gathered on his forehead. He finally made a phone call, not overly concerned if I was listening. Apparently, it was to Max Cohen likely at Ringside. He referenced me being in the office in front of him, asked Cohen if any deliveries arrived at the sports center, and then instructed Cohen to refuse any. Cohen's response was loud enough I could hear it through the line. In his most soothing voice, Helbert explained the consequences of both alternatives.

"Wise choice," I said after he hung up.

"Now what?"

It was easier to get forgiveness than permission. I grabbed Helbert's phone and got a hold of Clarence Mendenhall, giving him the skinny on what I believed was going on with Detective Hoeg. He would have a patrol car check out the brick building on North Arkansas while two detectives covered the fenced in former aircraft parts factory. Glick Helbert started shaking, probably in need of a glass of courage this early in the afternoon. Mendenhall would meet me at Cudahy in an hour to start pulling the pin on this grenade. It gave me the time to make sure no other parties would interfere. Glick could have his drink when I was gone.

I provided Charlie with the approximate address where I encountered Sibyl. My thought was they had been tailing me to keep track of the situation with Alonzo, even though they didn't know for certain where he was. I previously checked with Nicholas and his sons to make sure Alonzo had indeed stayed put. So far, all my ducks were in a row.

It didn't surprise me to find the blind lady and her boys with her. She smiled as I walked in the door, despite the fact no one had spoken a word. Perhaps she was psychic after all.

"You really need to change your cologne," she said. Right there, she gave away one of her secrets. She still had plenty more.

"Hanukkah present from my dad," I responded. "Same one every year." We both smiled.

I sat down at the table opposite her, hands in clear view. Charlie went so far as to remove his hat but stood stock still at the doorway. I explained everything in detail, never mentioning where Alonzo was keeping himself. She never asked. I laid out the plans as well as the hopeful resolution. If everything went as expected, the police would arrest Hoeg and there would be no further threat to the Washingtons.

"If it's okay with you," I stated plainly and respectfully, "I've got to go and check on Althea. Until this cop is put away, she might be in danger."

As I stood, she reached out her hands toward mine, holding them as gently as my father had. There was a strange sort of comfort in that.

"No need," she stated. "We've kept our eye on her." Perhaps the comment shouldn't have startled me. "Figured you've had enough on your plate as it is." The smile now gave off an aura of complicity. Whereas she desired to maintain control of her small kingdom, she would let me be a part of the crusade. For the time being.

My good foot was tapping a rhythm on the floorboard in the back seat. I was keeping time like a drummer, like Max Roach backing Bird and Diz. Only I was the bandleader, and the beat of the drum was like gunshots.

Charlie dropped me off at Cudahy where Mendenhall was waiting. He was grateful for the sawbuck and would have stayed further. I let him know quite clearly this was where he got off the train before it turned into a runaway. He nodded, likely thinking about his wife and daughters. At times, retreat was a wise course of action.

Chapter Twenty-Six

There was no doubt we would find Lautenberg at the packing plant on a Saturday considering what was going on was outside of normal business operations. Hoeg was on the move, and we needed to set the trap. Mendenhall's badge was better than a battering ram against one of those old European castles. The eyes of the security guy at the front gate bugged out more than Sam McDaniel. Detectives didn't typically prowl around a meat packing plant unless it was Marty Hoeg.

"Take me to Lautenberg," Mendenhall said coarsely. He didn't intend it to be a polite request, nor did it need to be.

Lautenberg was sitting with his feet up on his desk talking casually on the phone. For the briefest moment, his eyes were like those of the front gate guy, then quickly returned to laid back and sleepy. He must have thought we didn't notice. We did. He made a quick apology to the person on the line and then sat up straight, hands crossed before him like a good altar boy. I doubted he spent a minute in any church. A big phony politician's smile crept up on his face. He knew I knew. That, to me, was comforting.

"Gentlemen?" He didn't follow with the customary inquiry as to how he could be of assistance. He apparently was aware we would advise.

"Marty Hoeg." Again, Mendenhall was throwing

hard fastballs like Bob Feller. The question was whether Lautenberg was Hank Greenberg hitting them out of the park or Ralph Kiner swinging and missing.

"I'm sorry. Is there a question there?" His attempt at being a sly shyster was failing miserably. He was a two-bit scam artist posing as a swell with a reasonably responsible position. Beyond that, he had nothing backing him, except for Hoeg. And that was fading.

Mendenhall slammed his fists down on the desk and leaned in as close as he could get, pushing out fiery breath onto the lackadaisical face of Aaron Lautenberg.

"You're expecting Marty Hoeg, a detective for the Wichita Police Department, here today. You're planning on loaning him one of your custodians or cheap laborers as well as one of your trucks. Just as you've done many times before."

"I have no idea what you're talking about, officer." It was pure grease sliding out of his mouth, slimy and unappealing. He proved he could remain professional and aloof at the same time. Either Hoeg was generously rewarding him or scaring him into submission. In both cases, he would be a tough nut to crack. We had to be scarier to him than Hoeg.

"Detective Mendenhall has a complete file of your incarceration in Oklahoma," I bluffed. Clarence heard it in my voice and didn't flinch at all. "My guess is your current employers know nothing about your past indiscretions. Which means you obtained this job through false pretenses. Given this company has federal contracts, my guess is it would be a criminal offense. The kind the FBI loves to sink their teeth into. One way or another, you can say goodbye to this comfy life of yours. Are we getting through to you?"

Right then, Aaron Lautenberg was a cornered rat, a piece of cheese stuck in his greedy face, ready to run if the opportunity arose. It wouldn't. My bluff worked, and he now realized we were more powerful than a corrupt cop was. We had the Truth in one hand, Justice in the other.

"How does it work?" Mendenhall asked.

"He moves…merchandise. Here, there, wherever. I find a flunky to drive for him, not one of our regular drivers. They'd yap so loud. Just regular guys. Custodians, night watchmen. Guys who could use a buck, you know?" He said it as though it were supposed to be a golden opportunity, a blessing from On High.

"People like Alonzo Washington and Randy Mason?" I asked.

"Not Mason. He never drove."

"What happened to him?"

Lautenberg took a big gulp of air. His face turned white, and his eyes glazed over. It was like facing your maker and fessing up to your sins, knowing there was no salvation from your confession. This rat was going nowhere.

"He knew where Washington was. Wouldn't tell. Hoeg told me he would—"

"What?" I demanded.

"Take care of it." Based on the report by the medical examiner, Hoeg did a lot more than just take care of it. He relished the beating he gave to the poor scared Mason kid who gave his life protecting his friend.

Mendenhall turned his head and looked at me, a slight smile on his face. What I could do and get away with was different from the restrictions the law put him under.

"Is he coming here today?" Mendenhall continued.

"Yeah." Lautenberg's voice was breathless as though all the life had drained from him. There was nothing left but an empty shell. Maybe that was all there ever was.

"When he does, you tell him there is no truck and there is no driver."

As though a bolt of lightning had struck him, Aaron Lautenberg rose from his chair, shaking his head. There were practically tears in his eyes.

"I can't do that. He'll kill me, I tell ya. He'll kill me. You saw what he did to Mason."

"He won't kill you," Mendenhall said. Though his words were reassuring, his tone was still one of a drill sergeant. "Certainly not on company property. I need him panicked and on the run. I need him away from here. You do that, it goes easier on you."

Lautenberg's head swiveled back and forth, from Mendenhall to me and then back again. He nodded his head heavily. Cooperation might not get him off the hook completely, just at least away from a sentence of execution. I couldn't concern myself with his future, living or dead. Knowing what Mendenhall had in mind, there was a concern as to how Hoeg would respond.

We parked on the southwest corner of Broadway and Twenty-First Street. The crossroad was within access to any direction Hoeg might come or go. It was the latter that was of the most concern. Within twenty minutes, Hoeg's car appeared driving north on Broadway and then turned east onto Twenty-First Street. He turned down the access road to the meat packing plant and waited.

It was a further twenty minutes by the time his car roared back down the access road, back onto Twenty-First Street, and drove like a missile past us heading west. I knew he would be heading toward either the brick building or the old factory. He was without a large vehicle to move merchandise and, for the moment, any allies to assist him. The swagger he displayed was an act, and the real Marty Hoeg started showing himself.

"I think it's best if we take the brick office building," Mendenhall said. "I can send the patrolmen back to pick up Lautenberg."

"If he's still there."

"Oh, he'll still be there."

"How do you know this?"

"I handcuffed him to his office chair before we left." Mendenhall had a smile on his face as big as Harpo Marx did and as silent.

The patrolmen were apologetic to Mendenhall when we got to the brick building. They indicated Hoeg's car had slowed down as it approached and then raced on after noticing them. Despite the explicit instructions to stay out of sight, this gaffe became a blessing. It left only one place to go.

The detectives, on the other hand, were out of sight. They came up to us as Mendenhall slowed down. One was stocky with a thick head of gray hair. The younger guy was blondish with a moustache that would have been perfect on a Hollywood actor, if only he had looks or talent. He was the one who spoke and rather eloquently at that.

"He got the padlock open pretty darned quick and then drove on through. We figured on waiting for you rather than following."

"You figured right," Mendenhall responded. "How long ago was this?"

"Ten minutes. Tops."

"Clarence, you can't go in there," I cautioned.

"Why not?"

"It's private property and you don't have cause. You go in there and a wily mouthpiece will toss every bit of evidence you gather."

"What do you suggest?"

"I'll go. As a private citizen, you can certainly book me for trespassing. If you'd like." I smiled. The law was most certainly a balancing act, not too unlike the Talmud, that required judicious determination. Unfortunately, we didn't have the time for that right now.

There were several things to consider. I couldn't drive Mendenhall's car onto the property. It was a police vehicle and would have been as bad as he and the two detectives going to the factory. Typically, I didn't carry a gun. Perhaps it was my experience as a soldier that turned me against them. I had no doubt a gunfight would ensue if I were to take Hoeg by force. He would certainly be desperate. My best course of action was a surprise attack to incapacitate him and call in the reinforcements. At this point, faith was my only weapon. I instructed Mendenhall to give me ten minutes to create enough of a ruckus as to warrant the police to have the probable cause they needed.

From a distance, I saw Hoeg's car parked at the front door. Along either side were two bays each where trucks used to pull in for loading and unloading. None of the doors was open. There was no telling what he could have been after in there. My guess was it was documents that would tie him to the hijackings and illegal transactions. The depths of his operation were still a mystery to me. All I knew was this shady empire was falling apart and about to collapse into the Arkansas River.

My soft-soled shoes yielded a crunchy sound as I maneuvered on the gravel parking area. It echoed in my ears as though a nuclear bomb had detonated. At the same time, I could also hear my heart pounding out a fast tempo rhythm on kettledrums. It had been quite some time since I was in such a life and death situation.

I stood still in the doorway. The place was largely empty save for a pile of crates about six foot high over to my left standing ready near one of the bays. There were markings indicating whiskey from Canada. A partition on my right continued down about twenty feet. Off in the distance, there were sounds of scurrying, feet moving quickly, drawers being open and shut rapidly.

When I got to the end of the partition, I spied a dim light around the corner. This was an office, and the sounds were coming from there. There was no choice in the matter. The only thing to do was to rush him, hoping I could disarm him as well.

I pivoted and ran into the open room. Unfortunately for me, he was facing the doorway. In that brief instant, he pulled his gun from his belt holster. My arms were outstretched. One hand reached for his hand holding the gun. The other went for his neck.

I misjudged considering he was significantly taller than I was. My arm pushed his hand down. The gun fired into the opposite wall. I slapped his hand down onto the concrete floor, and he dropped the gun.

However, I only wound up grabbing his overcoat at the shoulder, his arm sliding free. The momentum of my attack caused him to fall backward. I lay on top of him. His left arm was able to move. A roundhouse left hook caught me on the temple, stunned me for a moment, causing me to relax. Without my aggressiveness, he pushed me off him harshly, throwing me like a dirty old sock.

Rather than pursue me, he tried to get up and move away. I grabbed his left ankle and twisted it in the opposite direction to the way he was moving. He fell again. As I went to fall on top of him and pin him to the floor, his right leg swung backward and caught me in the upper thigh. Despite the pain, I continued forward, falling on him, and taking his head in a stranglehold. By that time, Mendenhall and the other two detectives came racing in. The gunshot gave them the justification to do so.

While they handcuffed Hoeg, I walked around, limping every step of the way. There was my war injury limp, a sharp pain like a needle sticking into my heel, and my bruised thigh limp, not to mention the steady throb from somewhere near my ear. If you didn't know better, you would have sworn I was an extra in *Boys Town*. Clarence Mendenhall noticed the grimace with each step I took as he scanned files in various folders on the desk.

"Please tell me there's enough there to convict him," I said, grunting as I walked off the pain, hoping this was all worthwhile. He nodded, his lower lip pursing out in confidence.

"If nothing else, Hoeg was meticulous. No codes, no secret entries. Just dates of shipments and names."

"Names? Whose names?"

"A bunch of guys who have got a rap sheet from here to Topeka." He smiled, fully confident we got in a good day's work. I now had reassurance Alonzo Washington was safe enough to go back home. It was likely he'd need to find new employment but that was incidental to the more pressing matters at hand.

It was necessary for me to accompany Detective Mendenhall to police headquarters to file a statement after which I planned on heading to meet with Alonzo and let him know the good news. Unfortunately, bad news came first.

I had forgotten how long it took to file reports and take witness statements. I finally realized how hungry I was as well as how tired and how much pain remained. A couple of aspirin Mendenhall brought me didn't do as much good as the magazine ads proclaimed. Shortly after eleven at night, a desk sergeant cornered me coming out of Mendenhall's office. He had a perplexed look on his face.

"Someone mentioned you were working for Albert Whitman. That true?"

"Well, I had a simple job over a couple of weeks ago. Why?"

"His daughter was found dead in a house over on North Grove."

"What?" My jaw fell to the floor. "What happened?"

"Overdose." One word, like one bullet, shot through my heart.

Chapter Twenty-Seven

There were many things in life that surprised me by their very nature, but I expected them, nonetheless. I had several friends during my time in the service. It shocked me when I learned of their passing, but it was war and I would have been surprised if they hadn't died. In the field of battle, death is always inevitable. Caroline Whitman was caught in a place stranger than a circus funhouse, a place where the good guys weren't who I expected and the bad guys were supposed to be on my side. There was nothing I could say to convince myself her death made sense or if anyone expected it, despite what I knew about her father. I don't suppose anyone could figure if she were addicted to the stuff or if something more sinister was afoot. To me, none of it mattered. A caring and loving young woman was dead, and to my way of thinking, she shouldn't be.

The desk sergeant provided me the details, which were sketchy at the very least. An anonymous call reported a drunken party or brawl. The caller's voice was muffled and non-specific, except for the address. It was right around Grove and Nineteenth Street North, an area with several small homes, most of which were dark and unkempt. I remembered calls from there during my time as a patrolman, none were pleasant. Traipsing through the neighborhood was always fraught with uncertainty.

The officers responding found nothing loud or out of the ordinary. One house had the front door wide open and what at first appeared to be a fire inside. Upon investigation, they found only a young white female in a room filled with many lit candles. The girl had needle marks up and down her arm and was deceased. Detectives arrived and canvassed the neighborhood for all the good it would have done. For better or worse, residents kept their mouths shut and hoped the police would go away like a withering tornado. However, there was identification in her purse that allowed her father to be notified.

I reached out to Captain Harold Huckins of the vice division as this was a drug related death. Two factors made him inclined to back off the case. The first was the house was a known drug den from prior arrest reports. The second was this was the daughter of Albert Whitman. If everything was as it appeared, it made no sense to Huckins to drag the family's name through the mud or his either. He might have even pointed out the strong bond between father and daughter that Dale Walker and I both knew to be a lie. I surreptitiously mentioned a few bits of my prior investigation in the hope I could instill a sense of urgency without coming right out and telling what I knew and couldn't prove. His comment about "taking it under advisement" did little to make me believe justice would be served for anyone. Captain Huckins wasn't a bad cop. Maybe a little too cautious for his own good. For him, going after pro skirts, boozehounds, grifters, and junkies was a lot easier and a lot better for the public's peace of mind. Razzing a respected member of the community was a surefire way to earn the label "boat rocker", not an epithet he wished to adopt. He was close to his twenty and the word "pension" probably floated through his mind on soft billowy clouds.

Standing there in the station, a place that had been like a second home to me for so long, I felt like a complete and utter failure and all alone. I could not fathom why Caroline Whitman was dead. A wild and profligate young woman who fell in love with a colored jazz musician and used nefariously by her father was all a story for a cheap melodrama or pulp novel. It didn't add up to death and certainly not to murder. It bothered me I figured this all wrong.

Then it occurred to me how this would impact Dale "Big House" Walker, a sensitive and talented man who valued love perhaps more than his music. In retrospect, I could finally understand what the two of them had together. It was a connection I never touched or even got near despite my passion and desire. They floated above the cesspool that caught them and eventually dragged them down. The world they wandered in suffocated them in the end. I had to find Dale and ease him into the truth he was about to face.

I found Richie and had him take me to the Black Cat Inn. At his insistence, I allowed him to go in with me. While I tried to be a friend to a man who could use one, I realized I could use one then as well. A quintet was on stage. The drummer, bass player, pianist, and trumpet player stood in the background. Front and center in the spotlight stood Dale "Big House" Walker blowing the saddest version of "Lover Man" I had ever heard. He barely moved and when he did, it looked like he was ready to topple over. He rocked on his feet slightly, perhaps drunk, hopped up on dope, or in an uncertain emotional state. He had his eyes closed; the one time he opened them he stared into the spotlight. Maybe he thought Heaven was calling to him.

I swallowed hard and batted my eyes to keep tears from forming. I stepped up to the bar and caught the bartender's attention.

"He juiced?" I asked quietly.

"No, man. But he's been drinking all day. Lucky he can stand."

"He knows?"

"Yeah." The bartender stared at his feet. "He knows."

I felt like slamming my fist down on the bar. All that would do is add more pain to my broken body. It was nobody's fault. Selfishly, I wanted to be the one to give him the news. It was vanity to think my words made it softer or saner.

The tidal wave of emotion had already hit and washed over him. The only way to express his abject sorrow was through his music. That is, until I caught up with him after the set.

He finished the song and walked through the other musicians out the back of the stage. I gave Richie a dollar, told him to get a drink or two, and ran outside to catch up with Dale. I found him by the stage door, guzzling out of a bottle in a brown paper bag that was wet at the top from dribbling. He finally looked up and saw me. In a stumbling fashion, he came toward me, not in a straight line because his feet were following his brain's directions.

"You could have saved her," he yelled. He grabbed me by the lapels as much to hold himself up as anything else. He was a desperate and lost man. "You could have saved her."

"Was she using? Dale, was she hooked?"

"No." His hands slipped from my jacket, he doubled over, and then turned away, sobbing like a newborn baby. "No, no, no."

"What was she doing there?"

He turned and faced me, holding himself upright as best he could. His eyes were as red as fire. Snot and spit poured out of him as he yelled, "I don't know. She ain't never been there before."

I approached him slowly. As a policeman, I would have seen a wounded animal, feverish and ready to respond rabidly. My father would have me look upon him as a man in pain who needed a brother to comfort him. I recalled Lamentations 3:32, *But though he cause grief, yet will he have compassion according to the multitude of his mercies*. Dale was unsteady and ready to collapse. I caught him and held him close, allowing his tears of mourning to dampen my unsullied dryness. He cried and wept, his heart beating faster than the tempo of the song he had just played.

"Why?" he said.

"Dale, I've got to figure out why Caroline was in a known drug house."

"She called me and told me she had one more errand to run for her father. That was it. Then we'd go away together."

"What was this errand?"

"Deliver a package of junk to a guy who was going to sell it."

"Who was the guy?"

His face turned from an expression of uncertainty and exhaustion to a desperate bid at recollection.

"Latino name. Oscar something."

Then it struck me.

"Oswaldo?" He nodded. "Oswaldo Acevedo?"

"Yeah," he said, shaking his head like an enthused child.

What I considered was far too sinister for my imagination but not as evil as what I knew truly existed in this world. So many people had indicated Albert Whitman was a monster, a businessman solely interested in wealth and power. It was truly sad to contemplate the notion his own daughter was an impediment to his success. Either he and Acevedo were close partners or Whitman had a hold over on him. My anger was rising and overshadowing my sense of law and order, right and wrong. There was only Righteousness and Justice remaining. I was to be their instrument.

I asked Dale to give me until Monday evening to get this case into the hands of the homicide detectives. I was practically begging him so he wouldn't go off the deep end. He still had his music, and I hoped to help him raise the sail on that to continue with his life. Everyone has a special purpose inside, the reason they live and breathe. I still tried to figure out mine.

It was after midnight, a perfect time to catch the underworld where they felt most relaxed and safe. Richie knew Acevedo had a house along North River Boulevard because of several fares he had that complained of the uncouth Latino living in a predominantly white neighborhood. It was apparent his braggadocio allowed him to resist the pettiness of these old money residents. For me, it meant not having to deal with a house in a large compound with armed bodyguards.

The hack parked in front of the house next door. This time, I told Richie to stay put. A slight breeze blew through the trees. Crickets chirped and the serene sound of the Arkansas River gave everything a peaceful quality though it was the furthest thing from it. Evil has a way of sailing silently in the wind.

I rang the doorbell and waited. It didn't matter who answered because I would batter down the door regardless of the pain still wracking my body. Fortunately, that was how it played out. Acevedo fell backward and landed with a dull thud on the marbled foyer floor, a gasp erupting from him like the uncertainty of the unknown. Squinting eyes, the same one would get from a gut punch knocking the wind out of you, accompanied the grunt erupting like a bellows. I had already gone a round with a decidedly taller corrupt cop. This older desperado would not be any more of a challenge. For a moment, I felt the pain vanish into the ether. I knew it would return eventually.

"I need to know everything."

"What are you talking about, man?"

I leaned over him as close as I could get, baring my teeth to indicate I didn't want him to try to get up.

"You and Whitman. And his daughter."

"I don't know nothing about—"

"No. Don't even start. You know Albert Whitman. You're involved with illegal narcotics in the seedier sides of town. He knows all the ritzy people. Together, you're a heck of a team. Aren't you?" I paused, took in a breath, and then changed my tone. I softened a bit but everything I uttered came through a tightly closed mouth, pointed like an arrow and as piercing. "You're nothing. You're a two-bit punk who could never get out of the barrio. You don't mean anything to anyone. I want Whitman."

"What are you gonna do for me?" he said smugly.

I grabbed his lapels and pulled him close to me.

"I make sure the district attorney takes the death penalty off the table. Or I leave now and let Whitman know you cooperated. Either way I don't care what happens to you. *Chupamedias!*" It had been a long time an opportunity arose to use my limited Spanish vocabulary picked up from my days on patrol. Calling him a "bootlicker" slashed his ego to the core. The big Latino man was cut down to size by a shorter, younger Jew.

I called Mendenhall from an all-night drugstore on Douglas and recommended he hold Acevedo as a material witness in the death of Caroline Whitman. It might have been circumventing Huckins as he was the lead investigator. I couldn't allow Acevedo to tip off Whitman. Suddenly, I wondered what was happening to me. It would be easy to consider this a battle as part of a bigger war. Then, I could justify being a soldier again in service to a greater good. Or perhaps a holy war, spurred on by the archangel Michael, seeking out those who followed the will of Satan. But I was neither. I had transformed into the adversary of those who dwelt in the gutter, as low as their level, despite homes in North Riverside or Eastborough. I had for the moment lost what made me who I was, both from the teachings of my youth and my temple as well as my experiences in a global conflict. I was nobody then. And I grew weary and tired. It made me more dangerous than my adversaries could ever expect or anticipate.

Chapter Twenty-Eight

There was a time in boot camp when I experienced what it was like to be hung over. My youthful days and time on the force didn't quite prepare me for anything as dramatic as that. The guys in the barracks took me out to a dive notorious for serving, or perhaps over serving, the green soldiers stationed at the base. For them it was like a rite of passage, and it was quite easy to identify me as a novice. Twenty-five years old and nothing more than Magen David during holidays and festivals. Not even an after-shift get together with fellow beat cops at a local establishment. The following morning, after consuming ample quantities of an amber liquid purported to be whiskey, my drill sergeant insisted I clean the latrine. He figured the lack of sun blaring in my eyes would allow me to recover quicker. I wasn't sure if he realized the odors were churning my stomach. I figured this was like counting rosary beads if I were Catholic.

After a day of tracking down a bad cop and a night of comforting a lost soul, I felt almost the same. Worn out and dragged over the coals, I sought only a small way of repenting. Unfortunately, the incessant mewing of Lady Mittens and Sir Pounce did nothing to comfort me. I couldn't blame them for not understanding. They, however, were at peace once I filled their respective bowls.

I required ample amounts of food and coffee, and it didn't matter if it was greasy and unhealthy. When you are drained of any semblance of energy, anything will suffice for immediate sustenance. Jennie pouted sarcastically when I dragged myself into King's X. She immediately poured a cup of coffee and then assumed a viable order for me. The Sunday morning patrons fresh from church turned their eyes away and spoke in hushed tones. My appearance was such no one likely recognized me despite my many acquaintances in the community. I sat hunched over the counter, shoveled food into my gullet, and tried to make sense of the prior day. None was forthcoming. I felt lost and craved guidance. It was then I decided to visit my father.

My dad knew everything about me without ever once inquiring. Whether it was the tone of my voice, the look in my eyes, or my posture, he could tell what I was feeling and what kind of mood I was in. The details were the only thing left to supply. I had an entire *mashal* to recite to him.

"I shouldn't be surprised by corruption," I said. "I harbor no illusions as to its existence, even here. It's just that, right now, too many innocent people were hurt."

"Innocent people are always hurt. And worse. Remember, Cain killed his brother. It was so from the start."

"But it's the girl, Pop. She didn't deserve to die. Certainly not at the hands of her father."

"Need I remind you of the Book of Job? One of the penalties of this life is that virtuous men, and women, suffer. The great fires burn both the good man and the wicked equally."

"And we maintain our faith." I sounded defeated. The large portions of food and coffee might have filled up my body, yet at this moment, I was bereft of any strength, moral, physical, or emotional. I was certainly not as strong as Job.

My father nodded in acknowledgement.

"Perhaps I should go to temple and say Kaddish for her." Though I said it in passing, the moment I uttered the words, I realized it might provide me with comfort.

My father placed his cup of tea down on the small table beside him and leaned forward. We were already close enough I would hear him. It was just that he wanted me to understand.

"The first thing you wanted to do when you got home from the war was to go to temple with Rabbi Saperstein and say Kaddish for your mother."

"I remember." I nodded.

"Why?"

"Why?" My eyes squinted in a strained ability to comprehend. I couldn't believe he would ask such a question. It was obvious to me. "To mourn for Mom. To pay my respects."

"You have read all the books of the Torah and many of the Talmud. You have studied Maimonides and Spinoza. You know prayers, many of them. Tell me, my learned son. Where is it in the Kaddish there is a mention of death or a supplication for the soul of the dead?"

Very quickly in my mind, I recited the Kaddish: *Yitgadal v'yitkadash sh'mei raba b'alma di-v'ra chirutei... Glorified and sanctified be God's great name throughout the world which He has created according to his will...* And as it played out in my mind, I heard the words more deeply than ever before, felt them echo within my heart, even more so than when I prayed for my mother. They resonated in my ears as though Hillel the Elder were pronouncing them. I looked up at my father after my internal recitation. Reciting Kaddish was not for those who had passed but those still among us.

"Yes," was all I could say.

"It is the affirmation of our belief in God. When we have suffered loss, we openly declare our faith. The dead have no more worries, no more pain, no more grief from this world. They are fully at peace. It is we, the living, who must go on."

It had never occurred to me before. Growing up, Kaddish was always the prayer for those who had passed, one spoken while in mourning. Everything my father said was true, but I still wanted to pray for the dead. Randy Mason and Caroline Whitman, even Chris Peterson, were victims caught up in a game of much bigger men who thought nothing more of them than minor inconveniences in larger schemes of power and wealth. Inconsequential pawns, not even human beings. The least I could do was offer a sense of justice. With Marty Hoeg in jail, all that remained was to bring Albert Whitman down.

Then, looking into my eyes, as though he were reading my mind, my father frowned.

"You fight in God's name, sometimes with a sword and other times with a trumpet as Joshua learned. You do not mock or forsake the strength He has given you, like Samson. If you will not follow rabbinical teaching, be mindful of the laws you once served to protect. We do not choose the outcome. God does. It is His will."

Like an old balloon, my desperate passion had deflated. Hoeg was no longer a threat to Alonzo and Althea Washington. Dale Walker would become famous and successful or waste away like so many others before him. I would seek to ensure all was right and just in the small world around me. This was no longer my battle.

As I left, I turned and embraced my father in a deeper way than my simple departures at dinners. This was perhaps only the third or fourth time in my life I had done so. It was not that our family lacked emotion or the expression of our love for each other. I felt it was due on my part to a lack of commitment. Words failed me; the action itself said it all. That and the small tear in my eye. Despite this peaceful feeling of acquiescence, I made my way over to visit Bradley Wolrebinski. Svetlana greeted me at the door. It was rare not to encounter her in a smock covered with paint or sculpting clay. In this instance, she had her hair up in a bun, and she wore an apron. She was now playing the role of homemaker with a panache not found on Ozzie and Harriet.

"Ah, Harold," she exclaimed with exuberance. "Come in. I've made a batch of poppy seed hamentashen."

"Hasn't Purim already passed?"

"It is never too late to eat hamentashen," she responded defensively. She appreciated my endearing smile but could easily tell I was not there for her culinary delights. "I suppose you want to talk to my husband, the criminal."

"He writes crime fiction, Svetlana."

"It's the same thing." I could hear the silent "Oy!"

at the end of her proclamation. Her very presence lifted my spirits.

"I'll take a hamentashen," I offered enthusiastically.

"Don't placate me. It doesn't work." And then, after a pause, "I'll give you one just the same."

Every Jewish mother is the same.

She went upstairs, was gone for a moment, and then came back down before returning to the kitchen. Bradley ambled down wearing a tweed jacket with elbow patches. He combed his hair with his fingers and squeezed the bridge of his nose. His embrace was like a professional wrestler. In that regard, he could have been a criminal.

We sat in the parlor with a glass of sherry. As was typical for our encounters, we leaned toward each other. Every conversation was a conspiracy. As I laid out my dealings with Albert Whitman and the recent passing of his daughter, I began to realize Bradley's feelings were not paranoid delusions. The reality of the situation brought everything into clarity.

"How can I get this guy?" I finished, sitting upright and patient. He followed suit.

"You can't."

My jaw did everything but fall into my lap. Bradley had the look of a mortician after examining a body and declaring it dead. He was unrelenting. "You're not dealing with a traditional businessman. You saw all those newspaper clippings. You know who his connections are. He is beyond your sphere of influence. His strength is greater than yours."

"There's always a way. Look, even the Treasury Department was able to bring down Capone." I could hear myself grasping at straws.

"Yes, but they were actively pursuing him. It's doubtful anyone in any law enforcement branch of the government or any ancillary agency has heard of Albert Whitman much less knows where Wichita, Kansas is. The best criminals are the ones no one knows about. Capone sought out the attention and believed he was beyond reproach. This is why he was vulnerable. Whitman hides in the shadows, content with his invisible power. Men like this are far more powerful than those two-bit gangsters."

"This is ridiculous," I said to no one in particular.

"Yes," he concurred.

Morally, I could not bring myself to topple an evil man in a manner not in keeping with my religious beliefs. Legally, I had no recourse to bring the suspected leader of a criminal empire to justice. I felt caught in a kind of *gehenna,* what my Catholic acquaintances knew as Purgatory. To move forward was either a sin or a violation of the law. The correct recourse was to move on, much as my father implied. Everywhere I turned I was rebuffed.

Instead, I borrowed Bradley's phone and called Floyd Gunsaullus. It was awkward catching him right before the end of his shift with a long drawn-out story, but he had the patience of a saint. There were several grunts to acknowledge he heard every detail I presented. I detected minor scratching sounds and considered he took notes, given how elaborate I had been. After I ran out of breath, there was a brief pause before he responded.

"In terms of your job for him, you were done a while ago. He asked you to find his daughter. You did, and he paid you for it. Don't forget you're not a cop anymore. You know what your biggest problem was?"

"Didn't know I had just one."

He ignored my comment and continued. "You were a lot closer to being a rabbi than a detective. You were too passionate at times."

This could have easily turned into an analysis of my attributes and faults if I took this too personally. I needed to stay on point. "Do you have anything on this guy or not?"

A plaintive sigh followed a big deep breath. "Nothing tangible. However, everything you mentioned, the writing on the crates and the hidden invoices, makes a lot of sense. It ties in with things we've heard in the past even though we couldn't put a finger on any of it. Of course, right now, there's no active case on him." There was special emphasis on the word 'active' indicating he wasn't as unknown as I might have thought. "But if you'd like we can visit him on the pretense of his daughter's death. Maybe your gift of gab can get him to slip up." I couldn't be sure if this was Gunny's way of making me understand the wall he was up against or using me in an unofficial capacity. Either way, it was something to do.

"Great. You can pick me up at Wolrebinski's house."

"First, I'm leaving for the night. Second, I wouldn't step foot in that madman's house even if a murder had been committed."

Before saying goodnight, he indicated he would pick me up the following evening. It was then I would have a chance to face the Leviathan.

Chapter Twenty-Nine

It was my intention to let Dale Walker know my plans in as encouraging a fashion as possible. I fully realized he suffered a loss greater than I could possibly imagine, especially when I fully understood his relationship with Caroline. Perhaps it would give him hope, a sense of balance on the scales of Justice, or maybe motivation to continue with his music and give joy to others. Just as likely it wouldn't but I owed him that much, one man to another.

The problem was I had no idea where to find him. I had never thought to inquire as to his residence. At this point in the day, none of the clubs would be open. I called the Rustic Inn and the Black Cat hoping to get anyone in the office or maybe a janitor. As it wasn't even noon and jazz musicians were not typically "morning people", it didn't surprise me when the phone kept ringing. There was a slim chance he might be at the house way up on North Broadway where they brought me to meet him and Caroline when they were concerned about Whitman. Hailing a taxi and driving there was a long shot and a waste of precious time so I passed.

All I could do was follow through with Gunny and hope we could break Whitman, maybe convince Saundra Mooney to turn state's evidence if she really knew more than I thought she did. At the very least, we could shake him a bit, have him come to realize he could no longer live comfortably in the shadows. As cool and calm as he had been up until now, perhaps his comprehension of my awareness would cause him to slip up in some fashion, if not now, then in the future. It was too much to expect but Hope was a powerful motivator, and it was all I had left.

My head hung low. I shook my head negatively at my thoughts. He just about ordered a hit on his own daughter. No, we would not rattle this man. Another example of the odds being too high. Bradley was right after all. It was fortunate I was not a gambler.

As it was my solemn duty to complete this task, I did not allow anything to deter me simply because everything wasn't as ideal as it should have been. Nothing ever is. I read the Psalms for a while and then started *The Razor's Edge* by Somerset Maugham. It would wind up being my fourth time reading it. The story of a man who had been to war and was looking for deeper meaning in his life was a theme I could connect to in this real world. As many times as I read it, I could not truly understand what exactly Larry Darrell found. There was nothing tangible, a code or mantra or even a system. In the end, it is always too personal to share. Each person finds it for themselves and retains it deep within. Too often, a person is unable to explain it or codify it to the complete satisfaction of others, even those closest to them. But it does exist.

Of course, the epigraph of the book sounded an awful lot like one from the Talmud. Surprisingly, it came from "The Upanishads." *The sharp edge of a razor is difficult to pass over; thus the wise say the path to Salvation is hard.*

The temperature had dropped slightly, and the breeze blew harshly. It was an unforgiving spring evening. Still, I found myself leaning against the front door to the building when Gunny arrived. I jumped into the passenger seat, and we drove off. I quickly tempered my eagerness. There was no need for conversation. He didn't have to tell me this was a police matter, and I should allow him to lead the inquiry. This was all second nature to me. If and when appropriate, I would interject or certainly respond. He was aware based on my feedback of the necessity to lean a little harder to somehow throw this man off his game. Barring that, it would be a dead issue. We would go home and twiddle our thumbs, gasp and moan in exasperation, and move on to the next case. And there was always a next case.

The same well-tailored servant answered the door and didn't act alarmed by the presence of the police. From the parlor, the voice of Albert Whitman granted access for which we apparently should be grateful by the tone of his voice. He stood formally holding a file as Saundra Mooney lingered before him. Our eyes met. Hers were filled with a kind of trepidation, not so much at my presence but that she was truly concerned for her well-being considering recent events and not simply the continuation of her employment. The calm veneer of Albert Whitman hid an explosive personality.

"Captain Floyd Gunsaullus," Gunny announced as professionally as possible. "We're working on the death of your daughter."

"I am grateful for your attention to this, Captain. However, as I have been told, she appears to have died from an overdose of narcotics, yes?"

"While that is correct, sir, we believe there was a possibility of foul play."

With contempt oozing out of him, he looked at Gunny, then over to me, and nodded in a kind of casual understanding. He was not the least bit perturbed. His lazy response came across as apathy. I was almost nauseous.

"Do you think the same thing, Mr. Bergman?"

"Yes. I do." My lips and mouth were dry, and my throat clenched. My father raised me to fear no man. This personification of evil struck a dissonant chord in my heart. An imperceptible nod reappeared. He turned toward Saundra.

"And what about you, Mrs. Mooney? Do you think my wayward, spoiled, rebellious daughter died of anything more than succumbing to her own perverse vices?" His voice rose a notch with each disgusting description. Though his head was turned, and he faced Saundra, he meant the inquiry for us. His head swiveled back suddenly, staring at Gunny. "Captain Gunsaullus, I believe you're with the Traffic Division. How are you involved in a suspected homicide case?"

Gunny's mouth opened but Whitman's words closed them just as fast.

"My daughter was out of control and got into things she couldn't get out of. Not even with my money and influence. That's the end of it. The quicker you people drop this ridiculous investigation, the sooner I will be able to get on with my life."

The words struck me as being totally honest without revealing any illegal activity. Caroline was out of control. She had gotten into her father's business, or was drawn in, and couldn't get out. Naturally, Whitman wanted to resume his lucrative drug distribution operation. He would still have to deal with Saundra Mooney, Oswaldo Acevedo, and me. I wasn't aware in the least of the soft smile played out on my lips. They were dry no more.

"Is there something amusing in all of this, Mr. Bergman?"

"Yes." The smile dropped. My face went blank. "Caroline was in love and wanted only to live her life with the man who had her heart in his delicate hands. As far as being rebellious, I guess if a rich white girl has a thing for a colored jazz musician, any parent might feel the same way. It's an easy word to bandy about. Rebellious. You know, going against your race and your social status and all. Of course, to your way of thinking, that would make her rebellious. But you are wrong about her." I took enough steps forward to be within arms' distance of him. While he was taller, I was a stone pillar, the same kind that supported the blinded Samson. "And while the police might not have a case, I am personally going to get to the bottom of this no matter how long it takes. You see, I have all the time in the world. And if I can dig up anything that implicates you in any of this, it will be my unmitigated pleasure to crack you like Humpty Dumpty." I took a quick look over his shoulder at Saundra, then turned and left. Gunny followed shortly thereafter.

I was already in his car with my arms folded across my chest like an angry little boy. He got in and mimicked me before letting out a belly laugh.

"You happy? You got it all off your chest? Do you think it made a difference?"

My father never scolded me in that fashion

although I had several superior officers in both the department and the army who did. It meant less to me now as it did then.

"I wanted him to know I knew."

"Trust me. He knows. Now what?"

I uncrossed my arms, relaxed my shoulders, lifted my hat, and wiped my brow. I had the faith of David without the sling or the stone. It appeared the Philistine would win this battle.

An unidentifiable form moved in the darkness that I barely caught out of the corner of my eye. Light came from the area of the front door as though it were left open. Within a few seconds there was a gunshot followed momentarily by another and then a woman's anguished scream.

Gunny and I darted out of the car and ran into the house. The parlor was not as we had left it. Albert Whitman lay on the Oriental carpet on his back, a bullet hole in his neck pouring out blood. Three feet away lay Dale "Big House" Walker. A gun was near his hand, powder marks on his temple. Saundra Mooney had stopped screaming, although her mouth was still open, and tears poured profusely down her cheeks. She shook as though electricity surged through her body. Her silent response was now almost deafening. The butler stood in the doorway, eyes bugged out, frozen as an icicle.

Gunny went over to the phone and called the Homicide Division, requesting Clarence Mendenhall. I went over to Saundra, put my arms around her, and turned her away from the scene. I felt her shaking. She couldn't stop. Her tears soaked my shoulder.

It was approaching eleven o'clock by the time the

detectives were through. The butler did not see or hear anything as Walker burst into the house after watching us leave. Saundra's statement was simple and direct although it took a bit of time to get it out of her through starts and stops. Whitman heard the stomping feet, turned, and was shot almost at point blank range in the throat. He fell and did not move. He couldn't even make a sound. At the point, Walker put the gun to his head and fired. The entire time, he was almost unaware of Saundra's presence, wasn't concerned what she saw. Perhaps, subconsciously, he needed a witness to tell his story.

Gunsaullus and Mendenhall stood with me in the corner of the room. From my own experience, homicide detectives did not enjoy this part of their job. When a person was killed there was always a story, always a loss, always a tragedy. Even in the case of a man like Albert Whitman.

"I know this wasn't the outcome you were looking for," Gunny said, this time with a bit more compassion.

"Would you laugh at me if I said it was God's will?"

Neither one answered me.

I offered to drive Saundra home, but she declined. As politely as she could, she indicated these events were a sign for her to move on. She didn't know where it would be. I casually invited her for a drink in a nice proper place before she left. She smiled and nodded but didn't agree.

If there was one thing that put my mind at ease, it was the cats. When I claimed the apartment, they were part and parcel of it. We grew to need each other and take care of each other. I half expected them to be sleeping as I arrived home shortly before midnight. Instead, they were eager to see me.

I took off my jacket and hat, removed my shoes and tie, got a glass of water, turned on the radio, and sat on the sofa. Lady Mittens was up on my lap first. Looking at me with big green eyes, she seemed to be castigating me for an offense known only to her, like coming home too late. Perhaps I had placed myself in jeopardy and would no longer be able to take care of her. It might have been I spent too much time away from her.

Sir Pounce did his figure eights around my stocking feet before jumping up alongside me, fighting for equal attention. I rubbed their respective ears. Their purring was like a metronome I could fall asleep to and often did. I marveled at the Lord creating the sound of purring. It was normal to a cat and utterly transcendent to me.

The night was clear enough to allow me to pick up a station from Kansas City. There were mysterious saxophones, heavenly trumpets, syncopated drums, and painful reminders of the harshness of life and of its inherent beauty as well. I wanted so desperately to understand how a simple assignment to locate a missing young girl left three people dead and uncovered a vicious criminal enterprise in the process. It was no different than seeking out a deeper and greater meaning upon returning from the war. I was the living Larry Darrell, walking the razor's edge toward salvation. Unfortunately, I had found no answers.

And then Billie Holiday appeared like a specter, ruminating in a plaintive tone about love and betrayal, joy, and pain. In the end accepting whatever happened, willing to let bygones be bygones. And with that, there was no need to explain anything.

It was then I could say Kaddish for Caroline Whitman and Dale Walker and accept God's will. My faith was renewed.

Chapter Thirty

There was no surprise Marty Hoeg had a lawyer within thirty minutes of being booked. A shyster named Trevor Kingsley, the kind of guy who would sell his mother for two bits then call the police to report her as stolen. Edwin Maxwell would likely play him in the film version. It didn't surprise me this was who Marty would turn to. I didn't try to guess what their defense would be. I figured it would be a bit of legerdemain Jasper Maskelyne would be proud of.

The police doctor's report was that "suspect fell while attempting to evade law enforcement officers," and no one really questioned it. I was quite certain Detective Hoeg caused a few suspects to fall in his pursuit of them as well. It was all a game everybody played, and everybody knew the rules.

Unbeknownst to me, the mouthpiece made an emergency motion before a judge first thing Monday morning to move Hoeg from this jurisdiction to the Kansas State Industrial Reformatory up in Hutchinson. The reasoning behind this request was the notion Hoeg would not get a fair trial in Wichita or anywhere in Sedgwick County. The judge granted the request but only insofar as where the state would hold Hoeg until trial. He set a date to hear arguments regarding an actual change of venue. If the case was as strong as I thought it was, a change of venue might not have any impact. Then again, I remembered Sgt. Schwarzlander emphasizing the notion of "keeping them at home." It was out of my hands at this point. Even if I were still on the force, my voice did not extend to the machinations of the justice system.

I hadn't slept well, because of not only getting home so late but also the wandering nature of my mind. It was a restless night, dreams and images of guns pointing at me, hypodermic needles, the seedy vicious laughter of junkies, and the wail of a mournful saxophone. Burning candles as the only source of light and not much at that. Rats scurrying while making screeching cries. Or was it the young college girls as they were dying? It was like a Hieronymus Bosch painting of Wichita as a hellish world, caught up in the filth and muck created by those with cleaner hands. It was not the place I grew up in or called home. Nevertheless, it was real.

This above all was what bothered me. I came to truly understand the brutal nature of humanity while involved in a global conflict. My days as a cop were cartoonish in comparison. It was difficult to accept I had been so naïve to think that way. Had I remained a cop and became a detective alongside Mendenhall, I might have witnessed it sooner. There was no telling where my life would have gone then.

What if I had followed my father's long-time desire to become a rabbi? What aberrations of the human condition would I encounter? What other kinds of suffering, deeper and more profound, would I face? It would appear there really was no escaping it whatever profession you were so inclined to follow. While there was beauty and joy one could find, if you looked hard for it, the world was a dark place. We had forsaken the Garden of Eden so long ago. Perhaps we no longer deserved Paradise, and this was our lot.

It was Clarence Mendenhall that got hold of me late Tuesday morning. He thought it would be good for me on many levels to join him at police headquarters for the transfer. Without discussing it much, all police yearned for a sense of closure. They knew they maintained the law, caught the criminals, and allowed the courts to handle the rest. But there was a deep-down desire to see it through to the end.

Word had gotten out about the arrest of a cop, and Clarence expected the scene to be a madhouse. Reporters would certainly clamor for a juicy story. This was meat and potatoes to them. Those family members, friends, and associates of persons arrested by Hoeg in the past would want to know how his actions impacted those arrests. Chief Shepherd was likely pulling the hair of out his head and shaking his jowls. Now that the war was over and everything had become pretty well settled, this would be the kind of lurid action to bring out the curiosity seekers, bored housewives, and criminal neophytes.

A passing hack picked me up a block from my apartment and dropped me off in time to witness a throng gathering outside. The buzz of muffled words and shouted questions of reporters was like the whizz of artillery shells, only slightly less dangerous. From my vantage point, I saw only the backs of men's shirts and jackets and women's housedresses, hats and Kodaks, and one newsreel camera. Everyone was a carbon copy of each other, much like all the homes in Planeview. However, because of his height, a tall and lanky colored man caught my attention. It was Jason.

I moved slowly toward the crowd, weaving in between a crunch of reporters and citizens, getting pushed aside or pushed back. I hardly looked at my feet or the people I was making my way through. I focused on Jason who had his gaze glued to the door of the police station, not moving his head. He slid his hand into his jacket pocket, casually as though he were perhaps reaching for a handkerchief. There was no telling exactly what his intentions were, but I took a good guess.

I made my way to about two feet behind him. The crowd was too loud for him to hear me. If he had any instincts, he suppressed them, being far too caught up in his prey. Suddenly , two detectives escorted Hoeg out. Even now, Marty Hoeg had a smug smile on his face. The possibility of incarceration or execution was a fleeting thought in his head. The slight chill in the air didn't appear to bother him a bit as he looked toward the sun shining brightly. Anyone who knew him felt the real chill of his presence and attitude. Meanwhile, his lawyer kept up a steady barrage of "No comment" to the various questions thrown loudly in his direction.

Jason's hand moved deeper in his pocket, twitched for a moment, and then came out. He was surprised when I grabbed his wrist, his head swiveling, and his wide eyes a combination of both anger and frustration. His teeth clenched. The suddenness of my move turned astonishment into annoyance. This was his only chance, and I intervened.

"There's no need for that," I said.

"You think a white man is gonna get sent up for killing colored?"

"He's getting sent up. It doesn't matter for what, does it?" There was a pout on his face, like a disappointed child. As many times as I crossed paths with him, I came to realize that was pretty much what he was. "Let's go see Sibyl."

Not surprisingly, Cal Dutcher waited around the corner. Apparently, he was the getaway driver if this thing went down. At first, he didn't see me as I walked behind Jason. He started the cab as we got closer. I reached in and grabbed his left wrist, with a "tsk, tsk" to let him know what I thought. Cal was never a problem. He was an errand boy with a cab.

Without any verbal instructions, Cal drove to the house I visited before for a clandestine meeting with Sibyl. There was only the grumble of the engine. The three of us entertained our own thoughts separately. It occurred to me how odd it was I had never encountered Sibyl or knew of her previously as a policeman. It was a testament to the lady's ability to remain underground and yet wield the level of power she had. There would have been many who fell under her chariot simply by taking her for granted. I knew better than that now.

Jason stood beside me, head bowed in shame. Cal remained in the doorway, not looking directly at anyone. Sibyl, sitting at a small table, acted as though she could see the disappointment. I learned a long time ago never to wonder how a magician does his tricks, merely to accept the wonder of it. I hated to admit it but there was a level of respect between us.

"I hope you will accept my apologies," she stated softly, "at the ham-fisted efforts of my son. It was, however, at my behest. So if you have any anger, please direct it at me."

"No anger," I replied calmly. "Just…"

"What?"

"Confusion."

She took in a big breath, held it for a moment, and then let it out slowly. This was a confession, and I was her priest.

"There is a concern Detective Hoeg, in an effort to mitigate his sentence, might reveal information injurious to certain business partners." Then, it became clear. Helbert, Cohen, and Stiff were in collusion with Sibyl and her group. Who knew how long such arrangements had been in place? It was likely Hoeg stepped in unaware of this and pushed as far as he could until the coloreds pushed back. Whether or not this would have been resolved without my participation at the urging of Althea Washington was unknown. There were only the events of the last three and a half weeks to consider.

"I think it's safe to say Glick Helbert has been on the police department's radar for quite some time and will continue to be. I don't foresee anything Marty Hoeg can say that will undermine these, shall we call them, business relationships. And Glick, well, he knows how to keep his nose clean when he must. And right now, well, he has to."

She smiled. This time, it was warm and endearing, almost welcoming. I was not quite part of the family. At least I was no longer the black sheep. There was a fine and delicate balance they maintained. Good and Evil were as relative as Law and Order. There were degrees of injustice and shades of righteousness. I had to accept that, otherwise the deaths of Caroline Whitman and Dale Walker would become meaningless.

Jason nodded to me as I passed him on the way out. He finally realized I had no intention of wanting to be his enemy. It wasn't quite when Jacob and Esau met but at least we were quits with each other. Cal dropped me off at home, saying nothing, looking in the rearview mirror once or twice. Clarence Mendenhall was waiting for me, pacing outside the front door to my apartment.

"I thought I saw you at headquarters this morning. Where did you run off to?" His tone was not a formal police inquiry but largely a sly jab.

"Just errands."

"Oh? And who was the tall colored kid you were with."

"Just a friend."

"Just errands. Just a friend. All right. Be that way."

"You talk to the District Attorney about Hoeg?" I asked, quickly changing the subject.

"Their case is solid. They figure they can get thirty to life easily what with all the records at the abandoned factory and the files in that brick office."

"You think anyone is going to raise a ruckus over his previous arrests?"

"The chief has got a rookie from the new class, Urban Steinke, reading all Hoeg's prior convictions. If the kid finds anything, we'll jump on it before it jumps on us."

"Hate to think Marty gets off on any technicality."

"Don't sweat it. And you know, from what I hear, crooked cops don't really do too well in prison. You know about Lt. Charles Becker?"

"The chair got him, not the inmates."

"Yeah, but imagine if they hadn't given him the death penalty."

He smiled, started to leave, and then turned back.

"It's only a reminder but I'd still love to have you on the Night Detective Squad."

"I know."

He held his gaze at me for a moment while he tried to decipher mine. He nodded with a slight smile and left. He would always remind me.

Chapter Thirty-One

I went to temple that Friday night. By then, most of the pain from my melee with Hoeg had dissipated. It was my heart that was heavy. I couldn't remember, outside of my mother's memorial service when I returned home, exactly when I had last been to services. To be honest, I didn't know why I went. It felt like a compulsion, an unidentified need based on the joy and peace it brought me as a youth. The ultimate response I gave myself was I was looking for answers. I could get those as easily at the Pan American from King Mar, assuming I was Buddhist.

It was largely as I recalled it from the past. There were responsive readings followed by Rabbi Saperstein's *d'var Torah*, the message about the week's Torah portion. Several older folks who remembered me as a youth shook my hand or embraced me. There was a sense of welcoming as though I came home. It wasn't enough to convince me to change professions but certainly provided a suitable ending to this difficult last month.

My father was surprised and pleased to see me, as I had not indicated I would be in attendance. It was a last-minute decision. I learned Saundra Mooney had moved, left the city for parts unknown. Her landlord advised she had packed up several suitcases, called a cab, and went down to Union Station. She rented it furnished and likely had objet d'art from Whitson Imports to add to the ambiance. There was nothing there that made the place singularly her own or identified who she really was. I guess I never really knew her. It was my hope at least I could apologize for all she had been through. I realized I was lost. Friday night services were an amenable substitute.

While I felt uplifted, I understood I had not found all the answers I was seeking. I strongly doubted working as a detective would be any more ideal for such a resolution. In the meantime, I finally rejoined the world, so to speak, and could find some small pleasure in the communion of a congregation. It was strange to consider I felt the same way around Mendenhall and Gunsaullus. My choices were as diverse as they had always been.

My father invited me to dinner the following evening, but I indicated I had another commitment. Cal Dutcher picked me up and brought me to the small and quaint home of Alonzo and Althea Washington. Upon entering, the smell of a home cooked meal drew me as bees to budding flowers.

"I ain't never had a white man to my house for dinner," Alonzo said haltingly. It was a statement of fact more than a shocking revelation. I, on the other hand, sat at a mess hall table with coloreds, with Protestants and Catholics, with men who voted for Roosevelt and Alf Landon. War has a way of bringing disparate people together. So too, does adversity. I wondered why it couldn't be that way all the time. I smiled warmly and shook his hand as though we were brothers in arms.

Carrots and potatoes accompanied the pot roast. Mrs. Washington offered a chopped green salad and a pitcher of sweet tea. After all of this, a peach cobbler finished off a meal of incredible generosity. It was more than I was used to, and I was entirely grateful for the abundance of it. It is truly remarkable how those who have little so often unselfishly give all.

Alonzo and I sat on the front porch, enjoying the pleasant spring evening. I gathered he wanted to make a statement. By showing his acceptance of a white man in his home, it was an acknowledgement about brotherhood and humanity. Althea came out and joined us.

"What now?" I asked him.

"Figure on going back to Cudahy." He noticed my perplexed look. "Wasn't their fault about none of this. Just Lautenberg and Hoeg. They always treated me well."

I nodded in understanding.

"In the end, it's about all that really matters."

"What about you, Mr. Bergman?" Althea pondered softly.

I smiled and thanked them for their hospitality without truly answering. Cal came and picked me up. I had him drop me off at the corner of Central and Market. It was only a couple of blocks away from what I called home, but I wanted to breathe in the air and feel my feet on the pavement, limp and all.

Loss was unimaginable to most people and harder to deal with. The only thing I could do was determine what remained. I had to believe the Lord would not take something away without either leaving me with the strength to accept it or provide a greater thing to replace it. For most of us, the answers were hard to see. It didn't mean we should stop looking.

A swirling wind blew leaves up and about. The night was clear, and many stars danced in the deep blue sky. It was a watchful and peaceful omen. Perhaps it was my imagination, but I thought I heard a saxophone wafting in the breeze.

I locked the door behind me as I entered my apartment, wanting only to go to bed early for once and feel a sense of being home. I gave the cats their nightly meal. When they finished, they both gazed at me in anticipation although it didn't appear they were still hungry.

I crouched down, and their playfulness turned on in full force. While they appreciated being rubbed, they ran off and then back. In reaching for Sir Pounce, I fell over. I lay prone on the floor. Lady Mittens took the opportunity to jump on my chest and knead my shirt with her paws. Meanwhile, Sir Pounce butted his head against my ribs.

For a moment, I was a young boy again, innocent and giddy, grateful for the smallest blessings bestowed upon me. There was no war, no crime, nothing else but the simple pleasures of life. I was thankful and at peace.

A word about the author...

I studied film-making and creative writing at the University of Miami in the 80's, was involved in the Boston Poetry Scene in the 90's, and am a former president of the Kansas Writers Association. My work has stretched from crime fiction to poetry, screenwriting to experimental fiction.

I live in a 100+ year old Victorian home in Wichita, KS with my wife, Shelia, and Sir Pounce Alot (the orange manx) and Lady Mittens (the tuxedo manx).

http://tikiman1962.wordpress.com